A NOVEL

HERSELF

WHEN SHE'S MISSING

SARAH TEREZ ROSENBLUM

SOFT SKULL PRESS
AN IMPRINT OF COUNTERPOINT

Library of Congress Cataloging-in-Publication Data is available.

ISBN: 978-1-59376-437-1

Cover design by Elke Barter
Interior design by Maria E. Torres, Neuwirth & Associates, Inc.

Soft Skull Press
An imprint of COUNTERPOINT
1919 Fifth Street
Berkeley, CA 94710
www.softskull.com

Distributed by Publishers Group West

10 9 8 7 6 5 4 3 2 1

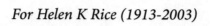

For Helen K Rice (1913-2003)

"The beginning is innocent:
everything that follows is just nostalgia."

—Haven Kimmel

Iodine

THE FALL

. .

Andrea's waiting for the Clark bus when she picks up Jordan's voice mail. Wind rushes in the background, wrestles Jordan for use of her phone.

"I know it's been a while, but I saw something you'll appreciate. I'm right behind a station wagon getting on the 134 when this Serb in an SUV cuts me off. Tinted windows, drug lord for sure. The wagon's a few cars ahead of me now. Wait, I gotta pass some idiot doing forty in the fast lane."

Andrea spots the bus's comforting bulk a few blocks down, slouching through five PM traffic. She clenches her phone to her shoulder, digs in her bag for fare.

"Sorry," Jordan's message continues. "Anyway: the wagon has this great bumper sticker. Shit, lemme remember it exactly. Okay, something like, 'The mother elephant was dying.' No, wait. 'The mother elephant was *drowning* and the other elephant just stood there!' Isn't that clever? Anyway, it made me think of you."

Andrea clicks shut her phone and joins the line of shivering people boarding the bus. This is the first she's heard from Jordan since a year ago, when she left for the second time.

The Criminal Mastermind loves reality television. When pressed she says she prefers *The Bachelor*, but with so many exciting options, she finds it hard to choose. She adores fish sticks, although she loathes seafood in any other form. Charmed by Keith Urban, Brad Paisley, she spends whole afternoons harmonizing to country music videos, sobbing into the couch's sturdy arm.

THE CRIMINAL MASTERMIND has a name, of course. Andrea repeatedly traces its letters, so crucial in combination, so insignificant when taken alone. She hears the name in dreams, and says it aloud in empty rooms, even guiltily imagines inking it onto her skin. Over the years, she's spent more time with the name than with the woman it indicates—certainly has given it more thought than the Criminal Mastermind, who sometimes doesn't bother to respond when she's called. Andrea's the one who waters and feeds it. If possession is nine tenths of the law, the name belongs to Andrea now.

Deep into the night the Criminal Mastermind lands for the second time on Andrea's doorstep, after a movie and two cab rides and hours of drastic sex, the kind that tears you down and rebuilds you, Andrea asks the Criminal Mastermind to say the name herself.

"*Your* name?" the Criminal Mastermind repeats, still sliding her fingers smoothly in and out.

"*Your* name. Say it, please?"

The Criminal Mastermind falters, a gold-medal athlete abruptly off her game. "You want me to . . . I don't . . . *what* do you want?"

"I want proof you're here with me. I want you to say your name."

The Criminal Mastermind looks suspicious but shrugs back into her role.

"Jordan," she says, eyes fixed.

"Again," Andrea whispers.

"Jordan," the Criminal Mastermind repeats, irritable this time, accelerating her thrusts.

"Again."

Jordan slaps a palm over Andrea's mouth. "Stop it." She works her other hand deeper and faster until nothing has meaning but fist against bone.

BEFORE JORDAN RESURRECTS their relationship, Andrea has two kinds of time in which to consider her: actual time and abstract time, the second a product of the first [Figure 1]. If Jordan were on an extended business trip, if she were doing research in Italy or opening a new McDonalds in Japan, if she were somewhere specific for a finite period, the time that pools around Andrea would feel circumscribed, discrete. But Jordan's absence is unbounded. With no reason to believe Jordan anything other than gone for good, Andrea's days widen and deepen. While everyone else dances lightly onward, wind riffling their careless calendars, Andrea sometimes doubts she'll make it through even a quarter hour.

THE CRIMINAL MASTERMIND adores movies. They offer whole casts of blank-canvas characters, surfaces Jordan can scrawl across.

Here are beautiful women she imagines winning; families whose fierce, hidden love earns their redemption; a cartoon fish that finds his way home. No surprise then, upon her arrival in Chicago, the first words Jordan says are, "A movie's just the thing."

At the snack bar, the Criminal Mastermind orders popcorn with extra butter and, even though it costs four fifty, a box of Twizzlers as well. Jordan's unexpected reappearance has Andrea so thrown she doesn't recognize her own reflection in the smudged glass counter, but Jordan's as excited about the glassed-in gummy worms as she is to see Andrea. "We gotta get some of these!" she says.

Right away, Andrea distances herself, thinking in three-by-five cards.

The Criminal Mastermind:
snack addict, broad-shouldered spendthrift, answer to two years and one month's worth of prayers. Never happier than at the movies.

Her mind snags on the oversimplification. The word "happy" fits the Criminal Mastermind like a pair of fat pants on an infomercial man finally at his target weight: Jordan occupies space inside the word but barely makes contact with its seams. Andrea figures a correct term exists for everything; her responsibility, to unearth it, which means she's constantly confronted with the space between the way things are and how she thinks they should be.

Often when she attempts to define something, her mind circles back to a Sunday school memory in which she wears a red plaid jumper, which means she is four, learning how when God asked Adam to name all the animals, Adam simply pointed from gazelle to tree toad and defined each one. Inside her, the story rings, a shrill bell. She recognizes Adam's impulse, far off but familiar, as exactly right and doesn't think to raise her hand, just stands and shouts, "That's me! That's me!"

"In this room we wait our turn." The pastor's thin-lipped wife tightens her bony fingers around her pointer. Ashamed, Andrea clenches and unclenches her toes inside her tight Mary Janes.

"Sit down," the pastor's wife commands. Andrea squats and wraps her arms around her knees.

"Class, how do we sit in this room?" The pastor's wife smiles before answering her own question. "We don't crouch so boys can see our panties. We sit like good little Indian braves."

Unmoving, Andrea sucks her fingers and stares at the pastor's wife, who says, "Bum on the floor, Andrea. You're taking up all of our time."

"Here sweetie." Jenny, the pretty high school volunteer, puts a light hand on Andrea's shoulder, urging her to sit flat. Andrea wipes her fingers on her thick wool tights and gazes at Jenny's Barbie blonde hair glowing butter yellow from within. At the time Andrea figures Jenny for an angel; later she understands the winter sun did all the work.

⁓

WHEN THEY FIRST meet nearly seven years ago, Andrea might call the Criminal Mastermind "mysterious," or "misunderstood," some word starting with "M" and implying an interesting inaccessibility. Her best friend Roslyn calls the Criminal Mastermind *meshuganah*. Roslyn has no patience with the intangible. At eighteen when Andrea unveils her burgeoning lesbianism, Roslyn dismisses it briskly.

"Now you'll waste even more time thinking about sex."

Even though her desire for girls feels, at the time, like some sort of specialty appliance—too many confusing attachments, the directions written in Japanese—Andrea takes umbrage.

"I have just as much right to be gay as you do to be straight," she informs Roslyn.

Roslyn taps ashes from her cigarette. "Obviously," she says. "Just that the whole thing sounds like another excuse for you to navel gaze."

Years later, when Andrea first takes up with the Criminal Master-mind and starts phoning Roslyn at midnight Pacific time, two AM for Roslyn in Chicago, Roslyn is characteristically frank.

"She sounds like a lunatic, kid."

Rather than argue, Andrea retreats to her trusty mental safe house, her thoughts aging sentinels trudging a worn path through her brain.

It's beyond embarrassing, the spacious home the Criminal Mastermind makes inside Andrea. She might as well be writing, "If only daddy would buy me a chestnut brown pony," or "Mrs. Andrea Elizabeth Wynn-Timberlake" in a pink plastic diary. The fact is she can't help herself. She continuously adds to her lists.

Jordan in Bits:

Exterior:
Cruel, ocean-eyed, hair like an *L Word* extra

Activities:
Drinking Coffee—luxuriant

(She'll settle for French roast, but a one-hundred-fifty degree Starbucks Venti Americano is her beverage of choice.)

Stopping at Rite-Aid intent on acquisition (Bottled water, remote controlled cars, nettie pots—she doesn't differentiate; any exchange of cash for goods revs her up.)

Driving—attentive but at ease (No talking when Jordan is driving, unless Jordan initiates.)

More Exterior:
Traditional Beauty (sloping cheekbones, full breasts, ~~slim hips~~, hipless, Anglo) meets Rough Hewn Masculinity (swagger, harsh mouth, hands like a miniature man)

Back to Activities:

Meeting new people—charming/shifty (Depends if the introduction is her idea or Andrea's)

Sleeping—uninhabited, small (As if she remakes herself daily through willpower, when not focused, her countenance transforms.)

Running—gangly and uneven (Lodged between puppy and adult, paws too big for body, ears at half-mast)

At the Movies—unencumbered (maybe free)

After two years devoted to thoughts of Jordan, years uninterrupted by Jordan's actual presence, Andrea ought to be capable of pigeonholing the feeling she gets when Jordan returns. Then again, it isn't herself she's studied. Also, it's one thing to think about Jordan, another to sit beside her, to dig her fingers into a jumbo box of popcorn just one seat over from Pure Evil.

THE CRIMINAL MASTERMIND is a thief and a man-hater; on these faults Andrea is clear. In the months after they first meet, as their liaison accelerates, the Criminal Mastermind borrows her girlfriend's car and they fly over hills and through canyons, the best parts of Los Angeles complicit in their affair.

Once at the foot of Runyon Canyon, fingers probing Andrea's open fly, the Criminal Mastermind pauses too long as a traffic light flips from red to green. Behind them, a silver Mustang, shark-squat and glistening, honks its indignation. The Criminal Mastermind takes one look back and puts the car in park. Fingers still inside Andrea, she smiles pleasantly as horns bray and cars pull around them, the Mustang driver, bearded, Armenian maybe, stubbornly flush to their bumper.

"Be right back." She flings open her door, leaving Andrea adrift in the churning sea of traffic. Andrea watches the Criminal

Mastermind yell through the driver's open window, "If only you'd been more patient, you wouldn't have missed your light."

The driver brandishes his fist, a living cliché, and Andrea laughs once like a cough as the Criminal Mastermind slips back into the car.

"Did you hear what that asshole said?"

Andrea shakes her head, buttons her pants.

The Criminal Mastermind attempts an accent, produces something Indian and Russian, a little German thrown in.

"My friend," she says, "you are a motherfucker. And probably a lesbian." She takes off with a squeal as the light turns green.

"Think he smelled your pussy on my hand?"

ANDREA WONDERS JUST what tugs a memory to the surface at a particular moment. She sometimes experiences the standard event/memory chain reaction.

For Example:

Walking to the El in Chicago->

She bites into an apple->

Recalls Roslyn's visit to LA (a four-day break for Andrea from writing her dissertation)->

Driving to Venice Beach->

Roslyn (sleek hair/teetering on cork wedges/fits in perfectly even on the West Coast) snapping a photo of Andrea in an apple green sundress, crunching on a Granny Smith the exact shade

But often memories that shouldn't be on speaking terms come to Andrea like spooning lovers, arms and legs entangled, impossible to unwind. The Mustang memory, for instance, segues resolutely into a second unrelated recollection: Jordan in Andrea's Westwood apartment in the early months of their first affair.

On her back on the living room floor, the Criminal Mastermind whispers into Andrea's hair.

"I want you to know everything about me, even if it makes me ashamed. I've never wanted that before, but I know you won't judge me. You're too sweet. You take me as I am. Patricia's not like that. I'm not myself with her; I'm on my best behavior. This morning she made me go all the way to the bathroom just so she could show me the wet towel I'd left by the tub. If you love someone, why does it matter where she leaves her towels?"

Andrea glances at the Criminal Mastermind's belongings, seeping from her open suitcase, puddled on the floor. Jordan's question out of context would seem boorish, but Jordan asks it like a child. Upon her arrival a day earlier, Patricia away on business, Andrea's apartment was poised and particular, not an item out of place. Now her off-white carpet is visible only in patches, heaped with layers of clothing, half-empty take-out cartons, and DVDs Jordan thinks Andrea *has* to see. That Jordan's whirlwind dislodges her possessions, her careful order, her lists, makes Andrea feel somehow at Jordan's mercy, a faceted feeling, untethered, dreamy, secure.

Sure cleanliness matters, she thinks, touching the heather-soft skin that girds the Criminal Mastermind's ribcage, *but so does passion.*

"There's more to life than an orderly house," Andrea says.

"You make me feel safe." Jordan traces Andrea's clavicle.

From what? Andrea wonders.

"So do you," she says.

"I've done stuff you can't imagine," the Criminal Mastermind continues, smiling. "Stuff you'd never do. The thing is, I issue my own paychecks. That's kind of an oversight, right? If the church were a company, I'd never have that freedom. There'd be rules to keep someone in my position under control."

Stop telling me this. Andrea thinks. Then, *Wait, tell me more.*

"It started when the old pastor went on a four-week vacation." Andrea pictures a man in a clerical collar on water skis; at that ice hotel in Finland; standing, arms folded, the Grand Canyon at his back.

"He left me in charge of the checks, then he was transferred. We had some Latino guy in the interim who didn't know his ass from his elbow. Probably a child molester. He never even glanced at payroll. I'm planning on paying it back; I just got a little ahead." She kisses Andrea's ear.

"We have about ten check signers, people in the congregation. Every week I print out duplicate checks, have one person sign one, a different person sign another, so I get paid twice, but see, I'm not forging anything, so it's not a federal crime. I'm going to stop, though. You make me want to be better. It's like Jesus preached: love and acceptance pave the way for change."

Jordan's mouth at Andrea's ear, the hush of breath against her cheek, these sensations blot out Jordan's confession; Andrea can't hold onto both at once. Later, too much later, she will deconstruct Jordan while Jordan's inside her; right now they're just too new.

Jordan/Fiction:

1. Though The Criminal Mastermind conveys an easy familiarity with Jack Kerouac, Toni Morrison, and Joyce Carol Oates, what she really loves are Clive Cussler novels. John Grisham will do in a pinch. She's made it halfway through Sue Grafton's alphabet, but Kinsey, she says, would be so much more interesting if she were a man.

2. During an episode of *ER* in which a schmaltzy "Some where Over the Rainbow" shepherds Dr. Mark Greene into the next world, the camera panning bereft over his abandoned eyeglasses, Jordan cries so hard her eyelids stipple with delicate burgundy blotches, blood vessels exploding beneath her skin.

3. She likes adventure movies; anything with a boy, a
dog, and a reason the two can't be reunited. A good
reason, but one that falls easily away sometime between the obligatory food fight and a surprise visit
to the boy's deadbeat father. Turns out he never knew
he had a son.

〜

THE NIGHT THE Criminal Mastermind appears in Chicago, two years after she stops calling Andrea and 2,016 miles from where she belongs, they see the second *Charlie's Angels* movie. Released more than three years earlier, it's inexplicably playing at a rundown theater in Logan Square. Andrea's not thrilled. Too old for Nickelodeon and too young to catch the show the first time around, she has neither nostalgia nor actual interest. Plus she hasn't seen part one. More important, she's spent twenty-five months stroking a mental map of the Criminal Mastermind's improbable return and their ensuing reunion, worn the fantasy into a specific shape, one involving deep tongue thrusts and Veuve, not a crowd of sassy teenage girls and a multiplex.

Just in from Los Angeles, the Criminal Mastermind is uncomfortable with public transportation, and the taxis that normally collect along Clark Street are strangely sparse. Finally, a sharp-featured Indian cab driver responds to Andrea's raised hand with a quick lurch toward the curb. When Jordan opens the car door, gestures for Andrea to climb in, Andrea realizes she's said next to nothing since stepping outside for her mail, finding Jordan instead.

"Towel Head," the Criminal Mastermind whispers gleefully. Andrea's half forgotten Jordan's casual racism. Even disapproving, she nonetheless fills with recognition, as if hearing a song she dislikes but knows well. Inside the taxi, she sinks into the sensation of the Criminal Mastermind's arm hooked firmly around her shoulders, the feeling overwhelming and proverbial, enough to halt Andrea's questions before they hit her lips. When she surfaces, they've missed the tiny discount theater and have to circle widely back, through one-way side streets and blind back alleys. By the time they slide into their seats, the previews have begun. On screen, Will Smith runs toward or away, chin thrust up and forward, muscles like raindrops on a windshield, skittering beneath his skin.

"Mmm. I loves me some of that!" A row of girls cackles. One takes a call on her cell phone. A woman with tight white curls puts a spindly finger to her lips.

"Whatsamatter? It's just previews." A girl in a sequined bandana uncrosses and crosses her pudgy legs.

"I think the previews are the best part," Andrea whispers—after two years of careful planning, not the first full sentence she hoped to speak. She envisions the can of tomato soup and leftover half-sandwich she'd planned for dinner. Before everything shifted, before she opened her door.

Throughout the movie, she keeps a careful eye on the Criminal Mastermind, not sure what she's afraid to see. The Criminal Mastermind only breathes, "Oh, cool!" as Pink rides through on a motorcycle, and shrieks with delight when the bad guys get their due. As the lights come up, she puts a butter-smeared hand on Andrea's knee, "That Bill Murray is a hoot and a half!" Mouth to Andrea's ear she whispers, "Now I'm going to take you home."

Falling asleep hours later, Jordan's collar bone sharp against her cheek, Andrea's mind alights on a memory: the rickety folding table at the back of her Sunday school classroom, blonde Jenny's tender arm hairs, delicate and feminine compared to her own. Andrea knows sex elicits haphazard recollections—something to do with release, she assumes. Whatever the reason, she craves the giddy launch into a memory-studded stratosphere. Usually she sees a state park, a grassy picnic area, or a wheel-rutted campground, each a fragment of a different family vacation. She doesn't consciously summon these visions, but there they are.

Once she asks Jordan if the same thing happens to her.

"Absolutely." Jordan doesn't hesitate. "Only I see the food court at the Beverly Center."

Now listening to Jordan's smooth inhalations, Andrea hears Jenny's voice.

"It's okay to identify with Adam." Jenny tries to catch her eye, but Andrea keeps her gaze like a prize, tight to her chest.

"God gave him an important job." Andrea stills as Jenny smoothes her hair, repositions her barrette. "We're all his children and our jobs are important too."

Andrea rubs her cheek against Jenny's chenille sweater. She watches an older boy double fisting windmill cookies, dunking each in orange juice before jamming it in his mouth. She knows Jenny doesn't understand, but she can't explain what she meant. She doesn't want to disappoint Jenny either, not when she smells so powerfully of lemons and the gold cross at her throat grazes her clavicle just so.

⌒

TWO MONTHS AFTER Jordan's arrival in Chicago and she has yet to explain. When pressed she widens her eyes, runs blunt-tipped fingers over Andrea's lips. "I wanted to be selfless," she says, sort of smiling. "But I guess that's not one of my strengths."

"What do you mean?" Andrea asks.

"You're young," Jordan drops her gaze and her hand. "I wanted you to have some kind of real life."

Wendy. Andrea grabs for the name like it's pepper spray, a thing she can use in self-defense. She won't be swayed by Jordan's explanation. Intrepid googling tells her Jordan's most recent ex-girlfriend is only thirty years old herself.

Jordan:
Perpetual college student, former parish administrator, lover of Mexican food, (the same woman who,

back in LA) keeps Andrea on the side for two years,
ultimately admitting that her girlfriend Patricia, a
gallery owner, is actually her "wife," at least in
Hawaii where they honeymoon, but (according to Jordan) avoid having sex, (she's the one who) cheats on
both Andrea and Patricia with a student intern at her
church, then abandons the lot of them to move in with
Wendy, the owner of a shabby (but exclusive) hair
salon in Echo Park

That afternoon at DSW, a store they frequent because Jordan can
never get enough shoes, Andrea scans a sea of footwear and spots
Jordan amid bent-over shoppers, each struggling like a bargain
basement stepsister to force her feet into clearance sneakers a size
too small. Eyes on Jordan, Andrea thinks, *shiny hair; ropey biceps;
ubiquitous sunglasses and Starbucks cup; essential oil: China Rain;
small, insistent fists; mean, perfect teeth.* The name "Jordan" doesn't
come to mind. Then, fighting a flood of tenderness she knows
will undo her, she thinks, "Criminal Mastermind." She has to do
something to resist, to make a category for Jordan, although how,
really, could there be one?

Renaming Jordan, marking herself as Jordan's creator, empow-
ers Andrea. So what if the empowerment is false? At least it
reminds Andrea with whom she is dealing: a woman Andrea has
known too long and too well to trust. Yet Jordan is also the person
who, in spite of experience, logic, and an otherwise intact sense of
irony, Andrea never stopped wanting. Now that Jordan's come to
Chicago to find her, Andrea discovers she misses her even more.

Andrea's Weak Spots:

1. Crying women. (Men too, probably, but she's never
been close enough to tell.)

2. Anything guilt-inducing: A. Homeless people B. Her
grandmother (who always says, "Oh, it's you," when
Andrea calls).

3. Roslyn's way with rhetoric. (She can undermine any
point Andrea tries to make.)

4. People who believe strongly in something. (Often
she pities them, but secretly Andrea believes they're
a kind of happy of which she can only dream.)

⌒

THE CRIMINAL MASTERMIND has a thing for kittens, a source of
tension because Andrea has nothing whatsoever for kittens. The
cashiers at Jewel-Osco have gotten used to seeing Andrea, stack of
lavender paper under one arm, tacking "Free Kittens!" flyers up on
the bulletin board. She's become adept at wording Craigslist post-
ings, and once she snagged a jogging-stroller-mom at a stoplight
and sweet-talked her into detouring past the apartment to collect
two mewling balls of fur. Andrea considers attracting the runner's
attention a particular victory; most joggers will race past a lynch-
ing, worried only about beating their time.

Andrea would like to ask what the deal is with the Criminal
Mastermind and kittens. However, having experienced the Criminal Mastermind's response to anything resembling criticism, she
hesitates. Each time she thinks to broach the subject, she remembers how Jordan stopped grocery shopping entirely when Andrea
noted that buying a quarter pound of ham and consuming only
two slices was wasteful, or how for weeks after Andrea requested
Jordan angle the dildo slightly lower during sex, Jordan brought
Andrea to the brink of orgasm and then pretended to fall asleep.

The fifth time Andrea comes home from teaching to find four
extra paws, one tufty gray tail, she pours herself a glass of Ben
Marco.

"What's the matter, babe?" The Criminal Mastermind asks
brightly, as if she can change Andrea from the outside in just by
pretending nothing's wrong.

"This is a small apartment," Andrea keeps her voice even. "We can't have more than one cat."

"But look how adorable she is!"

The kitten leaps madly at Andrea's curtains, hangs yowling by a single claw.

"Jordan."

The Criminal Mastermind disentangles the kitten. "I'm calling her Delilah. Isaiah is under the bed, but he'll get used to her. Poor thing was trapped under the neighbor's garage. You should have seen her matted fur."

"You need to get rid of her."

"She's my responsibility."

"She isn't."

"I'm the one who found her. I can't let her die."

"She doesn't have to die. Take her to that cat place in Roger's Park. It's no-kill."

"I won't let you die." Jordan whispers, pressing her mouth to the kitten's neck.

"Jesus," Andrea can't help saying.

"It's okay, Buttons." Jordan continues to caress the cat.

"I thought you said Delilah."

Jordan turns haunted eyes on Andrea, more forceful for their vacancy.

"When I was little I had a cat named Buttons. Not really mine, but I fed her. She lived on the street near my house. My parents wouldn't let me bring her inside."

Jordan weeps as she speaks, her words riding shaky sobs.

"One weekend I was going to a friend's birthday party and I wanted to say good-bye to Buttons before I left, so I called her and she came running across the street right in front of a car."

Jordan flushes pink. A vein trembles above her right eyebrow.

"It happened so fast I thought I imagined it, like maybe she hadn't been hit, and I ran toward her; the car was halfway up the block by then and Buttons lay twisted in the street, her head tweaked to the side, her eyes popping out of her head. I couldn't stop crying but my mom made me go to the party anyway even though the girl who invited me only did it because her father worked with mine."

Andrea can tell it's time she summoned a reaction. She's sure if she talks she'll say the worst possible thing.

"Since then I can't let a cat live on the street." Jordan inhales shakily, Delilah clutched tight in her hands.

"That sounds traumatic," Andrea says finally. "I admire your impulse to rescue them, but we can't keep every cat you find."

"I understand," Jordan rubs a finger under Delilah's chin. "Now that I think about it, I'm probably a little compulsive about kittens." She waits, maybe for Andrea to nod sympathetically. Andrea sighs, manages a slight tilt and a smile.

"I'll try to control myself." Jordan says, meaninglessly. Andrea is going to have to stay on her game.

Staying on her game has become a theme of sorts, the subterranean backbeat lending rhythm to her days. The good part is she feels alive in ways she hasn't before, alert to every sound and movement, star of her own thriller. The bad part is she's so exhausted that when she stands or sits suddenly, her vision floods with violet splotches. She's lost track of what's happening on her favorite television shows, hasn't read a book in seven months. Forget about calling anyone back.

Scott, a teacher with whom she used to linger in the break room, occasionally meet for coffee after work, asks her in passing, "Where've you been lately?"

"I picked up another job," Andrea lies.

She checks her e-mail one day to find a note from a student: "I waited outside your office for half an hour; did I get our appointment time wrong?"

Not only does Andrea not remember scheduling the meeting, she could swear she's never heard the student's name in her life.

No matter. The Criminal Mastermind demands this intensity of focus. No telling what she would do if it suddenly went missing, but Andrea places odds it would involve nudity or embezzlement of some kind.

Although Jordan's past justifications for thievery range from her former Episcopal priest boss's egocentric aesthetic ("She has photos of herself all over her office!") to a need to court Andrea in style ("Expensive as always, aren't you?"), Andrea thinks it has nothing to do with either and everything to do with boredom on a scale too vast for Jordan to identify, a restless dissatisfaction larger than Jordan's viewfinder, only one part visible at a time. This leaves Andrea zigzagging as if to snag a searchlight, forever responsible for foiling Jordan's fundamental ennui.

The Criminal Mastermind never actually says so, never threatens to cheat or leave or do something illegal if Andrea's attention becomes diluted by work or school or family or friends. She doesn't have to. Her departure is implied by her arrival, inevitable, like a cresting wave. Andrea can't understand how this crucial truth went undetected by her predecessors. It's clear to Andrea that the fast track to obsolescence is becoming Jordan's actual girlfriend. As soon as Jordan claims a woman, she loses interest, the woman plunging in value, a newly purchased car driven from the lot. Maybe Andrea sees what Jordan's exes didn't because while they lived and slept and ate with the Criminal Mastermind, the bulk of Andrea's interactions have been clandestine; quick change sex in the bathrooms of various Starbucks, staticy nighttime phone calls from dips between the Hollywood Hills [Figure 2]. All things considered, Andrea was satisfied with their arrangement. She banked on her outsider, crotchless-panty status to keep the Criminal Mastermind's interest. Viewed on the diagonal, she couldn't possibly lose her appeal.

If it were up to Andrea, the Criminal Mastermind would never have come to Chicago to make an honest woman of her. She'd have settled there with some current girlfriend, an accountant maybe, or a lawyer working sixty-hour weeks. The only true way to keep Jordan's attention, a thing Andrea wants so much she hates herself, is to be something spicy and extra, a girl just out of reach. Now with Jordan installed in Andrea's one-bedroom, she tells herself all of Jordan is obviously better than none. What's required of Andrea now is creativity. She's not like the others. She won't let Jordan's cross-country move diminish her; amuse-bouche to standing rib roast [Figure 3].

Things That Make Andrea Different/Reasons (This Time) Jordan Will Stay:

Unlike Patricia, Andrea refuses to add Jordan to her MasterCard/She's not a pushover

Andrea isn't/was never straight

They both love Cry Wolf, but not the way other lesbians do

(Andrea acts like?) She really needs Jordan

⌒

BACK WHEN ALL their hours are stolen, Jordan announces she's taking Andrea to a baseball game. About a year prior to the Christian intern, a year and a half before Jordan flees with Echo Park Wendy, when Jordan's still claiming she plans to leave Patricia and Andrea doesn't yet know better than to hope she will, Andrea isn't in the habit of saying no to Jordan, but privately she questions such use of their time.

"You'll love it," Jordan promises. "We can leave if you get bored."

"You'd just stand up and walk out?" Andrea asks.

"It's about the experience, not the game," Jordan runs her thumb along Andrea's jaw. "The food, the sun, the crowd. As long as we have fun, who cares how it ends?"

A pie chart of Andrea's daily agenda would show equally large chunks devoted to date preparation and post-date journaling, a small slice for actual dates, and an even tinier sliver for less exciting aspects of life: eight hours of sleep and anything whole grain [Figure 4]. Trying to look like the type of person who skips work on a weekday to drink plastic cupped beer and shout at men she's never met, Andrea nearly doubles her prep time. She winds up dividing her wavy hair into pigtails, dressing in a blue and gray baseball shirt and Capri jeans. Snatching her keys from the counter, she ignores an unfinished paper ringed with coffee stains, pretends to herself it isn't due the next day.

At Dodger Stadium, Jordan buys a Dodger Dog and nachos and beer. She buys peanuts and cotton candy and a pink racer back tank for Andrea, whose long sleeve shirt is quickly saturated with sweat. Although in the future the memory will be thoroughly mined, first blissfully between rendezvous and then more soberly after Jordan leaves and before she returns, Andrea will always thrill recalling the proprietary way Jordan rolls up the tank top, insisting Andrea show off her stomach.

"If you got it, flaunt it. And baby, you got it."

There are things Andrea won't remember: she won't remember who the Dodgers play. She will also forget the day of the week, and whether her flip-flops are red or blue. Likewise, she won't be able to pinpoint how the conversation about infidelity starts. She'll know she feels flattened by the heat, compressed by the relentless sun. The players on the field gather and disperse with no discernable explanation, and Andrea resents the surrounding spectators' easy knowledge of the game.

"Patricia hates afternoon baseball."

This is an early warning: say a negative word about baseball and risk her role as the anti-girlfriend. Andrea isn't sure if Jordan intends to be memorized, learned from, but each statement she makes feels like a carefully placed clue.

"Not just baseball, she hates watching anything in the afternoon. She'd rather be working, and since I do her books, she thinks I should be too." Jordan props her feet on the seatback in front of her. "I practically have to medicate her to get her to go to a matinee with me. She's so type-A she loses her shit. When we left the theater after *Air Bud* and she saw it was dusk, she started to hyperventilate. And forget about watching a movie on the couch or having sex before six PM."

Jordan glances at Andrea. "I mean, you know, when we were still having sex."

Andrea presses a fingertip into the scarlet skin on her shoulder. A white circle blooms. "I need to use the bathroom," she says.

"I probably sound like the classic adulterer: my wife doesn't understand me!" Jordan throws an arm around Andrea, and Andrea bites her lip, feeling her raw skin blaze. "Come on," says Jordan, "the bathrooms are this way."

In the bleach and beer-scented restroom, Andrea pees and flicks water at her face and chest. Outside, Jordan leans against a railing, staring out at the parking lot.

When Andrea thinks about it later, she won't be able to explain how she knows, more important, how she summons the courage to say it. Actually courage isn't really an issue because the words fly from her mouth to their mark before she has time to consider.

"You've cheated on everyone you've been with." The sentence ripples lightly back to Andrea, surprisingly careless to her ears.

"What a thing to say." Jordan matches her casual tone.

"It's true though."

"Well now, let me think." Jordan stretches her arms over the railing, thinking or tanning, Andrea can't tell. "Yeah, I guess I have."

Andrea tenses at the admission; no matter she already knew. Hearing the information feels different than inferring it, like seeing a friend walk away with money you offered freely but never thought she'd accept.

"Everyone but my first girlfriend," Jordan amends.

"Why not her?"

"We were thirteen. I thought she was my destiny. I never held back a thing."

Andrea at Thirteen:

    Still plays with Barbies

    Leaves sleepovers crying

    Never kissed a boy

"What happened?"

"Her parents walked in on us. Threatened to send her away. Wouldn't let me anywhere near her. Then she started dating Sandy Summers, one of her friends from choir. I found out because she invited me to her concert. I thought it meant she wanted to get back together, but at the concert she dedicated a song to Sandy. So she got sent off anyway, nothing to do with me."

"That must have been awful." Noticing she's biting her index finger, Andrea drops her hand to her side.

Jordan lifts her sunglasses, turning her high beam eyes on Andrea. "I swore I'd never feel like that again."

You got dumped by a thirteen-year-old so you've cheated on everyone since? Andrea struggles to transform the thought into something from which Jordan won't stalk self-righteously away. "That's no justification," she says finally.

Jordan leans back against the railing. "I just hold a little something back. No one wants everything I have."

Andrea clamps both hands on the railing. Trapping Jordan between her arms, she slowly leans in.

"What are you doing?" Jordan shifts between Andrea's outstretched arms.

"Making sure I have your attention."

"Alright?" Jordan tries to organize her face into an expression of amusement but only gets halfway.

"I want everything. Nothing you have is too much."

"That's what she said," Jordan quips, cutting her eyes away.

"And once Patricia is out of the picture, once we're really a couple, you're not going to cheat."

"I'm not?" No jest; Jordan really wants to know.

"No."

"What's going to stop me?"

"I am."

"You are?" Jordan's eyes glisten.

"You need some fucking boundaries," Andrea bad-cops, making it up as she goes along.

"And you're just the girl to give them to me?" The words are derisive, calculated to repel her, but Andrea sees Jordan's inadvertent expression—she looks like a contented child tucked up in bed.

"I know what you need."

Andrea scans Jordan's face. Odds are she's looking at a childhood need tardily met. She'll take a chance though, call what she sees love.

Another Memory, Somehow Related:

INT. JOAN'S ON THIRD—AFTERNOON

With a white handle bag hooked over her arm, Jordan pays for a lemon bar and then heads toward the door.

              ANDREA
      You gave him a five.

Andrea steps back to let an arid-faced woman, talking angrily into her cell phone, stride past.

              JORDAN
      Next time someone tries to cut in front
      you, give 'em an elbow to the ribs.

              ANDREA
      What about the sandwiches?

                        JORDAN
    What about them?

                        ANDREA
    You didn't pay.

EXT. JOAN'S ON THIRD — AFTERNOON

Andrea nearly collides with a tall, exquisitely dressed
mocha-skinned couple. They blink, lizard-like, and
regard her with languid scorn.

                        JORDAN
        Watch it, you two.

                        ANDREA
        It was my fault.

                        JORDAN
        You are a mess today.

Jordan slides her palm into Andrea's back pocket.

                        (Cont.)
        Good thing I'm here.

                        ANDREA
        The money.

                        JORDAN
        Guy forgot to charge me. Not my job to
        remind him.

Close up on Andrea; she knows what she is
about to say next. Externally she looks in
control, driven. Really, she can barely
breathe.

                        ANDREA
        Okay, *Criminal Mastermind.*

Cut to Jordan, happy to be caught, her wings pinned
back, a neat label written underneath.

⌐

HERE'S SOMETHING ELSE the Criminal Mastermind loves: cheese sandwiches. Actually she loves bread and cheese in any combination and form. In Los Angeles their dinners feel stylized; deep fishbowl glasses of red wine are swirled and sniffed, Andrea's silky skirt rides her thighs, and the Criminal Mastermind rolls wads of cash into the waiting hands of valets before fucking Andrea in Patricia's car. In Chicago, Jordan still tips lavishly, but the extravagance now seems suspect. Wherever they eat, the Criminal Mastermind orders a version of the same thing. At Reza's she gets fried cheese and flatbread, at Gioco, Gorgonzola gnocchi, at Clark's, grilled cheese and tomato soup, and at Taste of Heaven, macaroni and cheese. Andrea fears for the Criminal Mastermind's small intestine, begs her to eat something green.

On a particular Wednesday, as they leave Gioco, Jordan holding the door, patting Andrea's ass as she steps through, Andrea stumbles on the curb, actually falls to her knees. She's dizzy from lack of sleep. They're celebrating Jordan's acceptance into DePaul, the unlikely transfer of most of her humanities credits from UCLA, but all evening Andrea harbors a slow-burning anxiety she pins to a class she has to teach in the morning. Queasy with exhaustion and worry, she only prods the caprese salad wilting on her plate. This makes her feel guilty on top of everything, even though the most wasteful person she knows sits directly across from her, picking at the two entrées she's ordered, abandoning them both to slowly sip her wine.

Andrea knows she should be home preparing her lecture, or at least trying to rest. She's not dancing naked on a bar or anything, but sometimes she can't believe how far out of her comfort zone the Criminal Mastermind has delivered her. In college, when the girls on her floor were fucking frat boys, eating pizza for breakfast, and cramming all night for exams, Andrea ate protein every three hours, jogged along the lake at dawn, began researching term papers as soon as the semester syllabus hit her desk. It's a struggle to relate herself then, color coordinating her closet while ordinary co-eds filed date-rape charges, with who she is now: woman approaching thirty, deep in perpetual thrall.

Jordan has yet to fall into any sort of steady job, which means she has no reason to sleep. Lately between midnight and two AM, she teaches herself to salsa dance. She says she's studying Hebrew, thinks she may try her hand at web design. Just after midnight is also when the Criminal Mastermind hits her sexual peak. If Andrea isn't awake for her to fuck, she'll watch porn all night or have cyber-sex in the first chat room she finds, no matter the room's theme or its occupants' proclivities.

`Top Five Sites:`

`Jews for Jesus`

`Gay Kayaking`

`Not My Bible`

`Just Ass`

`I Heart Dakota Fanning, Do You?`

Andrea wakes sometimes to find the Criminal Mastermind asleep near the keyboard, head pillowed on her arms, and the computer screen cluttered with x-rated dialogue boxes, incriminating as condom wrappers.

There are worse pastimes, Andrea tells herself, wishing she could phone Patricia, find out her approach to Jordan's infidelity and take the least similar tack. But Jordan's online exploits aren't what keep Andrea alert, keep her spreading her legs when she's already sore and so tired she sleeps and wakes as the Criminal Mastermind fucks her, the whole experience taking on a hallucinatory hue. Andrea stays up because if she's not available when the Criminal Mastermind wants sex, the Criminal Mastermind could meet another girl and fall in love with her. She could buy the girl thoughtful gifts, more romantic for their simplicity. She could take up night walking, tell Andrea she's trying to gain some perspective, lose a little weight. She could spend her walks reciting Rumi into her cell, undeterred by Andrea's ready access to the records from their shared phone plan. The Criminal Mastermind could also leave her, but Andrea is more troubled by the banal subterfuge that comes before. She's uncomfortably familiar with the Criminal Mastermind's tactics, having not long ago been the girl on whom they were employed.

Leaving the restaurant's warm, candlelit interior feels like a loss. Although November, the outside air already harbors deep winter's scentless hush. For the first time since moving, Andrea misses Los Angeles. Season may weaken into season there, until husks of whole years are unwittingly shed, but the Midwest alternative seems suddenly more alarming. Here inevitable months, distinct and determined, line up and drop like stones. *Winter chases summer, no, that's not right,* Andrea thinks, pulling gloves from her pocket, *more like winter is summer shot dead.*

Having held the door for Andrea, Jordan turns to talk to the host, a woman exactly her type, one of them anyway. In her hand Jordan holds a thick wad of cash, as if brandishing her family crest. Halfway through the door, Andrea watches Jordan peel off a bill and hand it to the host, who smiles and flicks her long hair.

Like a cornucopia, Andrea thinks, remembering handprint turkeys and construction paper pumpkins, each tucked carefully in her backpack, Sunday school gifts for her mom. Since coming to Chicago Jordan hasn't made a move to find a job, yet with no discernable source of income, her pockets overflow.

Andrea isn't reckless enough to mention this, but the dull drone of curiosity, steadfast attendant to all their late-night dinners, rises now to an adamant roar. She fingers a square of paper in her back pocket, creased from repeated reads. She can't keep waiting to confront Jordan. It's long past time. Perhaps this understanding undoes her, or maybe she's too drained to both process and walk. Either way, she drops abruptly to her knees where sidewalk meets street, as if thought has struck her down.

As the shock of cold concrete beneath her knees gives gradual way to a hot, raw throb, Andrea remains on the ground out of preference; she could stand if she chose. On the sidewalk's eroded edge, hot trickle of blood oozing down her knee, Andrea has the next part memorized. How many times has she fallen in her life, from bikes and trees and once a slow moving car? She knows what's required: the unborn recovery implied by its precursor, the fall. Instead, slowly enough to pretend she hasn't, Andrea folds forward, lowers her cheek to the pock-marked cement.

Moisture seeps from the sidewalk. It hasn't rained since dawn, but the cement retains the memory of rain, offers it to Andrea's skin where it presses. She ran for miles by the lake that morning, no matter the ache in her heels or the wet. Now she wonders how she traversed such space so effortlessly, when the distance from the curb to her apartment, a class to teach in the morning, this Criminal whose scent infuses her sheets, seems unbridgeable. Someone else must have done it, some stranger sharing the accident of her name, because now the mere straight-legged distance from her face to the ground, as opposed to its proximity when kneeling, one leg bent under, rosy with blood, that distance seems measureless. How far exactly from here to there?

The first time Andrea meets her, Adrienne Anderson is unimaginably sweet. A longtime fan of Cry Wolf, Andrea thought hard before crossing the line from anonymous audience member to lurking fan. Backstage on a landing linking two narrow sets of staircases, she clutches a lump of tinfoil in her hand. The walls and low ceiling are layered with graffiti, and here and there Andrea can read a significant band name, a date. Open at the base of the stairs, the loading dock door lets in frosty gusts of air. Still, Andrea's so warm that rivulets of sweat trace the slope of her calves. She's beginning to feel she's been back here for hours; she was born back here maybe. Each time she hears heavy feet on the stairs above her, she opens and closes her hand around the foil, arranges her face into an innocuous smile. So far she's been ignored by two guitar techs, a pizza guy, and some man in a brown leather blazer, perhaps the manager of the club. That the next set of boots belongs to Adrienne, despite hours of anticipation, leaves Andrea unprepared.

"You waiting for me?" Adrienne asks, so close Andrea can see her pores.

"I'm sorry." Andrea steps backward, teeters on the edge of the lower set of stairs.

"Whoa now!" Adrienne grabs Andrea's wrist. "Careful," she adds, letting go. "Were you at the show?" Adrienne holds an open bottle of Coca Cola in her hand, the free one, the one Andrea can't still feel, clutching her wrist. Despite the chill, beads of moisture glisten on the bottle's long neck. Waiting for Andrea's answer, she tips her head back to take a sip.

"Yes." Andrea says, watching Adrienne's throat contract. "You were wonderful. You're always wonderful." She leans against the graffiti strewn wall, thinking of the words that overlap where her shoulder blades press.

"Thanks, babe." Adrienne wipes her mouth on the back of her hand. "Did you want something? An autograph, maybe?"

"I wanted to give you this." Andrea unwraps the ball of tinfoil. Inside she's placed a tiny golden hourglass, a delicate chain threaded through. "Because of your song," she says.

"I know." Adrienne sweeps her hair to the side. "Put it on."

"Really?" Andrea stares at Adrienne's bare, sweaty neck.

"Sure."

Fastening the clasp, Andrea notices the subtle lines radiating from the corners of Adrienne's eyes.

"Thank you," Adrienne says.

"I just wanted to give something back." Andrea moves past her, continuing up the stairs.

"Where do you think you're going?" Adrienne smiles. "You won't be able to get out that way."

"Right." Andrea starts down the steps. Halfway to the bottom, she turns back. "Thanks for everything you do."

"I won't take this off," Adrienne says, or that's how Andrea remembers it, anyway.

STEEPER
FARES

▪ ▪ ▪

The text exchange happens later. After Jordan leaves Patricia and Andrea, before Andrea flees to the Midwest.

ANDREA: But it can't be as good as us.

JORDAN: It's . . . different.

ANDREA: How?

JORDAN: She isn't you.

ANDREA: Is that good or bad?

No reply, if Andrea's memory is accurate, and by the next day, Jordan's number has changed.

WHEN JORDAN APPROACHES her for the first time, Andrea is sitting in front of Los Angeles's Troubadour, peering through her reading glasses at an early draft of her thesis proposal. She is waiting for a general admission Cry Wolf concert to start.

"Hey," Jordan says, squatting, "you go to UCLA, right?"

Andrea blinks. Tan Vans, dark blue Levis, waffle-knit shirt, secure behind mirrored sunglasses; Jordan's thin-lipped smile seems almost a sneer.

"Yeah. Do you teach there?"

Jordan laughs the throaty chuckle Andrea comes to know as part of her pick-up persona. Unchecked, Jordan's laugh is high-pitched, riddled with snorts.

"Nah, I'm a student. But thanks. Do I really look that old?"

Andrea feels her face go hot. "I'm not a good judge of age."

Jordan leans in to look at Andrea's paper. Reflexively Andrea shields it from view.

"I haven't chosen a major, but I'm thinking about religion," Jordan says, "How about you?"

"MA in English. I'll be done in two more years."

"I'm nowhere near finished. There's always something new I want to try." Jordan pulls her shirt away from her skin and Andrea smells something she describes to Roslyn the next day as unearthly. Later, unscrewing caps to browse essential oils, she finds it on special in the cosmetics aisle at Whole Foods.

"So." Jordan sits back on her heels, "I've been here since five and I really need a Starbucks fix. Why don't you join me in line, save our place, and I'll run and get us something to drink."

"You've been here since five AM?" Andrea glances ahead, counts four people between herself and the spot Jordan indicated, marked by a purple JanSport backpack, one person from the front of the line.

Jordan shrugs, "I was running late."

"When do you usually get in line?"

"Depends on the location. California fans are pretty fierce, maybe because Peter and Adrienne live here, plus the weather's so nice. There's one girl from the Valley who goes to every single concert on the West Coast. I'm on a mission not to let her get in front of me. If I hadn't had a fight with my girlfriend I'd have made it here before her today. This your first concert?"

"In LA, yeah, but I used to go all the time back in the Midwest. People don't get in line this early, though. I thought for sure I'd be one of the first."

"Well, at least you can be third. Grab your stuff. Come sit by me."

"Won't the people who've been here longer be angry?" Andrea asks, already gathering her things.

"Fuck 'em." Jordan winks, a move that strikes Andrea as a shade too corny.

"No one came with you?"

Jordan shakes her head, silver hairs glinting amidst brown. "My girlfriend can't stand Cry Wolf."

"You better revise your intake form. That's the sort of thing that should be divulged right up front," Andrea says, heart fluttering.

Jordan does the throaty thing again. "Before you move in together."

"Before introducing your cats."

"What about you?" Jordan checks her spot in line.

"Me?" Andrea folds her glasses into their case.

"You waiting for anyone?"

"No. It's too embarrassing," Andrea says, tucking the case into her bag.

"What is?"

"Being obsessed like this."

"Are you kidding? This isn't obsession; this is what makes us who we are." Standing, Jordan offers Andrea her hand. "Come on."

In the front row at the Cry Wolf concert, bodies crushed against the lip of the stage, Andrea watches Jordan and she watches Adrienne. She can't decide where to look. She's known Jordan for nine hours now—as far as she's concerned, the most crucial nine hours of her life. Jordan purses her lips and claps her hands; Adrienne smiles with her eyes closed, her whole body clenches when she holds a note.

"We thought about calling the band Peter and the Wolf," Adrienne says, adjusting the microphone so she doesn't need to bend to speak into it. Andrea sees her do this at every concert. The roadies always underestimate Adrienne's height.

"But he's Peter," Adrienne gestures at her sandy-blond haired brother who grins with half his mouth. "So guess what that would make me?" She does a kick ball change, scuffing her heavy boots against the stage. The audience laughs appreciatively, and Adrienne laughs along, her dark hair gleaming under the hot stage lights. Andrea has to admit Adrienne's banter verges on lame. Good thing she has that mouth, those biceps. They make everything she says sound better.

A woman directly behind Andrea lets loose with a whistle.

"Plenty of gym teachers in this crowd," Jordan says. She sees Andrea watching her and smiles, lines etching the corners of her eyes.

At that moment Andrea believes without reservation that Jordan is a gift from the universe. She will never be this certain again.

Something Similar:
In seventh grade, a beautiful Indian girl transfers into
Andrea's class. At the time she's mostly friendless;
Roslyn's father, having taken sabbatical, moved the family to Connecticut for a year. When Sejal, all whooshing
black hair and fragile bony elbows, shows up in school
and against all odds befriends Andrea, even though every
hearted-i-dotting blonde girl in the class wants her,
Andrea knows God is somehow responsible. He's made Andrea
a girl out of earth and bone marrow, someone to meet her
specific needs. Then Andrea sprains her ankle running to
the car with her Keds unlaced and has to miss two weeks
of school, and by the time she returns, Sejal has cut off
her hair and started eating lunch with Tara Sheffield,
the blondest of the blondes. During the time she has Sejal though, Andrea knows she is blessed.

Jordan takes Andrea's hand, "Enjoying the concert?"

Andrea nods, listening to Adrienne and Peter harmonize. She can't bear how alone she feels when, after a chaste squeeze, Jordan releases her hand.

⁓

UNWAVERING SINCE ANDREA turned nineteen, her crush on the lesbian half of Cry Wolf is by far the heartiest she harbors, surfing the crests and hollows of her life for a decade, occasionally drifting, but never capsizing, instead remaining reliably afloat. In contrast, her other crushes tend to time out at just under six months. If she were to write her memoir, which she does on a daily basis but only in her head, she'd credit Cry Wolf with saving her life. Early on, she confesses this to Jordan, a decision she comes to regret.

Jordan's eyes widen. She leans across the wrought iron café table to grasp Andrea's hand.

"Mine too!" she says.

"Cry Wolf Saved My Life," Andrea says, withdrawing her hand to bite her cuticle, "Sounds like the topic of a lesbian talk show."

Jordan sips her lemonade, swirling the glass as if aerating wine. "Kidding aside," she says, "I want to hear about you."

"Well," Andrea backpedals, "they probably didn't actually save my life."

"Let me be the judge."

Andrea thinks of that stupid joke about lesbians: one says to another, "Let me be frank," and the second replies, "No, let me be Frank."

"Tell me," Jordan says as Andrea dithers.

"Okaaaay," she extends the word, buying time. She's no good at anecdotes. Eager to provide essential details, she always starts too far back. She remembers in junior high, Roslyn saying, "Hey, why'd you switch from cornflakes to oatmeal last week?" Andrea's response: "It all started when I was five."

"I guess I was sort of anorexic." Andrea says. This seems a solid entry point.

Jordan gasps so theatrically Andrea thinks maybe Jordan is mocking her.

"Go on," Jordan says when Andrea remains silent, "please."

"I was like that awhile, maybe from fifteen to nineteen."

"That must have been hard."

"I don't know, it wasn't that bad. I mean, it's not like I knew what was happening when I was in it, I just sort of got through. But in my first year of college, my eating got worse, probably because I wasn't ready to be away from home and then—"

Andrea pauses, feeling uncomfortably histrionic.

"You have nothing to be ashamed of, you know." Jordan takes her hand again, this time refusing to let go.

"I'm not—"

"An issue like that," Jordan continues. She shakes her head, the movement releasing her distinctive scent. Andrea inhales, almost closes her eyes. "It just proves how sensitive you are, how much a part of the world. You should be proud, not ashamed."

Bullshit, thinks Andrea. Still, she smiles demurely; the frail Ophelia Jordan's description evokes.

"So your eating got worse," Jordan prompts.

"Plus I was a film major freshman year. I guess I'm mentioning it because I'd planned it since I saw *Some Like it Hot* when I was ten, but turned out I hated the program." Andrea presses a finger to the side of her water glass.

"You were going to tell me about Cry Wolf," Jordan says.

"Right. I also think I had all of these veiled lesbian urges. Not like I had a problem with being gay, but I was scared to admit it to myself. So, long story short, I went to a Cry Wolf concert with my friend Roslyn."

"The one you've known since you were three. What's she like?"

"Smart, determined, she works hard but makes it look easy. Beautiful. Dark hair, but not like mine. When I was a kid I thought she looked like Snow White."

"So you were at the concert?" Jordan says.

"Yeah. Anyway, it was the first time I'd seen them live."

"I'd love to relive my first time. Nothing's ever as good."

"When was that?"

"Eighty-five maybe? They'd just come on the LA scene. In the midst of all these hair bands, suddenly there's this pair of folk singing siblings. No one knew what to make of them, but I loved them right away."

In eighty-five I was in pre-school. Andrea stops herself from saying it, half believing Jordan won't notice their age difference if she swallows the words. She'll learn soon enough that nothing escapes Jordan's observation, certainly nothing as obvious as the nearly two decades separating them. In fact, it's that time which interests Jordan. With Andrea she starts out undeniably ahead.

"I did too. Especially Adrienne." Andrea's face warms, from the memory or the confession, maybe both. "She was up there doing exactly what she wanted, totally true to herself. And all that crazy energy, you know how frenzied she is when she performs."

"Good word."

"There's no way I could have played like that."

"What do you mean?" Jordan's eyes take on a new level of focus.

"I was eating, like, a grape a day. This thing that I started out doing to, I don't know, make me special, in control, whatever, it made me ordinary, incapable of doing anything real with my life."

The sharp lines of Jordan's face regroup, take on the soft look of compassion. *She likes the parts of me that are broken*, Andrea thinks. *She likes them the way a thief likes a loose screen.*

"That's most of it," Andrea watches her hands smooth her skirt. Deep in some mental filing room, her fingers don't look like her own.

"What's the rest?"

"Uh, there's the part about . . . you know."

"Ah, the crush."

"It's embarrassing."

"Hey, it's me."

She's known Jordan for something like three weeks, too brief for such intimate words.

"She exuded this crazy sexuality, totally direct. Not even Roslyn was immune. After the concert ended, in the parking garage, trying to find Roslyn's car, I was thinking it, but she's the one who said it. 'I was really attracted to the woman.' And I was kind of shocked, cause not only is Roslyn straight, she's totally closed-mouthed about that whole thing. Like she dates, but she never discusses her sex life, whereas I'm this open book."

"You are, huh?" Jordan leans back in her chair, hands folded over her belt buckle.

Aware of Jordan's flirtation, Andrea can't quite get there in time. She's stuck a few sentences back, working through Jordan's attraction to her weakness. Information she can't readily catalog, it sets guilt and giddiness circling inside her like sharks.

"So, I agreed with Roslyn. Then she said, 'She has this really masculine energy,' which I guess for Roslyn justified her interest, like if a woman is masculine, being attracted to her isn't quite as gay. But then she said, 'I could never sleep with a woman. Once the clothes come off there's nothing there I want.' And I was quiet because I was thinking, for the first time, really letting myself think, 'There's something there for me.'"

Andrea sits back in her chair, notices she'd shredded her napkin. She holds confetti in her hand. "It sounds phony, but the next day I changed the way I ate, then I changed my major. A few months later I told my parents I was gay."

> ("Phony," a word she can't say without thinking of Holden Caulfield.)
>
> **Other words/associations:**
> "Moses (Moses Moses)"(Charlton Heston/*The Ten Commandments*)
>
> "Elegant."("I think it's wonderful that you're married. I think it's just elegant." Marilyn Monroe/ *The Seven Year Itch*)
>
> Is no thought free from annotation? Is nothing just hers?

"That's incredible. I have goose bumps. Feel them." Jordan puts Andrea's hand on her arm.

"Tell me your story," Andrea says, thinking how a person drawn to weakness lays down her weapons never knowing she has.

"I will someday." Jordan catches their waiter's attention, gestures for the check.

Afterwards, constructing the myth of their origin, Jordan will both celebrate and minimize Cry Wolf's role. She'll wax poetic about the impact the band had on both of their lives, how at different times but in similar ways, through the grace of Cry Wolf, they both got saved. But she'll also claim to have had an eye on Andrea at school for months, say if they hadn't officially met at the concert, they would have met some other perfect way.

This is how Jordan credits their relationship with inevitability: she aligns it to Cry Wolf, a higher power, then breaks from the band like Martin Luther gone his own way. Dazzled by Jordan's flair for the epic, Andrea will come late to the understanding that labeling something destiny does not make it fail-safe. Now though, Andrea has yet to regret her admission, the power she unwittingly places in Jordan's hands.

Andrea's Letter to Adrienne, Age nineteen/The Most
Embarrassing Thing Andrea Owns:

Dear Adrienne,
In the early morning, invariably I am able to compose
the perfect letter. But only in my head. Then I fall
back asleep and wake hours later with no concept of
what seemed so compelling and brilliant to me. I guess
I don't have anything to say that you haven't heard
a thousand times from a thousand different fans, but
since I'm the one saying it, it feels important.
First I want to tell you I think your songwriting is
innovative and your songs so rich that one could fall
between the layers. Although I relate most readily
to Peter's lyrics, I feel more of a kinship with the
emotions that contribute to the driving force behind
your songs. I really admire your guitar style. Did
you take lessons or just pick it up on your own? I've
been a fan for about five years, but I saw you guys
for the first time recently. Since then, I've become
positively rabid in my devotion to you and Peter,

well, mainly you. I couldn't believe how generously
you gave of yourself in concert. And I loved that
thing you said about feminism. I get so angry when
I see how scared people are of that label. I have a
whole involved theory about why, but since I'm trying
to keep this letter short so it has a chance of being
read, I won't go into detail. However, if you're interested, I wrote two massive papers on the subject,
which, with no provocation whatsoever, I hold people
down and force them to read.

The main thing I wanted to tell you is sort of bi-
zarre and definitely really personal, so I hope you
don't think I'm nuts to tell it to a perfect stranger. Don't worry, I don't have some wacky fetish.
The thing is, I've always been pretty certain I was
heterosexual, except maybe for when I was in middle
school, but I was confused about most things then.
I've felt a tug toward some women before, but my
feelings were never strong enough for me to embrace
them and really focus on their significance. But then
I saw your concert; it was as if you were channeling
the music, along with this incredible sensuality, and
both were gushing from your every pore.

You're probably thinking, what am I supposed to
do about the fact that some random Wisconsin girl
has a crush on me? Well you could rescue me from my
humdrum life and let me be your love slave, which
I'd actually really like. Come on, I'm nineteen; a
fifteen-year age difference (or so) isn't that big
a deal. I'm actually sort of serious about this. At
least I could be your friendship slave, but that
doesn't have the same sort of ring to it, does it?
Seriously though, I feel close to you in many ways.
I'm aware this closeness is somewhat of an illusion,
but I want it to be legitimate and reciprocated. Besides being drawn to the person I want you to be, I
want to really know you. I wish I could just meet you
on the street and have no clue who you are so you'd
believe me when I say I'm drawn not to your celebrity

status or "icon-ness" but to you. Of course I realize
the chance of you taking me up on any of the above is
probably zero, so do you think we could correspond?
Short of that I'd love to get one letter from you.
If not that, then an autographed photo? Something?
Thank you so much for reading this. You really mean
a lot to me.

                    Your stalker (Ha ha, just kidding.),
                                        Andrea Wynn

THE FIRST TIME Jordan confesses her feelings for Andrea, she retracts her avowal, and then begins phoning Andrea after Patricia's asleep.

The Criminal Mastermind says she's a night owl: "I just don't have any other time to myself."

As far as Andrea can tell, Jordan's days consist of driving around Los Angeles. In addition to doing Patricia's books, she's picked up a job selling hair products to salons, is slowly transitioning out of her work at the church. Surely that leaves time before the sun sets to make a call. Also the term "night owl" evokes a midnight stamp collector, pipe brimming with fragrant tobacco; an old lady sipping Ovaltine. Jordan's nocturnal nature is more werewolf than stamp collector. But Andrea demands no explanation. She smiles into her pillow, assures Jordan she wasn't really asleep.

Looking back, Andrea stacks Jordan's late night calls under the heading, "strategic" rather than "coincidental." She's heard waking a hostage repeatedly is one of the most effective forms of brainwashing.

"I'm walking Sammie," Jordan says, or "I ran to the market for some wine," or sometimes, giddy, "I just had to get away."

Andrea clutches her phone tight to her ear; Jordan's every word an iridescent marble dropped into night's velvet bag. Once, Jordan sighs and Andrea shivers at the sound, chiding herself for her amplified response. It reminds her of when she first came out, how she languished in her dorm playing Cry Wolf songs, intent on hearing the squeak of guitar strings, every intake of Adrienne's breath.

"I used to do the same thing with David Cassidy," Jordan says when Andrea tells her; "I had such a crush on him when I was a kid. Heel, Sammie. Hang on a second, she sees another dog."

Andrea drifts, listening to the underwater sounds of a dog barking, Jordan and a stranger exchanging muffled words.

"So when you listen to Adrienne's fingers on her guitar, do you imagine how they look?"

"What?" Andrea's not sure from where Jordan's voice summons her, but she remembers popcorn and a Steve Martin impersonator, someone she instinctively knew wasn't Steve himself.

"Well, they're probably calloused from playing, and I'm sure they're really strong. And of course the muscles in her forearms, they way they ripple under her skin. Do you picture all that?"

"I guess so." At the time, Andrea views Jordan's support of her crush in contrast to her former girlfriend Linda's defensive response. A few months into their relationship, Linda pokes Andrea awake to tell her, "I had a dream we went to see *Rent* with that girl from Cry Wolf. The seats were made of dentures and you said you were in love with her.'"

"What did you say?" Andrea asks, taking shameful pleasure in her crush's power to penetrate the reaches of Linda's unconscious mind.

Linda taps her squawking alarm clock into silence.

"I said, 'Well, that's not obvious or anything.'"

"You've seen her face when she's playing," Jordan continues, her voice a low drawl. "Really beating at her guitar." She waits and Andrea hears a car honk in the background. "Intense, right?"

Andrea comes to her lesbianism by way of Women's Studies

and Madison, Wisconsin; she knows only from thick sweaters and androgyny, is first vexed and later exhilarated as the hidden complexities of gender expression and attraction are slowly revealed. With no exposure to the lightly penciled butch/femme rules, Andrea thinks maybe Jordan has a crush on Adrienne. She has no idea that would be like Dan Rather and Tom Brokaw admitting a mutual attraction, Derrek Lee and Derek Jeter falling hopelessly in love.

"They way she bites her lower lip, kind of juts her chin, jerks her hand along the neck of her guitar? Quit it, Sammie. Don't you think she almost looks like she's going to come?"

Naiveté no excuse, Andrea should suspect Jordan intends to arouse.

"I hadn't really thought about it," she lies.

"I don't believe that for a minute," Jordan murmurs. The next night she doesn't bother to say hello.

"Imagine you wander backstage after a concert and you see her at the end of a long dingy hall. Actually at first you don't know it's her, you think it's some guy, a security guard maybe. But as you get closer you recognize her and she spots you too. She looks pissed. Maybe the concert didn't go well. She's drinking a Corona and you can see beads of moisture glistening on the bottle's long neck. She tips her head back to take a sip and you watch her throat contract.

"All of a sudden you feel uneasy but you don't know why. You start to walk past her, continue down the hall. But she stops you. She says 'Wait.' No, what she really says is 'Where do you think you're going?' You don't know how to answer, so you shrug, and she says 'Come here.' By the way she says it, you can tell she's well past her first beer.

"You step toward her even though you think maybe you shouldn't. She runs the bottle down your leg, up under your skirt, all the time she's looking you dead in the eye. You feel the bottle against your inner thigh. By the way, you're not wearing any underwear. You know where the bottle's headed. You know what she wants to do."

Abruptly Jordan stops talking and Andrea tenses, thinking Jordan's heard her breathing grow strained.

"That's okay Camille," Jordan's cheer-infused voice bursts against her ear, "I was up anyway, I don't mind you calling. I'll make a copy first thing in the morning. You have a good night." The phone clicks and Jordan is gone.

"AND THIS TURNS you *on*?" Obviously Roslyn responds cuttingly when Andrea describes Jordan's monologue. Doesn't really describe it, makes distant circles around what Jordan actually says.

"I'm aware it sounds weird." Andrea drops her head to her knees and picks at her toenail polish.

"Weird doesn't begin to cover it. It's like some lesbian joke. I'm waiting for the punch line."

"It's nice to have a dependable source of derision." Andrea lodges her cell phone between her cheek and her shoulder and gathers her textbooks. A year in LA and she still forgets how abruptly the temperature changes when the sun begins to set.

"I know, then you brought yourself to orgasm by rubbing against a photo of KD Lang."

"That's A-plus material you got there, Bronstein. Forget law school, you gotta take that shit on the road."

"Hang on a sec, my roommate just walked in wearing a bolo tie; I think I'm gonna come!"

"I'm hanging up now." Andrea slings her messenger bag over her shoulder and heads across the quad. When she gets home she finds an e-mail from Roslyn.

You gotta watch what you admit to people. Some things aren't meant to be shared.

In almost twenty years of friendship, it's the closest Roslyn's ever come to an apology.

Andrea has a secret about the lines and charts that structure her days. Actually it's worn and universal, hardly a secret at all. She's in the company of addicts and lab rats, anyone who presses a bar for a pellet; still she pretends she's unique. As much as her compulsion to comment and quantify keeps her safe, she's realizing it also confines her. Like anything raised in captivity, she notes her cage's dimensions only in freedom's glare. The Criminal Mastermind runs two fingers over Andrea's throat, tells her she's a good girl, and the words and definitions flee like vampires from sunlight. She feels skinned, some outer layer cast off. Before Jordan, she has no idea her mind is a tightfisted lock, sex a sly, determined key. It isn't like this with her first girlfriend, Linda; she doesn't imagine it will be with anyone else. She can't lose this feeling. Although a fresh acquisition, it seems an elemental piece of herself.

⌒

JORDAN FIRST FUCKS her two months after they meet at the Cry Wolf concert; she takes her time. Although Andrea already suspects Jordan knows a thing or two about infidelity, she accepts Jordan's claim to be tormented—a by and large faithful partner, struck down just this once by unexpected love. Later she'll realize Jordan's anguished reluctance is manufactured for anticipation's sake. By the time Jordan calls Andrea from the base of her stairwell, Andrea has twice given up; she's cried more than once. When her cell phone rings, Andrea shakes her purse out to find it, heart accelerating.

"Hey," says Jordan when Andrea answers. "The thing is, I'm outside."

Later, breath still jagged, Jordan's fingers wound through her hair, Andrea sees herself, age eight, a Mr. Rogers album jacket tucked under her pillow.

Each night she reaches for the record cover, anxious to touch an object redolent of day, not night. Slumber at a stubborn distance, she holds the glossy square, tracing Mr. Roger's sympathetic face with a single halting finger. Down the hall, her father coughs. In the morning Andrea's mother will help with the difficult parts of dressing: pull up her tights and plait her hair. She'll dress the record too, slide it smoothly back inside its sleeve, placing it on the shelf between *The Care Bears' Christmas* and Burl Ives. Andrea knows this will happen because it happens every morning, but marooned in her room, daytime seems like a fairy tale, an infrequent visitor, *Brigadoon*. Staring directly into Mr. Roger's glossy eyes, Andrea thinks how lucky married people are; no one expects them to sleep alone. She likes how it feels to be close to his picture, which seems both him and not. She's connected to Mr. Rogers, but also safe and out of reach.

Once, her mother asks Andrea why she tucks Mr. Rogers under her pillow before bed. Andrea hesitates, unsure how to match words to feelings.

"Because," she starts, then stops, popping a finger in her mouth.

There are more feelings than there are words to describe them, that's what she remembers thinking, although when she looks at six-year-olds now, she can't imagine they have such intricate thoughts.

"You're a big first grader," her mother reminds her, gently guiding Andrea's hand away from her mouth. "Remember, what happens if you stop sucking your fingers?"

"I get to pick out whatever nail polish I want as long as it's not too dark," Andrea recites.

"That's right. Were you ready to answer my question?"

Andrea twists the hem of her skirt, sifting through thoughts. She wants to describe to her mother how she feels awed by Mr. Rogers but also known.

"Andrea?"

"He's a good man." Andrea says.

Her mother smiles in a way not quite happy, but pats Andrea's head. The answer's inaccuracy troubles Andrea, but it's all she can think to say.

Years after the event, but hours before the memory's appearance, lying beneath Jordan, Andrea feels for once fully present. She isn't thinking about Mr. Rogers, she isn't thinking about anything, an incalculable relief. Riveted in the moment, she feels free of her inherent running commentary.

Straddling Andrea, Jordan comes in her jeans minutes after she walks through the door.

"If I were a guy I guess we'd have a problem," she says, then reaches for Andrea's T-shirt, peels it centimeter by centimeter away from her skin.

"There's nothing you'd say no to." Jordan's lips brush Andrea's ear with each word. Andrea goes still, lust like an arrow arching through her to meet its mark.

"Spread your legs," Jordan whispers. She pins Andrea's wrists to her sides, eases her mouth slowly to rest between Andrea's legs, her warm breath the only thing to touch Andrea for an excruciatingly long time.

Reasons Andrea Might Believe in God:

1. The Internet. It's the collective unconscious made manifest; Carl Jung meets Philip K. Dick.

2. Milk Ducts

3. Minor Keys

4. The Mayans

5. According to an NPR expert, beavers build dams in response to the sound of water. How do they translate aural event to visual reality? How do they know a dam is required?

6. Startling fact: some people want to climb on top of other people, insert anything they can inside. Others have no interest. They prefer to lie helpless beneath; they only want to be filled. No matter the number of tops and bottoms in the world may not find their peg in the hole corollary; that would prove God's active involvement, determinism an unpleasant by-product. The God in whom Andrea might believe does not turn a key in our backs, set us on a skittery mechanical course toward our intended. But for those who crave a complementary counterpart, God certainly provides.

Making God complicit in Andrea's evolving sexual philosophy seems if not immoral at least improper, like inviting her grandmother to a drag show. However, born with an echoing interior, Andrea has few choices. She can find religion or court obesity; she can label her crisis existential or call it hunger or sexual desire. Of course, identifying the source of her malaise won't change the fact that her default state remains one of lack. Bottom line, something inside her is absent.

Jordan finds fulfillment (Andrea ponders the word's etymology. As a whole it means contentment. Is it coincidence that the word at its center is "fill?") in Church and through sex. Member of a liberal Pasadena congregation, Jordan has no problem conflating the two. Early in their relationship's first phase, before Jordan embezzles sufficient church funds to trigger a crisis of faith, she woos Andrea with quotes from poets and ecclesiastic wordsmiths, Thomas Merton and the like. Jordan especially adores a certain line of Jeanette Winterson's.

"Sex," Jordan says, leaning back on a pillow or, if they've ended up on the floor as is common, possibly a shoe, "lifts you out of yourself more cleanly than anything divine."

Other Favorites:
"All concepts of God are like a jar we break."
(Saint Teresa of Avila)

"I would like to be the air that inhabits you for a moment only. I would like to be that unnoticed and that necessary." (Margaret Atwood)

"If you bring forth what is within you, what you bring forth will save you. If you do not bring forth what is within you, what you do not bring forth will destroy you." (Gospel of Thomas, verse 70)

"Jeanette Winterson?" Roslyn says when Andrea regurgitates the quote. "She's like the love child of Anne Lamott and Woody Allen."

Although she worries she's betraying Jordan, Andrea laughs and agrees.

Andrea knows enough to nod solemnly, possibly say something astute or awed, never let herself fall asleep. The price of sex with Jordan is her post-coital proselytizing—one of the prices anyway. There are other, steeper fees, all of which Andrea is willing to pay. But the topic, Jordan's effortless acceptance of sex as a spiritual move, Andrea thinks somehow a cop-out.

Still, no star-pricked sky, no impassioned sermon, no ocean at dawn makes a sweet home inside her. The only sure thing to draw goose bumps to her skin is the perfect complexity of Jordan's protrusions, her own indentations, how they align. There may have been one set of footprints when Jesus carried her, but she feels for the first time one solid person when Jordan slides her fingers inside.

Smack in the middle of their relationship's second run, Andrea isn't sure when she first heard the word "bottom," when its accuracy became impossible to dismiss. As a term of identity, it seems valid in the way "lesbian" never for a minute felt. She assumes Jordan the source. Over time and geography and arrivals and departures she gives Andrea a greater understanding of herself than Andrea cares to admit. Either that or she plants insights inside Andrea then feigns discovery, cooing over personalized buried treasure, things only she requires.

Jordan initially volunteers "top" as a preferable alternative to "butch," a word that seems to both tempt and humiliate her. While Andrea doesn't immediately warm to its inverse equivalent, when Roslyn calls she takes the term on a test-drive. She's not sure what exactly she says. Most likely she unfurls her newfound identity like an accidental banner, presents it with the fake-carelessness of a Women's Studies major (*Well, as a newly identified bottom, I feel America's health care system leaves much to be desired*).

Roslyn's lack of response makes Andrea assume the call has dropped. Her reception throughout her Westwood apartment back then is spotty at best. She repeats "Hello" three times into the cell phone silence; a live silence with no relationship to any other, not a lull in conversation, not the hiss of a record before the music starts.

"Half the women who want to buy our NCLEX course are from the Philippines," Roslyn says finally. "What do you think that means?"

Andrea knows Roslyn is working part-time to subsidize law school. Knows she's selling test prep to foreign medical graduates, has an idea what NCLEX is, something to do with nursing or pharmacy, one of the two. She can't ask Roslyn to clarify, because while she doesn't remember the answer, she's certain she's asked the question before.

"The other half," Roslyn continues, "are from some tiny part of

Africa where everyone's last name begins with "Nk."Their first names are all Nannette; it's like their village was founded by Kurt Weil."

"Are you ignoring me?" Andrea asks.

"Actually I'm hanging up on you. My supervisor just got back from lunch."

"Bottom sounds so lowly," Andrea tells Jordan in Chicago, still struggling with the term. "Like I'm subordinate."

"You're not subordinate. Go grab me a Diet Coke." Jordan smirks and kicks her feet up on the coffee table, knocking a half-eaten Twinkie and a Phillips-head screwdriver to the floor.

"The way we are sexually, doesn't it affect your opinion of me?"

"Well, yeah." Jordan flashes a thumbs up. "High marks," she says.

"But how can you respect me when I let you, you know."

"What do you let me do?"

"This isn't foreplay!" Andrea actually stamps her foot.

"Maybe not to you."

"Can't you see how it's scary?" Wanting Jordan to intercept her, Andrea moves toward the front door.

"Hey," Jordan cheetah-jumps over the coffee table, catches Andrea's arm.

"It scares me too sometimes," Jordan cups her chin. "What goes down between us."

"Whatever," Andrea jerks her head back, but Jordan keeps hold of her face. "You've been who you are your whole life; I'm sure this is nothing new for you."

"You on your back telling me anything I do is okay?" Jordan's grip tightens.

"I hate how that sounds."

"I've never once had what we have. It's new to me too." Jordan releases Andrea, returns to her seat. "Now quit pretending you're going somewhere."

"You're sure you don't think less of me?"

"I think more of you. Do you know how much power there is in letting go?"

Andrea studies the dips and planes of Jordan's face. "I'm whole without you," she says feebly.

"Sure you are, but it's hard work isn't it? Come sit by me."

Jordan leans back on the leather couch she bought when she first moved into Andrea's Chicago apartment, guides Andrea's head into her lap. Jordan's tender expression should ease Andrea, but all Andrea can think about is Jordan's chin. Head bent, Jordan's chin dissolves, absorbed by the thin pleats of skin at her neck. From this angle Jordan doesn't look dashing or potent, just old.

ANDREA DOESN'T FOR a minute believe the thrall in which Jordan keeps her exists relative to anything else. Still, the amiability of her sex life with Linda might predicate how crazed with lust Jordan makes her feel. Both earnest Women's Studies majors, Andrea and Linda touch each other carefully, Linda keeping meticulous score of how many orgasms they each have. After Andrea goes down on Linda, Linda thanks her politely, then plops herself between Andrea's legs. "Scootch up," she says. Their mouths and hands have no relation to Bogart and Bergman, no connection to history or literary passion or anything greater than themselves.

Roslyn sums up Andrea's dissatisfaction neatly, ice rattling in her glass, "The problem with Linda was she respected you. When you were eleven you used to tie yourself up with the laces of your Keds. You don't give a shit about respect."

Andrea has no word to describe sex with Jordan; in fact, the act empties her of words. Their connection has little to do with Andrea's level of experience; it's about a third thing they create when only the two of them are present.

JORDAN'S PREOCCUPATION WITH menstrual blood takes getting used to.

"Trust me, I'll love it," Jordan says when Andrea resists.

"But why?" Andrea asks, thinking, *Does that mean I'll have to love doing that to you?*

"Uh, because I'm a lesbian. Are you?"

Andrea turns her face to the window, sees black outlines of palm trees against pale morning sky. They've been sleeping together two and a half weeks now, each encounter an exchange, Andrea parceling out bits of her soul to Jordan—who knows what she's getting in return?

"Come on, it'll be you, only warmer and wetter." Jordan skins off Andrea's panties and with something like greed, eases open Andrea's legs.

Andrea holds her breath, tries not to think about her underwear, on the floor in a shaft of streetlight. She's pretty sure they're stained.

```
Regrettable Facts:

  Barring famine or tapeworm, Andrea will never be a
  size two.

  No matter her age, whenever she ascends from any
  basement, she'll always have the urge to run.

  Without sex with Jordan to release her, it's
  likely she'll die alone here, caught inside.
```

THERE'S A CRY Wolf fan couple Jordan loathes, a ridiculous puppy dog pair.

"They met through an online fan forum," she tells Andrea. "At every concert, they wave this banner with a timeline relating important events in their relationship to Cry Wolf's career highlights. If you end up behind them, you're fucked."

"Self-indulgent." Andrea uses thumb and forefinger to force her eyes open, imagining she's the kid in *A Clockwork Orange*. She has a nine AM meeting with her advisor tomorrow, but no way will she kick Jordan out.

"I've heard them at the tour bus. They must've told Adrienne their story fifty times. You and I met through Cry Wolf too, but I'm not gonna scrapbook about it." Jordan plays with yesterday's newspaper, making rapid tucks and folds.

Andrea yawns; she can't help it.

"Am I boring you?" Jordan asks, voice disproportionately cold.

"Of course not." Andrea's pulse skitters against her neck. She thinks how Jordan kissed her for seven solid minutes when she arrived. She knows because when the kiss started, she happened to look at the clock.

"I should go." Jordan slaps the triangle of newspaper on the kitchen table and grabs her jeans from the floor.

"Home?" Andrea watches Jordan button her pants. This is maybe the fifth time she's offended Jordan without meaning to and they've only been sleeping together five weeks.

"Yeah." Jordan bends, scooping up her car keys and some change.

"When will I see you?" Andrea tugs her nightshirt over her head, then, still feeling exposed, grabs her running shorts from the hamper.

"I'll call you." Jordan opens the front door.

"When?" Aside from Jordan showing up late at night to fuck her, they haven't established much of a routine. Suddenly afraid she'll never see Jordan again, Andrea feels tears pooling in her eyes.

"Hey, what are those for?" Jordan strokes her knuckles across Andrea's cheek.

"What if you never come back?"

"You think I could stay away?" Holding Andrea's face in her hands, Jordan stares so hard at Andrea she has to look at the floor.

"I'm sorry, rough week. Patricia's having money problems at the gallery, so she's on my case about every little thing. Plus I had one of my seizures. Nothing to worry about; it's my first in almost a year."

"A seizure?"

"They're kind of interesting, actually. I had one on my motorcycle once, though. Not something I'd recommend."

"What did you do?" Andrea pictures Jordan helpless, motorcycle skidding through gravel and stones.

"Pulled over when I had the memory. Woke up under my bike." Jordan takes a tin of Altoids from her pocket, slips one into her mouth.

"Were you okay?" *Dashing and tragic*, Andrea thinks. *So much to contend with, I'd be temperamental too.*

"Sure, but the guy who found me called the cops."

"Did you go to the hospital?" Andrea pictures herself finding Jordan, instantly reverses the vision; imagines she's had the seizure and Jordan's swooped down to rescue her.

"Couldn't take the chance. I hopped on my bike and high-tailed it out of there."

"Why?"

"No insurance." Jordan crunches into the Altoid. Andrea can smell peppermint from two feet away.

"You can't drive without insurance." In retrospect, Andrea views the disclosure as watershed, a red flag she spotted instantly, thereafter observing Jordan from a more distant point.

"Sure you can." Jordan hands her an Altoid. "Try one. I'm obsessed."

Jordan's Top Three Flavors:

    Mint

    Butter

    Artificial smoke

"Do you know what causes them?" Though she hates mint, it never occurs to Andrea to refuse. She chews and swallows. In truth, Jordan's disclosure intrigues her, no matter what she later wants to think.

"Someone once told me that coke altered my brain chemistry." Jordan looks the way she does whenever her history with cocaine comes up, like a kid who got into her mother's makeup, half guilty, half proud.

"They say strobe lights trigger seizures. You should always be careful. You know, at plays or at clubs."

"And I could get hit by a bus when I walk out this door." Jordan says, touching Andrea's cheek. "Anything is possible. That's what's so great. You look exhausted. Sleep late tomorrow. I'll call you at noon."

"Promise?"

"Yeah." Andrea relaxes as Jordan kisses her. Whatever was wrong now isn't. Andrea knows if she opened her eyes she'd look straight into Jordan's; she never shuts them when they kiss. She claims she doesn't want to miss a second of Andrea, the romance of the statement almost mitigating the experience, but not quite. Andrea always feels she's kissing in a combat zone, kissing a bald eagle or a tiger crouched in a tree [Figure 5].

After Jordan leaves, Andrea turns off the light in the living room, fills a glass with water at the kitchen sink. Sipping, she straightens the pile of notebooks and folders on the table, gathers the papers that fell to the floor when they fucked. In the middle of the table she sees Jordan's discarded newspaper. She's made a perfect paper hat.

⌒

I'VE NEVER DONE this before," Jordan tells her late in the first year of their affair. She's lounging on Andrea's floor in Westwood, passing an anatomically correct dildo from hand to hand.

I don't believe you, thinks Andrea. "Oh," is what she says.

"You don't believe me, do you?"

"I mean, you've had like a billion partners, it seems weird this hasn't come up." The amount of energy Andrea expends restraining herself from saying anything moderately offensive to Jordan causes her to say something incredibly offensive one time in ten. Luckily Andrea's more blatant lapses support Jordan's perception of Andrea as clumsy and genuine, and thus generally strike Jordan as sweet.

"That's right; you'd think one of the legions of women I've been with would have made a request." Jordan smirks, thwacks the dildo against her palm. "Have you used one?"

Andrea hesitates. She regrets every sexual tidbit Jordan coaxes her to reveal. She can't predict what will later enrage Jordan, no matter how compassionate she initially appears. Once, over ice cream, Jordan asks Andrea if she's thinking of her high school boyfriend because she knows he took Andrea for ice cream on their first date.

"No," Andrea answers truthfully. She's actually been thinking about how much she liked to step on ants as a child.

"Could have fooled me," Jordan spits. "You're like all women, always thinking of cock."

"I tried using a dildo one-time," Andrea says finally. "It didn't go well."

"With whatshername?" Jordan refuses to admit she knows Linda's name.

"Linda?"

"The fat one," Jordan confirms.

"Yeah."

Linda isn't the least bit fat, and Jordan knows it, she's seen pictures; still Andrea lets her comment slide. "We didn't know what we were doing and I wasn't turned on."

"Patricia used to beg me to buy one and fuck her with it." Jordan waits to see how Andrea responds.

"Why didn't you?" Andrea asks, playing with a loose thread on her couch.

"I guess I didn't feel safe. I just figured she wished I was a man. You know her history."

"Just men, right?"

"But you're my little virgin, aren't you? You'll only be thinking about me."

"I always am," Andrea says, and means it. Her low belly warms as if tethered to Jordan's slow-creeping smile.

⌒

CLICHÉS ARE CLICHÉS for a reason, Jordan sometimes says to justify her racism, not in relation to sex. But Andrea finds the explanation useful in illuminating her sudden affinity for items on display in West Hollywood storefronts, ball gags and the like. She's embarrassed to be drawn to these tired tropes. Still, she finds herself craving the feel of metal binding her wrists, the lightning sensation of a thin strip of leather licking her back. It's not that their sex life necessitates executioner masks and leg restraints, silver necklaces with the word "slave" brushing the indentation at the base of one's throat. But sex with Jordan suggests the accoutrements even in their absence, the dynamic between the two of them unmistakable, stark.

The first time Jordan spanks her doesn't compare to the first time she strikes Andrea full in the face. By then they've been sleeping together for over a year. Jordan has reserved a room at The Standard Hotel, the perfect place to celebrate anything illegitimate, a business deal, an affair.

Andrea feels cowed by the hot pink-infused lobby, the Kate Moss clone working the front desk. She's out of place in her tank top and nondescript sandals. Surely this establishment calls for cowboy boots, numerous necklaces, a small dog in a large purse.

Everything in their room is sleek and low to the ground, 1970s chic. Jordan taps the sheer glass shower stall, indicates the pair of flat, carpeted stairs leading up to the bed.

"When we move in together, we gotta get a place like this!"

The first night they fuck for hours, until all Andrea, aching and hungry, can think of are different kinds of meat. At two AM they sprawl on the bed eating cold Thai food, flat slippery noodles, scallions and thin rectangles of beef. Jordan has rented a DVD player and brought along a copy of her favorite movie.

"It's called *Pillow Talk*," Jordan says when she slips it into the player, "with Rock Hudson and Doris Day."

Andrea knows at some point before the next thing she remembers, the sun rises and sets. However, in her mind, the two AM movie dissolves into late the next night, Madonna's new album on endless repeat. Jordan keeps getting up to skip past the first song.

"I couldn't fuck you while Madonna was rapping about lattes," she explains later.

The way Andrea remembers it, Jordan sports a lime green dildo, impossible because all Jordan's cocks are flesh-toned. True, one of them is chocolate brown; that's something else altogether, though. Aside from her penchant for racial role-play, authenticity is Jordan's primary concern. Anything patterned or shaped like a dolphin never makes the cut.

"Keep that lesbian shit away from me," she says.

Andrea doesn't know why she thinks the dildo Jordan uses that night is green, the color of the one she and Linda shared. She's confident all related memories are accurate, to this day, clear and precise; still what does it mean that a vision of something that never happened bounds happily alongside them, tongue lolling, masquerading as truth?

Here's what's real, what doesn't fade with time: Jordan, solid above her, cock plunged inside Andrea, fingers in her mouth, then rearing back, eyes on Andrea's, her arm raised to strike. When Jordan's open palm makes contact, Andrea's both solidly anchored in her body and floating deliriously above. Her face explodes with sensation: numbness follows heat follows pain. Her body responds instinctively to some clarion call. Instantly she knows she'll do anything to recapture this feeling, anything Jordan tells her, anything to make her stay. At home the next day she touches a bruise as she showers. The light ache tugs her back to the moment the slap landed, evokes the sensation of almost being somewhere, losing where she's been.

An Abbreviated Register of Andrea's Celebrity Crushes (In Order of Appearance):

LeVar Burton

Tony Danza and Alyssa Milano (Andrea loves them both so much that despite the incestuous implications, she sort of wants them to hook up.)

Katharine Hepburn

Not even one of The New Kids on the Block

Steve Martin (It all starts when Andrea dreams she's his personal assistant. She shows up for the interview in a red silk pencil skirt, and right away his daughter doesn't trust Andrea. She gives Andrea a tour of the property anyway, because Steve is enamored with Andrea, so what can she do?)

David Duchovny and Gillian Anderson

Melissa Etheridge, Ellen DeGeneres, Al Pacino, and Gina Gershon (All in rapid succession, right before discovering she's queer. In its own way each of the four makes total sense.)

Although Andrea still recalls every twerpy boy-in-her-class crush, one or two per year until age eighteen, after coming out the list bores her. It seems irrelevant to the person, the *queer person*, she's become. But of course that's inaccurate. Worse than inaccurate, it's revisionist, superficial, an easy way out.

Q. Why superficial to dismiss the boy crushes?
A. That they don't relate to her current sexual identity doesn't render them meaningless. Why should
her present self be realer than a self gone by?
She lives inside who she is now, but who she was
lives inside of her.

~

ANDREA HAS MEMORIZED Jordan and Patricia's address, type-written on a bill on the floor of Patricia's car. She's kidding herself to believe restraint keeps her from spying sooner. If Jordan carried a driver's license, Andrea would have made note of her address long ago. (Why Jordan has no license is a question Andrea knows better than to ask.) The mail on the floor is irresistible. Committing the address to memory takes less than a minute; she's finished and front-facing by the time Jordan returns to the car. From there, a half hour drive to Pasadena later that week is nothing; Andrea concentrates on the mountains, scarcely thinks as she drives.

Now, parked one street over from Jordan and Patricia's, Andrea is surprised by how normal the area appears. Upper class normal. Odd considering Jordan's told her she and Patricia rent their house for eight hundred dollars a month. The vast lush lawns, the upscale shops, the proximity to Caltech—this is not an eight-hundred-dollar-a-month area. Maybe Jordan has one of those out-of-touch landlords who inherited the property from an estranged relative. She's an environmental lawyer or she runs a nonprofit. Making money isn't her priority; she never bothered to research how much she could charge.

Andrea slouches in her seat. She's wearing sunglasses. She thought about wearing a wig. Now that she's here she doesn't know what to do. Glancing at her left side-view mirror, she instantly suffuses with sweat. Behind, a tall, horsey woman approaches; naturally cool, fresh like a crisp-leafed plant, or a slim, elegant tree. She wears loose denim shorts belted low on her hips, a worn gray T-shirt, and soft brown sandals. Her long golden-blonde hair is woven into a braid.

A young Candice Bergen, Andrea decides, Heidi Klum, Christie Brinkley, someone WASPy and effortless whose cheekbones have launched a thousand ships. No matter Andrea herself is Christian. Her Christianity came by way of Italy and Poland; Ellis Island bullies changed her grandfather's name.

Andrea pictures a sleep-away camp scenario, her grand father vs. the cool kid in the top bunk.

"Wisnoozki? I can't pronounce that; from now on I'm calling you Wynn!"

Uncertain whether to be flattered or offended, her grandfather backs away twirling his lanyard.

This woman, on the other hand, her ancestors skated right through.

An old German Shepherd mix lopes beside the woman, tethered by a battered leather leash.

The dog probably shops the Sundance Catalog, Andrea thinks. She's going to have to wring out everything she's wearing, also possibly her hands.

With each step the woman takes toward her, Andrea feels herself grow swarthier, somehow nameless, indistinct. The woman's alongside her car now, and Andrea notes the gold cross sparkling at her throat. No way this isn't Patricia; still, she has to know for sure.

"Excuse me." Andrea's voice sounds out of practice.

"Can I help you?" The woman pauses, a pleasant look settling on her face.

Andrea has a positive ID now; she recognizes Patricia's voice from messages Jordan's scowled and played her. "This is what I have to put up with," she says.

"Do you need directions?" Patricia asks, giving Andrea a perfect pretext.

"Uh, I'm sure it's right around here, the Caltech campus? Do you know what street it's on?"

Patricia must answer, her lips definitely move. Andrea misses what she says though. The next thing she knows she's parked in a driveway several blocks over. She hopes she went in the direction Patricia indicated—no reason to arouse more suspicion than she may inadvertently have. Andrea works to calm her breathing; there are better places to pass out.

Why All Her Crushes Are Relevant:
They ease her as sex does. Running a finger along a face in a yearbook, or a glossy celebrity cheek, she feels gloriously outside of herself. They give her something she lacks: a direction in which to waft her needs.

⌒

"PATRICIA'S EX-FIANCÉ WAS a black man," Jordan tells Andrea. "Our first two Valentine's Days together she insisted on sending him a card."

Andrea and Jordan have been fucking for almost a year now. The parts of Andrea's life that don't involve sex with Jordan stand frozen as Andrea pulls down a long twisted driveway. They wave hazily from behind a thick pane of glass.

"She said it made her sad to think of him lonely."

Sometimes she can't even concentrate on Jordan; she's preoccupied remembering her rather than focused on the live moment.

"That's nice of Patricia, I guess." Bottom line, sex with Jordan consumes Andrea, everything unrelated seems a lie.

Jordan's lips tighten which means she's narrowing her eyes which are hidden behind her sunglasses.

"You'd hate black cock, you know."

"Now you tell me." Jordan never responds well to sarcasm, but sometimes a little bit of Roslyn falls out of Andrea's mouth.

"I'm just saying. You're afraid of snakes, aren't you?"

"Yeah." Andrea checks out Jordan's profile, sharp and stoic as something carved in stone.

"That's what black cock looks like, snaky." Jordan wiggles a finger.

"How do you know?"

"How do you think I know?"

"You only slept with those five guys."

Andrea has memorized Jordan's male conquests. Not just as a means of protection, but because it turns her on.

"Which five?"

"Your softball coach, Doug from high school, that guy you slept with because Tess did, that actor you met when you were a gofer, and your friend, David." In neat chronological order, Andrea offers up her information.

"You sure do listen, huh?"

Andrea flexes her toes in her Converse, trying to warm them.

"I may have underestimated slightly." Jordan tilts her head back against the cement wall behind them.

They are the first two of a long line of fans blocking the entrance to the San Francisco post office. Cry Wolf has a two-night gig at The Fillmore, one door down. Determined to be first in line, Jordan's been in her spot since three AM. Andrea joined her at seven. At ten AM, other less crazed fans began to arrive. By two PM, countless irate post office patrons have tripped over Andrea, and the line for the concert stretches to the Kentucky Fried Chicken halfway down the block.

Jordan is characteristically rude to the people who step on them, vigorously attentive to those in line.

"You never know when we might need a favor," she whispers to Andrea, and laughs heartily when a muscular woman in a navy camping chair tells curious passersby they are awaiting the release of a new postage stamp.

"John Denver," the woman tells certain people, "Marilyn Manson," she sometimes says.

"Underestimated how?" Andrea shifts uncomfortably on the two-person camping couch she and Jordan share.

"Maybe I slept with a few more than five," Jordan says in her I-dare-you-to judge-me voice, "most of them when I was doing cocaine."

Andrea focuses on the first part of Jordan's sentence. "How many more?"

"I'm really not sure."

"How is that possible?"

"The more experiences you have the fewer you remember. You'll understand that when you get to be my age."

"It's not like you're eighty!"

"And what are you going to do when I am?"

"You must have some idea how many."

Jordan scans the sky where it peeks from behind clusters of buildings.

"I hope the storm holds off till after they open the doors."

"Can't you just estimate?"

"Jesus, babe, I don't know, more than fifteen less than thirty?"

"But you knew you liked women from the time you were fourteen."

"Yeah but, you know, women are complicated. Sometimes you just wanna fuck."

There's nothing Jordan likes more than a line buddy, a short-term acquaintance she can dazzle and promise to keep in touch with before never making contact again. Today she's targeted Jan. If Jan were anything short of Harvey Keitel-butch Andrea would be on red alert, like at the last show when she came back from a coffee run to find Jordan chatting up an eight-foot-tall blonde. Thankfully, Jan's voice grits under two decades of cigarette smoke. Her gut has its own address. She's Andrea's type, not Jordan's: she's old and seriously flawed.

When Jan lumbers off to buy smokes, Jordan pinches Andrea's cheek like an Italian grandmother gone horribly wrong.

"She's got something, huh?"

"What do you mean?"

"Hey, I'm not threatened." Jordan spreads her hands. "She's an old bruiser. I bet she'd like a piece of you."

Before Andrea met Jordan she can't ever remember blushing. Now she spends half her time baboon-ass red.

"You'd like that wouldn't you?" Jordan cocks her head.

"What about Sarabeth?" Andrea glances at Jan's nondescript girlfriend who's been quietly knitting for most of the day.

"Who?"

"The girlfriend, or didn't you notice?"

"What about her?"

"Like, the fact of her existence, for one."

"Meaningless." Jordan dismisses Sarabeth as easy as sweeping away crumbs.

"Meaningless?"

Meaningless Things (According to Jordan):

    Time

    Recipes

    Small dogs ("rats on a string," she calls them)

```
A place for everything and everything in its place
Annual dental appointments
Later: Andrea's MA
```

Andrea can't help but admire the power implicit in Jordan's denial of any person or rule for which she finds no immediate use. Her intolerance for protocol doesn't bode well for Andrea in the long run; just now it's exactly what Andrea craves.

"You think Jan wouldn't throw her over in a second for a chance at you?"

"I have no idea." Blushing again, Andrea examines her knees.

"I talked to Jan while you and whatshername were in the bathroom." Jordan rummages in her backpack for her water bottle. "Want a sip?"

"What do you mean, you talked to her?" Andrea shakes her head.

"I asked her what the deal was with her and the girlfriend. I didn't exactly say she could do better, but hey, we all know it's true."

The second time they're together Andrea fears the ease with which Jordan separates people from their life stories. Right now she's simply impressed.

"What did she tell you?" Andrea asks.

"She got out of a ten-year relationship about a year back. Her ex broke her heart, dumped her ass, took the cats. Whatshername was there when Jan needed her. I get the sense the ex was a hot one. Figure she's slumming with this girl. Look at her, she's no threat."

Andrea watches Sarabeth turn a page in her novel, something by Jennifer Weiner no doubt. A block away, Jan ambles toward them.

"She got that limp in the army." Jordan watches Andrea watch Jan.

Andrea darts a look at Jordan.

"True fact." Jordan nods.

"Thanks for keeping an eye on our spot. This one wouldn't be able to defend it alone." Jan indicates oblivious Sarabeth.

"No problem." Jordan stands to bump fists with Jan, who's about a foot taller. Next to her, Jordan looks eager and cartoonish, not powerful at all.

"What do you think?" Jordan asks later. Jan's sleeping, her cap tucked over her eyes. "We get her back to the hotel room; both do you at the same time?"

Electricity flits through Andrea, as if she's mistaken an electric fence for an ice cream cone, taken a nice long lick.

"How serious are you?"

"As serious as a heart attack."

"Do what you want." Andrea eyes Jordan steadily; if this is a challenge, she's not backing down.

At the concert Andrea rides a wave of adrenaline. She always enjoys her concerts sober, but tonight's effervescent wash of anticipation feels alcoholic, makes her wonder what she's missed.

"Man, I had the wine glass in hand," Adrienne says before the second encore. "Pete was just about to hop in the shower!" A cluster of shrieks blossoms from front row stage right, the area in which Peter's fans congregate.

"It's not as exciting as it sounds," Peter says, tuning his guitar.

"How old are you, darling?" Adrienne moves stage right, addressing a long-necked redhead. "She's sixteen," Adrienne reports. "Must be one of yours, Pete. Mine skew older. And they've got shorter nails. Alright, we're gonna play one of Peter's songs before we send you on your way."

As they walk back to the hotel after the concert, Jordan assures Andrea, "I'm gathering information, tomorrow night's the night."

Later she forces her clenched fist inside Andrea, subdues her with a hand to her throat. When Andrea wakes the next morning, Jordan's been in line for hours, but her scent still hangs in the room.

"A NEW STAMP," Navy Camping Chair Lesbian confirms, nodding. "In honor of Aileen Wuornos," she adds.

"Who?" The redhead from last night scrunches up her nose.

Jordan and Jan are deep in conversation when Andrea shows up, slap-happy with exhaustion, balancing a tray of coffee. Andrea hands Jordan her Americano, Venti, with waterfalls of cream. Like all of Jordan's appetites, her need for caffeine is superhuman. Usually Andrea drinks an even eight ounces of coffee, but on concert days, she allows herself more. Offering Jan the black coffee Jordan instructed her to buy, Andrea blushes as Jan winks at her, then settles herself on the ground in front of Jordan, leaning back against her knees.

"Why is this night different from all other nights?" Jordan says, indicating Andrea's medium-sized coffee. A line plucked from a Jewish holiday, this comment is a ritual for Jordan. At first surprised to hear Jordan say it, Andrea's gotten used to her snatch-and-grab tendencies. She borrows from every religion she can. "Because on this night, Andrea breaks one of her little rules."

Is the quote from Rosh Hashanah or Passover? She'll have to call Roslyn to check. Flicking on her iPod and lodging the buds in her ears, Andrea lies on her back, glancing at Jordan from beneath lowered lids. To someone else what Jordan and Jan are having might look like an impromptu chat, but each move Jordan makes is deliberate; Jan's approval scrolls across her face. Andrea watches it like a silent movie. As much as she'd fight the comparison, Jan makes a fine damsel in distress. Jordan's every mustachioed villain, smiling as she ties Jan to the tracks. Andrea marvels at the way Jordan wears her villainy. On her it looks heroic. Maybe Jordan *is* some kind of hero, or maybe a magician. "Here," she says drawing attention to her right hand, "this is how I see you." Meanwhile her left hand is hard at work.

Watching Jan, all puffed up and beaming, Andrea feels a tug of hypocritical scorn. She knows exactly what Jordan is doing, parading before Jan, with a flourish delivering Jan's favorite forgotten self.

To Jan's left, Sarabeth sags forward, drowsing. Her khaki pull-over is hiked up around her stomach revealing a milky expanse of slack skin. In sleep she seems more china doll than woman, or maybe that's just what Andrea needs to believe.

That night she does her part, the events of the evening skidding like a computer slide show, each static, isolated but thematically linked.

There's the moment when Andrea tries to distract Sarabeth, pick her off from the rest of the pack. Jordan's hard at work on Jan, buoying her with beer and compliments; soon Jan won't be able to discern her will from Jordan's—she'll do anything Jordan suggests.

Another moment: Jan throws an arm around Andrea. Blinking like a startled bunny, Sarabeth actually snatches at Jan's sleeve.

Before or after, Jordan pins Andrea against the stage, runs her hands over Andrea's body, bites at her neck. Next to them Jan stares, glassy-eyed, Sarabeth nowhere in sight.

Still later, as they leave the concert hall with Jan, Andrea pictures herself and Jordan, cutting a swath across continents, taking what pleases them, a lesbian James Gang of two. She remembers watching Adrienne press her lips to her micro-phone, how she closed her eyes like she was making a birthday wish. Mouth to Andrea's ear Jordan whispered, "I could get her for you, too."

Things Andrea's Ashamed Of:

She believes if Adrienne got to know her, she'd love Andrea just as much as Andrea loves her.

Once, babysitting, Andrea spit her gum on the sidewalk. "You littered!" Her young charge said, eyes round.

She sort of hates Roslyn for eating without deli-beration yet remaining effortlessly slim.

When Andrea touches herself sometimes she pretends
she's Jordan.*

* She's not exactly ashamed.

~

A BOLD MOVE on Andrea's part, toward the end of her time at UCLA, she starts dating a classmate.

"I mean, dating like our grandmothers dated, not dating like anyone born after 1921." Andrea selects an orange and tucks it in her basket. "Have I ever told you how great I am at choosing fruit?"

"I've received entire voice mails on the subject. But back to you dating, how did you meet her? When did this start?"

"I've had classes with her this whole time. Something just clicked." Andrea tucks the phone under her chin and counts out ten protein bars.

What clicks is Jordan's freedom to both sleep with Andrea and eat the gourmet meals Patricia concocts, plus a comment of Jordan's weeks ago, standing in line to sell back their books.

"Thank God for summer." Jordan stretches her arms luxuriantly, her books stacked at her feet. A Midwesterner, Andrea can't quite generate excitement about a season change as subtle as hot and smoggy versus kind of hot and clear. As far as she can tell, the primary difference between June and January in LA is in January women wear Uggs with their shorts.

Andrea looks where Jordan's looking, at a tiny blonde girl in cut-offs and a yellow tank, a green bikini top peaking from beneath. Noticing Andrea, Jordan grins widely, "See? How great is all this flesh?"

"It's fabulous." Andrea says sotto voice, and the next day she asks the green bikini girl out for coffee after their final exam.

"So, how far exactly did women born in the '20s go?" Roslyn asks. "You're what, getting factory jobs together and drawing your nylon seams on with eyebrow pencil?"

"More or less." Andrea dodges a tall guy with a popped collar juggling three cases of beer.

After coffee, a long walk a few days later, more coffee and an impromptu dinner out, Green Bikini leans against Andrea's doorframe, trailing a hand down Andrea's chest.

"I'm new at this."

"What, dinner?"

"You know what I mean."

"I'll go slow." Andrea moves in to kiss her. She's thinking about Jordan. Wishing she would show up right now.

"And you like her?"

"She's very pretty. I'm kind of shocked by how pretty she is." Andrea adds sliced turkey and reduced fat cheese to her basket.

She and Green Bikini have lolled around kissing a few times since, Andrea behaving as if she's doing the girl a favor when she refuses to move faster. Although Andrea wastes little time analyzing her feelings about Green Bikini, she does wonder if her lack of attraction is caused only by her preoccupation with Jordan. Are her emotions just caught up elsewhere, or is Green Bikini's femininity getting in the way?

"What's wrong with pretty?" Roslyn asks.

"Nothing. Just that I feel like I'm kissing Cameron Diaz—fuck off," she adds as another popped collar kid lets out a whistle. "I'm talking too loud," she says into the phone.

"Wait, Cameron Diaz is gorgeous, why is that bad?"

"She's not bad, and this girl isn't either, she just has no edge."

"You mean she's not butch."

"Well."

"But you chose this chick, you must be kind of into her. How did Jordan take it when you showed her the door?"

At first it seems enough to do like Jordan, keep a little something on the side. Pretty soon, Andrea decides she needs Jordan to know what she's doing, so she starts to drop subtle hints. When subtle doesn't work, she follows some advice in Cosmo, sends herself a bouquet of flowers, signing Green Bikini's name. Jordan doesn't say a word when she's at Andrea's apartment, though Andrea sees her glance at the card. She also knows Jordan notices the photo of Andrea and Green Bikini she's tacked on her refrigerator. Taken at a late night study group months back, the photo means nothing, but when Andrea happens to find it, she crops out two other girls, and voila, connotations abound. Jordan leaves without kissing her, and around three AM, the sound of Andrea's phone snatches her from sleep.

"How long have you been seeing her?" Jordan's voice is surprisingly calm.

"Just a few weeks." Things are moving too fast for Andrea; she suddenly sees all she stands to lose.

"You like her?"

"She's alright."

"I didn't exactly ditch Jordan," Andrea tells Roslyn, looking for the register with the shortest line.

"But you want to be with her." It's a statement the way Jordan says it. Though she yearns to, Andrea doesn't shout, "I only want to be with you."

"What do you mean, you didn't ditch her?" Roslyn's voice is shrill.

"Here's the thing, babe, I know the way things are isn't fair." Jordan sighs into the phone.

"I guess I'm sort of seeing them both." Andrea places her groceries on the conveyer belt.

"No." Andrea agrees. "They aren't fair at all."

"Damnit, Andrea. I thought you were finally getting out." Andrea hears Roslyn light a match and inhale.

"And I know that." Jordan pauses. "Look, you can leave me all you need to, but I'm here to stay."

Andrea's pretty sure the line is care of some singing lesbian, the brunette Indigo Girl maybe, but it gets her right where she lives. Somehow Jordan's shifted things. She sounds desperate yet long-suffering, waiting for Andrea to make up her mind and commit.

Andrea hands the cashier her credit card. "Not by a long shot," she says.

⌒

THE CRIMINAL MASTERMIND tells Andrea that she wants only to drive at night through the canyons, rhythmic profundity pouring from her speakers, her fingers dangling, stroking sweet temperate air. If she lacks gas money, she'll settle for curling in a car in the driveway, doors open, music spilling out. If she lacks a car, she'll settle for an expensive stereo system. But without the car, she claims, it's really not the same.

Courtney Love says something about summertime and rock and roll and cars and sex, about innocence and transgression, which Andrea can't exactly remember, has never directly experienced, but when she reads the quote the hairs on her arms stir like aquatic plant life, so she suspects it's a profound human truth. She thinks her way around the quote whenever she rides with the Criminal Mastermind, which she realizes hasn't happened in at least a year.

Jordan's Top Five Songs:

1. "Beast of Burden"—The Rolling Stones
2. "Essence"—Lucinda Williams
3. "Slide"—Ani DiFranco
4. "Tony"—Patty Griffin
5. "You Wreck Me"—Tom Petty

More Favorites:

"I Will Always Love You"—Dolly Parton

"I Feel the Earth Move"—Carole King

"Mysterious Ways"—U2

"Stand By Me"—Ben E. King

"Similar Features"—Melissa Etheridge

"Goodbye Earl"—The Dixie Chicks

"It Was a Very Good Year"—(As sung by Frank Sinatra)

"This Love"—Maroon 5

SOON AFTER JORDAN moves to Chicago, they rent a car, drive to Wisconsin and Minnesota, catch four Cry Wolf concerts in six days. Riding shotgun, Andrea marvels at Jordan's small hands casually gripping the wheel. She thought she'd never see those hands again, but here they are, at ten and two, precisely where she's seen them so many times before.

"What are you, my girlfriend now?" she asks.

Jordan glances at her. Amused or wounded, on Jordan sometimes the two look the same.

"This is the second time you've asked me that."

"What?"

"Don't you remember?"

Andrea shakes her head.

"It meant a lot to me," Jordan does an impatient lane change. "It hurts my feelings that you don't."

Andrea shifts in her seat, the car's been theirs for all of five hours and already a textured quilt of debris blankets the floor. She kicks a drained Diet Coke can under her seat and remembers watching Jordan empty Patricia's car after a weekend spent together, Patricia in Phoenix for her parents' thirtieth anniversary. Jordan takes Patricia's nightly calls on Andrea's tiny patio, sometimes turning away so Andrea can't see her face, sometimes rolling her eyes at Andrea, dropping a rueful smile.

"There are only four good hours per week: Fridays between three and seven PM.*"*

Roslyn says this to Andrea when they're in middle school. Unpredictable the statements that endure to become gospel, Andrea remembers those she thought she'd outgrow, will never be certain which ones have slipped away. Roslyn's words still resonate, though. As a child, Andrea's weekends sullied as soon as she stepped through their Saturday morning doors. Her pilfered days with Jordan invoke their memory; each one ends so wrenchingly, it's hard to believe the way it starts, promise glinting off its edges like rays of sun. Andrea knows Patricia's return will temporarily render Jordan inaccessible; it always does. The first few hours will be excruciating, but by the fourth day, Jordan's calls will start again. "She just wanted my attention." "Sorry babe, I couldn't get away."

Andrea prods a pile of shoes and CDs Jordan's deposited, watches Jordan, in up to her shoulders, birth the dregs of their weekend from Patricia's car.

"Why not just clean as you go?" Andrea crosses her arms over her stomach. Long shadows score the sidewalk, the air beginning to cool.

Jordan hoists a garbage bag full of El Pollo Loco containers, crumpled gym clothes, and soda cans onto her shoulder. "It's too much work," she says.

Now Andrea looks at Jordan's sharp profile, cows and falling-down barns glide past her nose.

"Remind me."

"We'd made love for the first time a week earlier and you didn't want to get off the phone. Patricia was waiting dinner on me and I was a block away with Sammie."

"Whatever happened to Sammie?"

"Patricia took her, you know that."

"She must miss all those walks."

Jordan rests cupped fingers on Andrea's thigh. "You said, 'wait, don't go yet, I have a question.' You always had just one more question."

Andrea opens her window. The dead winter air hangs heavy with the scent of manure. She closes it again.

"I said, okay, one more question. And you said, 'What do I call you?' I asked what you meant, and you said, 'Can I call you my girlfriend?' It about broke my heart."

"What did you say?"

"I said, 'I'd like that.'"

"I wasn't your girlfriend. Patricia was. Or maybe Wendy; it's hard to be sure."

"But you were so adorable, just the way you asked."

Andrea remembers every detail of the conversation. Listening to Jordan retell it makes her feel as if Jordan is stealing her clothing item by item, tossing each piece out the window onto the highway behind. She isn't adorable. She's a child.

"There's an elevation to popular music that is the sound of the summer spilling out of someone's car and

the moment you break up with somebody and the moment
you first get sex and it is as impenetrable a memory
in someone's brain as a great still from *Gone with
the Wind*." (Courtney Love, quoted in *Rolling Stone*
"Women of Rock Issue" 1997)

The quote, when found, disappoints.

Driving to Milwaukee, Andrea remembers a trip they take to San Diego. On the way to Madison, she recalls a drive to Ventura. All those quests seeking Cry Wolf, satisfying and meaningless, consequence of a modern life: stores stocked with frozen dinners, no wild boars in sight. In Nevada they hit a raccoon, in Seattle Jordan finally lets Andrea drive. Memories spiral like snowflakes; there is no pure present, just this white expanse of all instants combined.

One insistent snowflake: two months before the pastor discovers the Criminal Mastermind in the supply closet with an intern, Jordan and Andrea drive to Berkeley to catch a show at The Greek.

"It's rough; I'm not going to lie." Jordan adjusts the rearview mirror, "being with someone who doesn't understand how I feel about Cry Wolf, it's like she doesn't understand some vital part of me, you know?" She glances at Andrea, "Course if she did like them we wouldn't be here, now would we?"

Almost two years in, no less enamored, much more tired, Andrea reclines her seat.

"Tell me again how you started listening to them."

"You always want me to repeat the things I tell you. You writing a book or something?"

"I want to know everything about you," Andrea says. Specifically she wants to trace the ways Jordan's stories fluctuate with each telling, which aspects remain static, which ones change.

"You do, huh?" Jordan taps the brake as the highway plunges downward, the ocean unfurling alongside. "You must really love me," she says.

Andrea smiles and touches Jordan's arm, unimaginably soft like the chamois cloth her dad uses to polish his Rambler.

"I was about twenty-five," Jordan says. "You know my parents were drunks, but I'd always tried to live clean. After high school I moved from Alta Dena to Silver Lake for a little while. I was with Tess, this nightclub singer. She had a bunch of slick friends, industry folks, you know? One time, this was before she was famous, we ended up at Melissa Etheridge's house."

New information. "What was she like?"

"I only really saw her from behind. That was the first night I tried poppers. Someone held one up to my face and I literally fell backward into a chair. Fast-forward a year and I'm doing as much coke as Tess. She's fucking her manager, I'm into a couple girls from work, we go our separate ways, and she ends up sober, married to some policeman, but I couldn't shake the habit.

"One night I'm out of my mind paranoid, sitting on my bathroom floor, I'm thinking I can't take much more. It's like I'm the only person who ever walked the earth, for sure the only person who feels how I do. I look in the mirror and there's this skull superimposed over my face. I'd lost a lot of weight, I might have been hallucinating, but I know the skull was a warning. When I saw it I panicked, thinking how I just needed something, any one thing to get me from this moment to the next. There was a tape on the floor in the hallway, a gift from some girl I was fucking. A song on it reminded her of me. Like I was hypnotized, I stuck the tape in the boom box. The first thing I heard was Adrienne. I listened to the song until it got light out. Then I flushed the last vial down the toilet. Her voice gave me the strength."

"You'd never heard Cry Wolf before?"

"Nope."

"I thought they started out playing all those West Hollywood clubs."

"Somehow our paths didn't cross until it was necessary. I wouldn't have survived the night without them. They made me feel . . . what's a word that means solid, but implies being connected to something too?"

"Substantive?"

"Yeah, like I didn't have to be lonely because there was something bigger than me. That was maybe my first taste of that feeling. I felt the same way when I started going with Patricia to church. I thought I loved her, but maybe I just loved God."

"Which song was it?"

"What's that?" Jordan stares through the windshield, past, not at, the road.

"The one that reminded the girl of you."

"That was like, ten years ago." Jordan runs a hand through her hair.

"But if you listened to it all night, if it got you sober, you must remember which song." Andrea's agitation mounts.

"Do you remember the first Cry Wolf song you heard?"

"Tarnished," Andrea answers.

"You're so precious." Jordan laughs.

"Why?"

"You haven't had much of a life yet. Relax, it's not an insult. I'd love to be where you are."

"I still think you'd remember something that significant."

"I know." Jordan squeezes Andrea's knee. This time she's left out the part where Tess dies.

Alternate Versions:

   -Tess lies for hours on the bathroom floor at The Palms before being found, face down, in a puddle of vomit and blood.

   -Having contracted HIV from her manager, Tess moves to Dallas where she now owns a Build-a-Bear franchise.

Thanks to an extensive daily pill regime, her T-Cell
count is high.

-Tess checks herself into rehab where she falls in
love with the wife of a famous producer. When the
two are discharged, Tess moves into the producer's
carriage house.

-Tess disappears into the desert. Months later her
car is found.

-She's a pediatric oncologist in Portland. Crazy
how someone can turn her life around.

-"Tess? We went our separate ways."

⁓

"WHAT IF YOU knew someone without a job who always had
cash?" Unplanned, Andrea's question alarms her. In front of the open
refrigerator, she waits a beat before turning, though she's already
found her yogurt and the circus of smells makes her throat constrict.

"I know tons of people like that. I'm from the Southside."
Unruffled, Scott squeezes a wedge of lemon before plopping it in
his tea. "What's the matter, work spouse?" This is something Scott
and Andrea call each other, in reference to an article Andrea read
explaining coworkers' tendency to partner up.

"What do you mean?" Andrea focuses on opening her yogurt,
afraid to meet Scott's eyes.

"You were staring at my tea all funny. You want some?"

"I'm just really tired."

"Help yourself. It's herbal though." Scott shifts the pile of
papers he's grading several inches from his mug.

"No, I mean, I was thinking, you precut a lemon, put it in a
plastic bag, and brought it to work."

"You calling me gay?"

"I'm calling you capable. I bought yogurt at the 7-Eleven on the corner where my bus drops off, only because I was in there already buying Advil. I left the whole bag on the counter. The cashier had to call me back in."

"You must be having some crazy sex."

"Well, yeah." Andrea spoons yogurt into her mouth. "Damn."

"What?"

"Cherry."

"What's wrong with cherry?"

"Tastes like cough medicine. I meant to get raspberry."

Sitting back in his chair, Scott interlaces his fingers, resting his head where they join.

I could predict his every gesture. Andrea stares at Scott's elbows, poking from behind his head like elephant ears. One of those people who sets a finger to his lips when thinking and taps his wrist to tell you it's getting late, Scott borrows liberally from the vast American library of visual cues. *Comforting*, Andrea decides.

"She's been in Chicago what, six months now?"

"Eight. You want this?" Andrea slides the yogurt across the table. Scott picks up her spoon.

"What?" Andrea props her feet on the chair next to her. Almost three years teaching, and she still can't align her self-concept with a person who'd wear navy flats.

"You're getting too skinny. Ever since you girls hooked up."

You girls, Andrea thinks, *Jordan would love that.*

"I'm not skinny."

"Don't give me that white girl shit. You're ten pounds down from when I met you. You stumble around here like this aunt I got who sleepwalks, and if you keep skipping staff meetings, you're gonna get fired."

"Okay, okay." Resting her cheek on the table, Andrea wonders whether Jordan's awake yet. Maybe she should call.

"You listening?" Scott puts a hand over Andrea's.

"You know my heart was empty, baby / till I saw you standing there / So lean right up against me, baby / Got some love I want to share."

"Shit," Andrea scrabbles through her bag, feeling for her phone. "Hello?" Answering, she silences Adrienne's voice mid-word.

"Guess what, babe," Jordan says. "They added another Madison date, totally last minute."

"We're going to the Wednesday show."

"Now we can see them tomorrow, too. If we leave by eight AM, we'll definitely be first in line."

"Jordan—"

"The confirmation from the website said all tickets are will-call, but I know a guy at the venue, and he told me some people already have theirs. There might be two lines, so we'll have to strategize."

"I have a staff meeting at noon tomorrow." Andrea says softly, glancing at Scott.

"What now?"

"A staff meeting. I have one."

Although Scott has his back turned, rinsing the yogurt cup, Andrea knows he's taking in every word.

"They don't really expect anyone to show up for those things. I gotta go, I'm getting another call."

"From who?"

"Remember to pick up cat food on the way home."

"Who's calling?" Silently, Andrea counts out ten seconds. *One Mississippi, two Mississippi,* just like her Sunday school teacher taught her. When enough time has passed she tells the dead phone, "Your mom? Okay, well, I'll see you tonight." Pause. *One Mississippi.* "Love you too."

"Scott?" Closing her phone, Andrea runs her thumb over the keys. "Cover for me at the meeting tomorrow?"

"Andrea," Scott sighs theatrically, shaking his head in the exact way Andrea knew he would.

"Please?"

THE CRIMINAL MASTERMIND is always happy to catch Cry Wolf in Madison.

"It's just like Berkeley," she says.

"I didn't know you liked Berkeley." They are in the front row as usual. This time the stage is only hip-height; they place their palms flat and lean forward, taking the weight off of their heels.

"I'm getting too old for this," Jordan rolls her shoulders, tilts her head from side to side.

"Age has nothing to do with it," Andrea says. "We've been outside in the rain for ten hours. Anyone would be worn out."

"I don't know why they always have an opener. That's like forty extra minutes on our feet."

Andrea gazes behind, over the dense wall of bodies. At the merchandise table, she can make out the opening act, a tiny Asian girl who spent the duration of her set giggling nervously and standing too close to the microphone. "Sorry, sorry," she repeated the whole time.

"Probably got herself a DWA on the way here," Jordan says following Andrea's gaze. Andrea understands Jordan means "Driving While Asian."

"Berkeley?" she prompts. Her chest feels strangely hollow; she knows there's a story here.

"I used to drive there and back at least twice a week."

"When?"

"Patricia and I had just gotten together. It always seemed like a good idea Friday night, but the drive home Monday was a killer."

"Patricia was working up there?"

"No." Jordan squats. "Man, did you hear that? My knees never used to make that sound."

"Why did you keep going to Berkeley?"

"I was fucking a radiology technician who'd moved there."

Andrea feels herself blink rapidly, all her consternation collecting in her lids.

"Here we go!" Jordan rubs her hands together as the club lights fade. As always Andrea warms, uncoiling gently when Adrienne and Peter enter, waving. So what if Jordan's a hot mess? At least Andrea has this.

"How's it hanging, Madison?" Adrienne hoists her guitar, rolls up the right sleeve of her shirt. Andrea notes Adrienne's guitar strap, brown leather with purple stitching. She's never seen it before.

"We've got a bunch of new material for you later, so let's dive right in."

Pockets of audience applaud. They've memorized Adrienne's patter; they know what she's going to sing. She breaks into "Swimmer," a surprisingly up-tempo song about a childhood tragedy, one of the Andersons' neighbors who drowned.

"It's all kinds of November out there." Adrienne says, later, sweat glistening where her collar gapes. "Here's an old song everyone can relate to right now." She leans into the microphone, *"All the leaves are brown . . . "*

Peter waits a breath and then joins her, his sweet tenor chasing his sister's dark alto down and around.

"California dreamin' on such a winter's day." Their voices tangle around each other, knit together into something new.

"Why do you tell me these things?" Andrea whispers to Jordan who glances over, eyes sparkling, expression glazed. "About Berkeley," Andrea clarifies.

"I'm committed to being honest with you." Jordan says, lifting her head as if for a congratulatory pat.

In the spotlight, Adrienne cups her hands around the microphone, shakes her head from side to side.

"You got gypped, didn't you?" Jordan says. "Ended up with me instead of her." When Andrea turns to dissemble, Jordan's eyes are on the stage.

"WHEN WAS THE last time you came home?" Roslyn's calling from her parents heated back porch. The creak of their glider is practically iconic, backdrop to all holiday memories. If Roslyn hadn't mentioned her location, Andrea would still have known.

> -Plates cleared from Passover dinner, Roslyn's father hides the afikomen, Roslyn covers Andrea's eyes.
>
> -Christmas Eve. Before heading to the early church service, Andrea stops at Roslyn's. They perch on the glider, exchanging gifts, Andrea's hair slipping from a floppy red bow.
>
> -Andrea, Roslyn, Margo, Beth, Jenny, and Tilda at Roslyn's twelfth birthday party, giggling and heaped together. In the background, Roslyn's mother presses palms to cheeks, afraid the glider's chains will snap.
>
> Is she recalling events or photos? Andrea can't be sure.

"I was going to come home in August, but Jordan surprised me with tickets to a bunch of Cry Wolf shows." In the background Andrea hears the low ripple of voices; she's pretty sure she can pick out Roslyn's father's laugh.

"It was one thing when you were in Los Angeles, but you're less than three hours away." Andrea pictures Roslyn, feet pressing the wall opposite the glider. Andrea's certain she's wearing the sky-blue pajama bottoms she keeps at her parents' house. Face bare of makeup, her short hair is held back with a white cotton headband.

"Jordan can't be alone at Christmas." Andrea checks the time on her phone. If Jordan isn't back in twenty minutes, she decides, then she can worry.

"Can't or won't?"

"The effect is the same."

"Bring her with you."

"Aren't we too old for this?"

"I'll never be too old to watch free cable and have my mom make me breakfast. Drive up tonight. Your parents would be thrilled."

"Even if I could still rent a car, Jordan's out Christmas shopping. I don't know when she'll be back."

"Leave her a note, she's a grown woman."

"That's pretty much homophobic."

"How do you figure?"

"You wouldn't say it if she were my husband."

"If Jordan were your husband . . . " Roslyn stops. "My mom just got back with the Chinese food. I gotta go."

~

DURING ANDREA'S LAST year at UCLA, Jordan convinces Andrea to spend Christmas in Los Angeles.

"Patricia will be in Phoenix with her family. We can go to Crystal Cathedral, or the light festival in Griffith Park, or the Reindeer Romp at the zoo."

"My parents would be really upset."

"Come on, you're an adult. Stay here with me. We'll go to Disneyland. They make it snow at night."

"Christmas is really big for my mom. She starts planning what cookies to make in October."

"It's big for me too. I always wanted it to be perfect, but my parents never rolled out of bed till three PM. One year they forgot about Christmas until I reminded them. My dad sent me to the corner liquor store with his credit card and told me to buy myself some baseball cards and a pack of gum."

"What if you came to Wisconsin with me?"

"And say what, you took pity on a spinster teacher and brought her home? Stay with me. We'll make it special; it'll be like a rehearsal for our new life."

An accurate promise, Andrea thinks, looking back. She doesn't remember feeling surprised when, on December twenty third, Jordan called to say Patricia's plans had changed.

Alone in Los Angeles, Andrea drives without thought. Traffic is thin on Gayley, Christmas only one hour away. Eleven PM in LA means one AM in Wisconsin, her parents home from church, the streetlights flashing red. Outside of Whole Foods, employees shout their good-byes. One, a thick-haired surfer type, plays hacky sack with a Santa hat. Paused at a red light, at first Andrea thinks something's caught his ankle and he's aiming to get free.

Third row, left side of the lecture hall, she realizes, recognizing him. Late every day, though he took notes like he meant it. He looks older without context, but the seminar she assistant taught last semester was an intro class. He can't be more than twenty-one.

> Door flung open behind her, cars honk and swerve
> as she runs to the surfer and buries her head in
> his chest.
>
> "Mom's making a goose," he says, stroking her
> hair. "Come for dinner. There are always extra
> presents. Stay the night."

On Le Conte, the Geffen courtyard burbles with theatergoers. Spilling through the doors under tiki-torchlight, their wine goblets glow like the future held in one's hand. Red to green and Andrea accelerates, skipping in front of a convertible where three teenagers sort through a bag from In-and-Out-Burger, unaware the light has changed. Andrea glides from the 405 to the 101 before she grasps where she's going. Lowering her window, she inhales, a mild breeze icy against her sweaty skin. The rickety 134 always unnerves her, so she pretends it's Disneyland's Thunder Mountain, all shaky loops and hairpin curves.

"Oldest highway in the US," Jordan says, proud like she owns it. All of Los Angeles is her own private playground. She once gave Andrea a tour of skid row.

Still and dark, Pasadena feels like a dense quilt Andrea can't find her way out from under. Heading toward Del Mar Boulevard, she sees a cop car. Something, perhaps a cat, skitters across the sidewalk in front of Jordan and Patricia's house. The street is packed with cars, which seems odd for midnight, odd for a suburban street on Christmas Eve.

Later, when leaving seems essential, Andrea will ransack her pockets, frantically search the block and a half of sidewalk between the house and her car. She'll have almost given up when she finds her keys right where she left them, in the car's ignition.

God bless Pasadena, she'll think, more than tapping the bumpers of the Jeep and the Beamer between which she's sandwiched, recklessly dislodging her car, desperate to flee.

Now, approaching Jordan's house, Andrea finds she's tiptoeing, though the street echoes with voices and low laughter; no chance she'll be heard. She recognizes Patricia's beat up BMW tucked back in the driveway, three other cars blocking her in. When she presses, the front door swings open, an obedient servant striving to please. Jordan and Patricia's tree, strung in golden chord and speckled with red bows, must be eight feet tall. Andrea remembers Jordan saying she didn't bother getting one. It seemed pointless with Patricia out of town. A linen-covered table extends the length of the living room. Heaped with red plates, a cut glass punch bowl, chafing dishes, and trays of tiny hors d'oeuvres, its attracted clusters of murmuring guests.

"Excuse me," an elfin man wearing thick round glasses steps back as Andrea turns suddenly.

"Sorry."

"Merry Christmas." He tips an imaginary hat as he passes. Just another unknown part of Jordan's life, Andrea wants to punch him in the nose.

In the backyard, tiny white lights thread through low bushes, and paper bag lanterns line the flagstone path. Andrea swipes a flute of champagne from one of several small tables and joins a huddle of partygoers.

"Better than last Christmas," a chestnut-haired woman says.

"You say that every year." Andrea can't find the voice's source, maybe the hefty woman in blue.

"Fantastic couple." A man with a handlebar mustache sips champagne.

"Half of it anyway." This time Andrea's certain Hefty's spoken.

"Patricia," Chestnut catches the elbow of a familiar blonde.

"Margaret, how long have you been here? Hello, Janice." Patricia kisses Chestnut and squeezes Hefty's arm.

Realizing she's staring, Andrea lets her hair fall over one eye. Serene and beautiful as the last time Andrea saw her, Patricia wears a slippery forest green sheath. The dress's thin straps graze her jutting collarbones, somehow reminding Andrea of trailing strings on a runaway kite.

"An hour or so. We knew you'd make the rounds." Chestnut smiles. "You know, Rusty thought he wasn't invited."

"That's absurd," Patricia's white-tipped nails glint in the lantern light. "I sent out invitations right after Thanksgiving."

"It's his own fault for spending half his time in Argentina," Hefty puts in. "Last time I went over there, his mail was stacked hip-high in the foyer."

"Where's Jordan?" A slim man in capri pants asks.

"Talking to Gretchen's hairdresser, I think." Patricia laughs. "You know how excited she gets about new people."

Andrea's already begun to back away, but she's pretty sure she sees Hefty and Capri exchange a look. The crash when she hears it doesn't startle Andrea, nor does she immediately connect it to herself.

"Will we be at this all night?" The elf man from the front door bends to look at her.

"What?" Andrea realizes she's fallen. Champagnes trickles down her ribcage between her breasts.

"We can't seem to stay out from under each other's feet." Reaching out a hand, the elf helps Andrea up.

"I wasn't paying attention," Andrea says, glancing back at Patricia to find she's staring directly at Andrea, her expression opaque. Andrea smiles, vaguely, and turns to link arms with the elf. "Help me find the bathroom?" she says, herding him toward the side of the house.

"I'm afraid I don't know where it is," he says, slowing to adjust his glasses.

"Oh, fuck off." Andrea lets go of his arm as soon as they're out of sight.

Don't run, she tells herself, crossing the front yard. *Soon, not yet.*

Glancing back at the spacious porch, Andrea thinks she sees Jordan. The posture is right, though it looks like she's wearing a flowered skirt, something she can't imagine Jordan deigning to do. One palm resting on the wall, she leans in to talk to another woman, gesturing expansively with her opposite hand.

After a moment, Andrea runs.

The first time Andrea meets her, Adrienne Anderson makes her feel like shit. Andrea's waiting in line for the bathroom, a bottle of Corona clutched in her hand. She's had barely two sips, but she needs something to hold. Linda's been gone for ten minutes now, but Andrea feels no urge to follow. She's trying to summon the nerve to talk to Adrienne, laughing with three Frat-ish lesbians, all tequila shots and madras shorts. One Andrea recognizes as a roadie, the others are probably local friends. Andrea just wants to check her lipstick, make sure there's nothing between her teeth. After that she'll approach Adrienne.

Behind her, a broad-shouldered woman joins the line. After a beat Andrea realizes the woman is Adrienne; offstage she's aggressively lean. Facing forward, Andrea holds the beer bottle to her lips, beads of moisture glistening on the bottle's long neck. Tipping her head back as if to drink, she even remembers to make her throat contract.

"Excuse me," Adrienne taps her arm, "would you mind if I cut ahead?"

Andrea turns. Inches away, Adrienne looks like herself in a photo, not the person Andrea feels she knows.

"Hello?" Adrienne smirks, "You speak English?"

"I love your music," Andrea says.

"Hey thanks," Adrienne steps around Andrea, "then you don't mind doing me a favor, right?"

"No, please," Andrea moves aside, conscious of her shoulder blades brushing the wall behind.

"Thanks. Too many beers." Adrienne turns her back.

"Great show tonight." Andrea can't let their contact end.

"The sound system was for shit. It's always like that in these Podunk towns." Adrienne runs a hand through her hair. "Nice of you to say though, I guess."

Just do it, Andrea thinks.

"So, maybe when you're done in there, maybe later I could buy you a drink?"

When Adrienne laughs, her teeth glisten, her bare
throat curves as she throws back her head.

"Of all the people in here, you think I'd actually
choose you?" Adrienne says, or that's how Andrea remembers it, anyway.

SMALL HARD
TRUTHS

∎ ∎ ∎

■ ■ ■

Andrea remembers something about the Santa Monica Pier but
she's not sure what.

■ ■ ■

ONE EASTER, ANDREA'S parents come to Chicago.

"You haven't been home for almost two years," her mother says when she calls.

Andrea pulls the back door closed and unclips her tiny iPod from her sports bra. A gift from Jordan, Andrea hasn't gotten used to how light the device is, practically weightless against her collarbone.

> *"I already have an iPod," she tells Jordan.*
> *"Come on babe, that thing's two years old. Plus you're a runner, you need something lightweight."*
> *"I run, I'm not a runner."*
> *"You're more of a runner than half the jokers on the Lakeshore path, and they're not wasting time doubting what they are."*

"Won't you want to be home for Easter?" Andrea adjusts the phone against her sweaty ear.

"Holidays are about family. We'd much rather see you."

Standing at the rear of her railroad-style apartment, Andrea feels she's peering through a paper towel tube.

As a child, she has a peculiar affinity for cardboard tubes and yellow twist-ties, connective tissue of household life. The red mesh covering strawberry

boxes is a particular obsession, at eight she rescues
them from the garbage, keeps a Kleenex boxful under
her bed. (Kleenex boxes are another item it seems
a shame to waste.) She figures the mesh will make
a handy hairnet if she dresses as a 1940s girl for
Halloween, or less likely, gets a job on an assembly
line. Whatever happened to all those Kleenex boxes
and twist-ties, all the doilies slipped from under
restaurant coffee cups and smuggled home? Strange,
her childhood affection for useless objects, things
she'd barely glance at today.

"Andrea?" Her mother's voice snaps her back to her hallway. Rundown and narrow, it opens into a living room filled with bookcases, most piled with random objects: scraps of paper, soda cans; Jordan deposits her trash in any convenient place. She kicks off her running shoes, wondering if Jordan's finally awake.

"My apartment's really small. . . . " Walking past the moist, towel-strewn bathroom, Andrea notices Jordan's left not one, but two days worth of coffee cups balanced on the edge of the sink.

"We're already booked at a bed and breakfast. The Internet says it's less than two miles from you. Hold on, honey."

Andrea hears her father's voice in the background.

"Did you try the upstairs linen closet?" Andrea's mother asks.

In the kitchen, Andrea tosses a soda can into the recycling bin, returns Jordan's half and half to the fridge. *She* has a linen closet; it's where they keep extension cords and colored pencils, things lacking a more appropriate home. Actual linens are either in use or in the laundry, never some designated spot.

"Sorry dear, I'm back. We'll drive up Friday."

Andrea pictures her parent's elderly station wagon, blue with wood paneling. Practically a family member, the car's still hanging on after almost twenty years.

"I know you haven't been going to church regularly, but I found one in Evanston with a sunrise Easter service. That's not too far, is it?" Andrea's mom stirs something as she talks. Andrea can hear the scrape of a spoon.

"Twenty-five minutes, probably less at that time of morning. What are you making?"

"Chicken soup. Your father thinks he's getting a cold."

In the living room, Jordan sits in a pile of laundry, curled on the couch reading a book. It's the second in a series about time travel and Scotland, saccharine if you ask Andrea, but Jordan says she can't put it down.

"My parents are coming," Andrea mouths, tapping Jordan on the leg.

"We can't wait to see you," Andrea's mother tells her, as Jordan mimes slitting her throat.

"PARENTS HATE ME, fathers especially." Jordan says this back in LA.

"Not my father." Andrea's chopsticks hover above her sashimi.

"No man likes the person fucking his daughter." Jordan scoops up a cucumber roll and says, chewing, "Just how it is."

"That's reductive."

"Oh, really, college girl?"

"And like, weirdly sexist." Andrea mixes wasabi and soy sauce.

"Have I told you about Martha?"

"No."

"I was banned from her family reunions."

"Why?"

"Not exactly banned, but definitely unwelcome." Jordan watches Andrea eat. "How is it?" She extends a finger toward the vivid spirals of raw fish.

"Amazing."

"If you gotta eat sushi, this is the place to do it." Jordan sips sake.

"Were you the first woman she'd been with?" Andrea knows Jordan is most people's first.

"That wasn't the real issue. I met Martha through her cousin, Julia." Jordan pauses for a reaction.

"So?"

"Julia and I'd been dating for two years."

"Will you have enough to eat?" Andrea's not in the mood to give Jordan the response she wants.

"The smell ruins my appetite. Don't worry about me."

"Why did you take me here if you hate sushi?" Andrea ticks her chopsticks together.

"Because you," Jordan pauses, "love it, and I," another pause, "live to serve."

PLEASE BE REAL with them," Andrea says Saturday morning. She and Jordan lean against the brick outer wall of m. henry waiting both for their name to be called and for Andrea's parents to arrive.

After dinner with her parents the night before, Andrea finds Jordan reading another book in the Scotland series rather than at a study group she swore she had to attend. The disparity between her parent's effortless normalcy and Jordan overwhelms Andrea. At dinner when her father sneezed, her mom rummaged in her purse for tissues; Jordan has the TV cranked and the radio blaring. Every light in the apartment is lit. If that's not enough, the concept of parents has caught Jordan's attention; she wants Andrea to call her daddy when they fuck.

"Real?"

"Just, don't put on a show." Andrea pulls her hound's-tooth scarf away from her throat. It's one of those indecisive April days. She keeps thinking if she just unzips one thing or buttons another she'll find equilibrium, but she's consistently either too hot or too cold.

"You think I put on shows for people?"

"Well, yeah." Most likely a mistake, Andrea says it anyway. It's been a while since she tossed off some not-all-that-perceptive note about Jordan's character. When they don't offend her, Jordan's a devotee of such observations. She says they're proof of Andrea's intelligence, proof she knows Jordan better than anyone. More likely, Andrea's the only person brazen enough to occasionally speak her mind. It'll backfire eventually, she's certain; it's just a question of when.

A gray-haired couple Andrea's watching becomes suddenly unambiguously her parents.

"Mom, Dad, hi," Andrea says.

"Mr. and Mrs. Wynn," Jordan drops her slouch and moves smiling to shake Andrea's father's hand. "How do you like the big city?" she asks Andrea's mother, tilting her head solicitously to one side.

Later, the weekend blurs in Andrea's memory, but certain incidents stand out.

During breakfast, Jordan stuns Andrea's fiscally conservative parents by ordering grapefruit and cranberry juice, coffee and Diet Coke, two kinds of toast and pancakes along with her meal.

"She must have been very thirsty," Andrea's mother comments later, when she and Andrea are in the bathroom washing their hands.

Convinced Andrea's parents will love Wrigley field, Jordan hails a cab after breakfast, herds the Wynns inside. A doomed venture, Andrea's certain. Her father cares about two things: cars and gardening. Her mother's never attended a baseball game in her life.

"How can you function without trees?" Andrea's mother asks, standing in front of the stadium.

"Closer," Jordan says, looking through her camera's viewfinder. Andrea sidesteps toward her mother. Across the street, her father leaves Starbucks holding a paper cup. Tea, Andrea guesses, most likely mint.

"But I suppose Chicago is better than LA." Her mother smiles for the camera.

"Trees are fine," Jordan says, slipping the camera into her pocket, "but what about culture?"

"Oh, well," says Andrea's mother.

"Which way's the lake?" her father asks when he arrives.

Later, at Belmont Harbor, Jordan whispers, "Your father acted like Wrigley field was some big inconvenience, but that's the kind of thing tourists love!"

"He doesn't like having his picture taken, that's all." A few yards away, her parents gaze out at the water. "He was really interested in the stadium's history. You saw him reading that plaque."

Andrea's mother points as a seagull swoops toward Lake Michigan's glassy surface. Her father sips his tea and pats her back. Watching, Jordan says, "What is it with your parents and nature anyway?"

Jordan tries to charm Andrea's father by talking cars with him, a subject she knows very little about.

"She says she had an AMC Spirit back in '77," Andrea's father says, helping Andrea hang a shelf in the bathroom. "She must be confused; those didn't come out till, oh, I'd say '79."

At the sunrise service there's a moment so sun-drenched and peaceful, Andrea can't figure how it relates to her life. The pastor, a plain man in his sixties with absurdly fashionable glasses, reads from Romans six: "But if we have died with Christ, we believe that we will also live with him. We know that Christ, being raised from the dead, will never die again; death no longer has dominion over him. The death he died, he died to sin, once for all; but the life he lives, he lives to God. So you must consider yourselves dead to sin and alive to God in Jesus Christ."

As a kid Andrea believed the passage magic, an enchantment summoned to frustrate death. Though she hasn't heard it in years, she mouths the words, each phrase evoking seasons of memories like crystalline rock candy, endless and multifaceted with no clear beginning or end. To her right she sees her mother nodding. Her father takes out a navy bandana and gently blows his nose. On Andrea's left, Jordan seems engrossed in the sermon; she clutches a soft-skinned hymnal in her hands. When the congregation rises to sing, Jordan whispers, "My heart is so full," and Andrea feels suddenly distant and nauseated, like Jordan snatched fulfillment from her hand.

"It was nice to meet you, Jordan." Andrea's mother says, Sunday afternoon, and unexpectedly, Jordan goes in for a hug. Over Jordan's shoulder, Andrea sees her mother's wide brown eyes. Her hands hang rigid at her sides.

"She's Lutheran," Andrea says later. "She's never even hugged Roslyn and they've known each other for over twenty years."

"She was so stiff." Jordan stares through the rain-streaked living room window. "I'll never make myself vulnerable like that again."

～

"THE HOT ONES are always crazy," Jordan says, to make her feel better whenever Andrea has one of her spells. The wrong term, "spell" implies smelling salts and a fainting couch, when what happens to Andrea is an ocean rising, a dark creeping wall.

"I'm not okay," she remembers telling her mother, back against her pinewood headboard, sheets clutched in her hands. Four years old and sleepless, she's just made the connection between her grandmother who arrives the next morning and something she overheard a babysitter say into the phone.

"It was Nickels's time." When she hangs up, her babysitter's face is bright in a way Andrea recognizes.

"You look like mommy when she watches a movie."

"A sad movie?"

"What?"

"Is the movie your mommy watches sad?" The babysitter plops on the floor next to Andrea.

"I don't know." Andrea cuddles into her lap.

"I'm sad because my boyfriend's dog died."

"Why did it die?"

"Because he was old."

"What do you mean, you're not okay?" Andrea's mother puts a hand to Andrea's cheek. "Your skin is cool. Does your throat hurt?"

"Die means never again, right?" Andrea's eyes burn, so she rubs them, but it doesn't help; she's already crying, her chest both taut and full.

"How do you know about dying?"

"The news."

"It means the person who dies goes somewhere different. No one knows exactly where."

"Why?" Andrea cries harder. She shrugs a shoulder, using her nightgown to dry her neck.

"Only God knows what happens. People aren't powerful enough to understand."

"I don't want Gramma to die."

"Andrea, Grandma is perfectly healthy. She's not going to die for a long time."

"But she's old. When you're old, you die."

"Don't worry about your Grandma. You'll see her tomorrow, she's fine."

Andrea's not sure why, but what her mom says makes the crying get bigger. Her mother's arms around her don't help; her body belongs to the crying now.

"I don't want to die!" Andrea sobs.

"Some people believe after we die we get to live with God. That sounds nice, right?"

"I don't even know God! I want to live with you!"

"Shh. You need to calm down now. You're going to be exhausted in the morning."

"But Mom," Andrea says and then keeps saying, "I'm not okay, I'm not okay."

Later, anorexia's meditative tunnel vision chases away the panic. Andrea concentrates only on weighing her food. Her crushes help, too. In college the studying mediates, also running, which lets Andrea feel momentarily as if she can escape the wall of water, though she knows it's always a few steps behind.

Linda has no idea what to do with Andrea, sitting up in bed beside her, trying to hold back the flood.

"Why are you crying?"

"I don't know. I think maybe the movie."

"*Titanic*? That was hours ago."

"I know."

"You said the whole thing was corny."

"It was."

"So now you're crying for Jack and Rose?"

"No."

"What then?"

"The scene where the dining room fills with water and all the dishware starts to float."

"What about it?"

"It . . . I . . . it felt like my insides." Saying the words bursts a dam; there's no controlling her tears.

"I don't understand where all this is coming from." Linda says, crossing the moonlit room to stand by the door.

"Can't you just, I don't know, help?"

"I don't think so. I don't like big emotions."

"I can't change what I am."

"Me neither. Sorry." Linda leaves, closing the bedroom door.

That Jordan seems to understand the dark water, that she knows exactly how to react surprises Andrea. Once when it hits they're driving into downtown Los Angeles, the air soft and warm, the buildings endlessly tall against the dark sky.

"I know," Jordan says, without looking at Andrea.

"What?" Andrea surfaces. She's fighting the current though she hasn't said a word.

"It's all too big and too much, but beautiful too. Makes you lonely, or not lonely; it makes you want something without knowing what."

"I'm so scared of dying." Andrea says.

"Me too." Jordan's hand, warm, small, strong, covers Andrea's. She relaxes as the waters recede.

Another time in bed, Andrea's overtaken. She sits up, panicked, needing more air. Awake beside her, Jordan sits too.

"I'm sorry." Andrea pushes her forehead into the heel of her hand.

"For what?"

"I get like this. I know it's weird."

"What can I do?"

"Please," Andrea feels the tears coming, "just please don't leave me alone."

Jordan urges Andrea's head to her shoulder. "I won't let you die," she says. The part of Andrea that never stopped being four, that part believes Jordan won't.

⁓

ANDREA IS SACKED out on a camping couch in front of some theater in Ventura, California. It bothers her that she can't recall the name of the venue, but not enough to open her eyes and check. Jordan's been on a bathroom hunt for twenty minutes now, but Andrea doesn't mind her absence; in it she has space to relive the previous night. It's the second leg of the same Cry Wolf tour at which she first encountered Jordan, four months since that show at the Troubadour, their first time seeing the band outside of LA.

The siblings live somewhere in Venice, so each time Cry Wolf goes out on the road they start in or around Los Angeles. Andrea noticed the trend back in college; realized Southern California fans got to see double the shows. Andrea's parents believed her when she cited UCLA's English MA program the best in the country. She'll never admit why she really came to LA.

Actually, Andrea knows exactly where Adrienne lives. She reads enough articles, does enough sleuthing, once even follows Adrienne's black Jeep after a gig at McCabe's. From four car lengths back, Andrea sees Adrienne wedge the Jeep between a rusted out Volkswagen Beetle and two precariously balanced Vespas, leaning into each other like tipsy college students on a first date. Pulling over, Andrea douses her headlights, watches Adrienne walk heedlessly to her front door.

After that she doesn't do worse than drive slowly past the house, never more than once every few months. Not at all since meeting Jordan. For now, she holds her knowledge aside and in reserve, but someday when she wants to impress Jordan she'll reveal it. She can't imagine telling Jordan less than everything—that's the stage she's still in.

Sunlight tickles Andrea's closed lids and she twists on the couch trying to ease the ache in her neck, result of staring up at the stage last night, also later, from Jordan's grip on her hair.

I love her, Andrea thrills at the words, her participation in something so universal and profound. Part of what she loves about Jordan is her ready acceptance. It feels unconditional. Linda once says, "You're great at first, but later, when things are supposed to settle down, you're still just as intense."

"Patricia called me intense when we first met," Jordan says when Andrea tells her. "She still does, only it's not a compliment anymore."

The sun's heat is possibly the best thing Andrea's ever felt, but then every sensation exists in superlatives lately. She remembers last night's concert, Adrienne in the blue spotlight, her low voice and clenched fists. She remembers Jordan's moonlit silhouette, the detonation of feeling that ignited between her legs and mushroomed to her fingertips, her brain.

Andrea doesn't realize she's sleeping until she isn't. She opens her eyes to find a familiar line-waiter sitting next to her, the couch sagging under their combined weight.

"So you're the new one." The girl tucks a hank of white-blonde hair behind her ear. Andrea tries to remember if she knows the girl's name. Hanna? Tanner? Andrea's never spoken to her, but the girl is usually second or third in line.

"Aren't you going to say something?" The girl fingers a broken heart she wears on a chain around her neck, "BFF" engraved in flowing script.

"I'm sorry?"

"You never noticed everyone either stares or looks away when you two walk by?"

Andrea stays silent as the girl narrows her eyes like a cartoon character; they actually transform into mean slits.

"She's been through half of us," the girl says, and Andrea understands at once what she means.

"You?" Andrea asks.

"No thanks!" The girl shakes her head, the sharp ends of her hair whipping from side to side. "I like guys. My friend Nelly though, we're both from the Valley? Ever since their fling she can't handle it if Nelly is first in line."

"Oh."

The girl stands. Andrea looks up at her, shading her eyes from the sun. She's sure there's something she should be saying, but all she can think about is the spreading tightness inside her chest. The girl shifts her weight from one foot to another.

"Was there something else?" Andrea finally asks.

"No." The girl seems disappointed. She's looking for some drama to break up the monotony of the wait. She turns to go then stops. "If it makes you feel better, she's stuck with you the longest. Most last about a month."

After the girl leaves Andrea stands and stretches, sees Jordan ambling slowly up the block. Soon Jordan will be kissing her. She'll rummage in a plastic Rite Aid bag, unveil a chocolate rose and place it in Andrea's hand.

In the moments before Jordan reaches her, Andrea makes a decision. She'll use this new information to shore up her defenses. She won't let it frighten her away.

Peter's Fans:*

Average Age-Range: 15-25

Likely tall, hawk-nosed, and gawky

Standard Ensemble: bejeweled jeans, tank top w/ peek-a-boo bra straps, hoodie, and ballet flats/ Converse/Uggs/knee-high boots (footwear dependent on year/state)

Typical Hairstyles/Headwear: long (dreads, pony tail, sparkly barrettes, newsboy caps, trucker hats, stocking caps)

Most Common Names: Mandy, Madison, Dylan

During Long Line-Waits, Most Likely to Pee at: Star- bucks (Drink: tall Frappuccino-Light with extra whip)

Favorite Cry Wolf lyric: "Oh girl (yeah girl) Let me take you home / Oh girl (yeah girl) You are not alone"

Top Line Snacks: fries, chips, nothing, Mountain Dew

Wallet Contains: photo of Peter/photo of fan plus Peter, cash, fortune from cookie, ID, debit card, Victoria's Secret credit card, ticket stubs

Most Cherished Memory: that one time when Peter, like, winked at her. Yeah, it was from the stage, but like, her friends swore he was looking right at her!

Adrienne's Fans:*

Average Age-Range: 21-45

Likely short, pug-nosed, and obese

Standard Ensemble: painter jeans, message T-shirt, hoodie or fleece, and Tevas/Doc Martins/Converse (all footwear possible; no concern for trends)

Typical Hairstyles/Headwear: short (dreads, buzz cut, baseball caps, trucker hats, stocking caps, bandanas)

---

* [Figure 6]

Most Common Names: Chris, Nic, Dylan

During Long Line-Waits, Most Likely to Pee at:
Starbucks (Drink: Venti latte/No drink; fight the
man, she's peeing for free)

Favorite Cry Wolf lyric: "What's freedom?
Freedom's what you choose."

Top Line Snacks: chili cheese fries, trail mix, vodka

Wallet Contains: photo of Adrienne/photo of fan
plus Adrienne, cash, three major credit cards,
library card, ID, photo of pets, ticket stubs,
lottery ticket

Most Cherished Memory: the time she and her girlfriend kissed and Adrienne totally gave them the
thumbs up

⌒

ANDREA THINKS OPENING her arms to Jordan again is possibly the most forgiving thing she could do. (Jordan: "You opened more than your arms, darlin'.") For Andrea the line between forgiveness and wretchedness is brittle as a gray hair. In mercy's aftermath, she becomes prone to angry lapses, moments in which she loathes herself for being not merely the latest in a line of women to whom Jordan sold swamp land, but the only one to ask for more.

Interrogating Jordan sometimes almost puts her mind at ease. Jordan's memorized the answers Andrea requires: "Yes I love you. No I don't think less of you. No you're not pathetic. Of course I'll never leave you again."

An unguarded moment: Andrea, head on Jordan's chest, confesses, "Before you came to Chicago, I'd watch reruns of *MacGyver* and cry thinking about you."

"MacGyver and I have so much in common. You should see me disarm a bomb." Jordan lightly strokes Andrea's upper arm.

"I mean, all the scenes in jungles and deserts, all the Mid-East villages and hostage situations, they're all shot in Griffith Park. So I'd see hills we used to hike or those falling apart cages in the abandoned zoo where you fucked me that time, and I'd think of you."

Andrea listens to Jordan inhale and exhale, hears the light whistle of air through latticed cartilage, a result of Jordan's foray into cocaine.

"Hm." Jordan's fingers thread through Andrea's hair. Their motion should soothe Andrea, but absurd as it seems, Jordan's fingers transmit boredom. Andrea thinks she remembers Jordan touching her like that right before Echo Park Wendy. If only she had some sort of imprint recording, a way to double-check what she thinks she knows. She vows constantly to trust her instincts, but a relationship with Jordan compels the opposite. Accustomed to squelching her intuition, Andrea feels sometimes like a runaway train.

"Whenever I heard anything about Wisconsin and serial killers, right away I thought of you." Jordan smiles as she says it; Andrea can hear it in her voice.

Andrea sits up, tucks her legs underneath her, crosses her arms over her chest.

"Watch those elbows, woman." Jordan rubs her hip. "What's wrong?"

"That's a shitty thing to say."

"Come on, babe. You aren't where you're from."

"It's not that."

"What is it?" Jordan's using the voice she pretends to think is supplicating; Andrea's pretty sure she knows it's condescending as fuck.

"It's like, I extended this olive branch and you set it on fire."

"Hey, you're the only one I ever went back for. Besides, you know it's not that deep."

Andrea thinks it's probably even deeper, but then, she thinks everything is.

MOMENTS, RUNNING, ANDREA feels certain of her borders, her fingernails seem an example—sharp, and definitive, they delineate Andrea from the surrounding air. In the lean slice of time between six AM and seven-thirty, Andrea is whole, an interesting byproduct of running until her feet go numb.

In the late spring, when Chicago's Lake Shore Path floods with seasonal joggers, Andrea retreats to a neighborhood cemetery. Almost three square miles, the cemetery's high cement walls defeat any wind. Inside it's still like a world created then forgotten, reminding Andrea of *The Secret Garden*, *A Fine and Private Place*, every book she loved as a child. Not only won't Jordan enter a graveyard, she'll drive blocks out of her way to avoid one—strange for someone Andrea thinks of as fearless. This is good; this keeps the running just hers.

Andrea's looped once around the road bordering the cemetery's wall, has cut through the grounds, planning a few circuitous laps, when she realizes she's being summoned.

"You can't run here."

"What?" Removing an earbud, she jogs in place in front of the squat funeral parlor.

"This isn't a playground." Comb-over sniffs, which seems so clichéd that later Andrea wonders if her imagination added that part in.

"Do I look like I'm playing?"

"You need to find another place to do," he gestures dismissively, "that."

"I see, so once you deposit my check, I'm no longer your responsibility?" Andrea finds herself oddly aroused, eager to take on a good fight.

"Sorry?"

"How dare you judge the way I mourn?"

"Oh, please."

"Don't you roll your eyes at me." Crying is easy, Andrea finds. "This is my last connection with my mother, and you want to take that away?"

"You need to leave." He's less certain this time, Andrea can tell.

"I start every day knowing she's gone, and every day I come here, before work, and for just an hour, maybe two, it's manageable, the grief." Ridiculous to note she's still running in place.

"Oh, please," he says again, but he's stepping back as he says it, turning to go inside.

"My pain is just as painful as theirs." Andrea flails a hand toward the airless building, watching him retreat.

Bisecting the cemetery's core, Andrea wonders at her defense, white hot and fully formed. She barely remembers a word. She wasn't herself with Comb-over, she was someone better. She'll take Jordan's arrogance, her defensiveness, her knack for manipulation. She'll take all of it. She's learning by example, whether she wants to or not.

～

PATRICIA'S NAME BLIPS across Jordan's caller ID five times before Andrea makes her move. Back in LA, she has little opportunity for detective work; Jordan controls what she sees and doesn't. Now, Jordan's belongings spread throughout the apartment, Andrea ought to have ample occasion, but Jordan's schedule is less than predictable. Today, however, she's certain of Jordan's whereabouts. Having rented a car for an Indiana Cry Wolf show the next day, she's driven Jordan to a three PM dentist appointment.

"I left some papers I need to grade at school," she tells Jordan. "Call me when you're through."

At home, Andrea starts with Jordan's closet, still stacked full of boxes Jordan says she'll unpack "next week." Lifting the cover from the top one, Andrea reminds herself to memorize the order of its seemingly haphazard contents, just in case the mess is a wily sort of trap. In the unit above, the neighbor's dog howls, and Andrea twitches, dropping a pile of yellowed loose-leaf.

First Box:

Deck of cards

Ticket stubs

One pack Juicy Fruit

Photo: Jordan in a ridiculous brown velvet pant-suit, Patricia wearing an ivory dress. They hold hands in front of a man in a clerical collar, the sky behind them, turquoise, like a swap meet ring.

Term paper, A+ (red pen)

Five bare notebooks, college rule.

One white sneaker

Video tape, "Queer as Folk" (black pen)

Second Box:

Books Books Books

Third Box:

Same

Three cartons down, she's found nothing alarming, though the boxes seem packed by a meth addict. She checks her cell phone. The bad news, it's already three thirty, the good, Jordan's just texted: "I've been stuck in the waiting room for half an hour. The only magazine this joker subscribes to is Log Cabin, Illinois."

"Sucks," Andrea replies, then opens the fourth box.

Fourth Box:

Two broken crayons

One tin of Altoids

Keys

Rite Aid receipt (Evian, string cheese, *Us Magazine*)

Shoebox filled with cassette tapes, mostly homemade

In the kitchen, she digs through Jordan's tower of cookbooks, purely decorative as far as Andrea knows. Probably bought to impress Jordan's ex from the late eighties, a celebrity personal chef.

"You don't cook; can't we put these in the basement?" Andrea asks once.
"I cook." Jordan rests a hand on the stack.
"Not since you've been here."
"I used to make Wendy dinner every night, but you're impossible to cook for." Jordan tosses a book from hand to hand.
"It looks like we have a poltergeist. Can you at least put them on the shelves?"
"No butter, no cream, what's the point?" Jordan scoops up her keys. "I'm running to Starbucks. Want anything?"

Five from the top, Andrea extracts a floppy paperback: *Moosewood Restaurant Cooks At Home.* Flipping pages, she finds a ragged envelope tucked between two soup recipes, "Spanish Potato" and "Sweet Pepper," both of which she wants to tell Jordan she would happily eat.

The envelope's most pertinent details become only belatedly obvious. Like a slapstick detective, Andrea takes in the particulars last to first.

1. No return address

2. American flag stamp

3. Andrea's name in unfamiliar blue hand.

She jumps when her phone goes off.
"Come and get me." Jordan texts.

⌒

HERE'S THE PROBLEM with sharing interests with your partner: when you separate, the same simple things that once made you happy instead make you unbelievably sad. Not only does the person for whom you're accustomed to unzipping your skin now recoil from the sorrow pooled inside you, but when she packs up, she takes Kung-Fu movie marathons and ballroom dancing with her, or worse, she strips them of solace, then leaves them behind.

If Andrea transcribed all the Criminal Mastermind renders useless the first time she leaves, the list would come with a magnifying glass and a low pedestal.

One Version, Heavily Abridged:

Diet Coke

Rabbits

Runyon Canyon

Lemon meringue pie

Guaranteed, their affiliation ruins exactly nothing for the Criminal Mastermind. A magpie of a woman, Jordan filches the most interesting aspects of her girlfriends, efficiently incorporates them into herself.

In Chicago, Jordan and Andrea spend Sunday mornings reading the paper at Metropolis Coffee. More accurately, Jordan reads the paper. Andrea tries to act like a responsible adult and prepare her lesson plan at least a day in advance. She used to be a pro at preparation, getting a rush setting goals and meeting them, never turning in a paper late. But life with Jordan desiccates her adrenal glands; her concentration is totally shot. Plus there's something

disheartening about watching Jordan live without apparent consequence. Andrea remembers Jordan procrastinating her way
through UCLA then charming her teachers into giving her exten-
sions, even A's. Disheartening and tempting, Andrea wants to get
away with things too. Despite new information, today she's on
a mission to prove she can have both Jordan and a normal life,
and for once she seems to be succeeding. The lesson plan expands
logically in front of her. She may actually finish without cutting
corners, maybe even on time.

Only lightly aware of Jordan's presence, Jordan as concept, as
live-action hero, as daily companion, as innately out of reach,
Andrea might be on her back on the beach in the Bahamas, that's
how relaxed she feels. She hums through her teeth and makes a
note, jumps when Jordan taps her on the wrist.

"Hear that? Those lyrics?" Jordan asks.

Andrea notices that with which she's been harmonizing: Ani
DiFranco singing about regret.

"Sort of."

*"We met in a dream / We were both nineteen / I remember where
we were standing / I remember how it felt / Two little girls growing
out of their training bras / This little girl breaks furniture / This little
girl breaks laws,"* Jordan recites. "That's us." She smiles widely, a
sesame seed lodged between her front teeth.

"Not nineteen, neither of us. Especially you." Andrea's surprised
at the gruffness of her response.

"Me, I'll always be nineteen." Jordan flicks to an article in the
sports section, folding the newspaper in on itself as she turns.
Andrea watches Jordan's hands on the desecrated pages. As on
every Sunday, Andrea will have to go section by section, collating
the sheets before it's again fit to read. She glances at the words
like obstinate insects on her computer screen. Irrelevant whether
there had been a logical trajectory—when her attention shifted it
fell away.

"I can't concentrate," Andrea says, louder than she intends. A man at the next table glances up from his bran muffin and frowns.

"Excuse me, sir." The Criminal Mastermind reclaims the man's attention by knocking her foot against his chair. "Can you tell me where to find the book drop?"

"What's that?" The man leans forward, more irritated than before.

The Criminal Mastermind continues, "Seeing this is a library and all . . . "

"This isn't a . . . I'm afraid I don't . . . "

"It's not? Well, then I guess we can talk as loud as we feel like." The Criminal Mastermind beams as if her Little League team has just won the big game.

The man inhales loudly. Gathering his plate and his coffee mug, he makes a show of bussing his table, then flouncing toward the door.

"Faggot." Jordan returns to her paper.

"That'll teach him," says Andrea, thinking of Jordan's daily battles. Would she be so quick to strike if she had less to hide?

"I love the shit out of Ani," Jordan says as the singer's ululations trail off. "You've heard of her, right?"

"Yes," says Andrea, remembering as a child thinking that when a song fades at the end, it means the musicians are leaving with their instruments, actually walking away.

•I'M THE ONE who introduced her to Ani." Andrea presses her cell phone to her ear. She's on the second of two buses she takes to get to work. What she really wants to discuss is the letter, but how would she even begin? "And here she is asking me if I've heard of her? How could she forget something like that?"

"Did you remind her?" Roslyn's voice in Andrea's ear sounds alien. Maybe it's been longer than she thought since they've talked.

"No. I was too angry. Or maybe I was scared."

"Angry, scared—if it's bothering you, mention it. Hey, did I tell you about this case they have me on at work?"

With Jordan in her life, Andrea's guilty of taking from Roslyn more than she gives, so she commits herself to listening. Roslyn's words come through in spurts and snatches, though. Right away Andrea is deep in her head.

She knows she's overly concerned with the concept of credit where credit is due, wants always to be recognized for her contributions, never confused with anyone else. Of course she too accumulates other people's interests, but unlike the Criminal Mastermind, she specifically recalls just who gave her what.

```
Pertinent Examples:
    Linda teaches her the name of those flat decorative
plates that contribute to a place setting but have no
functional use. If not for her, Andrea wouldn't know
to call them "chargers." Their romance may not be
otherwise noteworthy, but from Linda she also learns
to roll her debt onto a single credit card, the one
with the lowest APR. This comes in handy much later,
after the Criminal Mastermind gets hold of her Visa.
    Roslyn opens Andrea's eyes to Nirvana, although as
a fourteen-year-old feminist, Andrea prefers Hole.
    Andrea's college roommate loves old school coun-
try music, uses it like white noise to lull herself
to sleep. She cites obscure trivia when sober, cries
over Charlie Poole's tragic life when she drinks. As
a result, Andrea develops a fondness for Patsy Cline.
She can recite Hank Williams's career highlights if
ever she's asked.
    Andrea's high school boyfriend teaches her how to
knot a tie, a skill that works in her favor when she
first comes out and assumes "butch," the only avai-
lable lesbian model.
```

"It could definitely lead to a promotion," Roslyn says as Andrea tunes briefly in.

```
Jordan brings to their relationship an obsession with
bodily fluids, one which disgusts and pleases Andrea;
one which she occasionally happens upon growing inside,
a lazy weed threaded through traits she takes pride in,
pointless and unappreciated when Jordan leaves.
     "Spit in my mouth," Jordan whispers once when
they're fucking, fingers pushing into Andrea's tem-
ples, which Jordan knows Andrea absolutely hates.
     "You're kidding?" Andrea says but Jordan either
doesn't hear or pretends not to, so Andrea gathers
saliva as Jordan lets her lips go slack.
```

Clearly then, Andrea, like the Criminal Mastermind, hunts and gathers, but she swears there's something more underhanded about Jordan's means of acquisition. Jordan's a grave robber, not an anthropologist; furthermore, Andrea wonders whether stripped of the habits Jordan assembles, she would exist at all.

At the end of the line Roslyn is silent.

"I'm proud of you," Andrea says, aware her rhythm is way off.

"Listen, just talk to her." Roslyn sounds tired. "I don't know what you've got to lose."

At any moment Andrea might lose everything; she's the girl who Jordan's been with longer than anyone else. There's no point explaining this to Roslyn, so instead she inquires after Dave, a guy Roslyn's been dating for some time.

"He found a better job in DC."

"When did this happen?"

"A few months ago. Remember? One of us said I was better off without him and the other agreed. I'm not sure who said what, but at least I remember the conversation, which is more than I can say for you."

IF THE CRIMINAL Mastermind were a two-term president, it's obvious who she'd be. She has Clinton's way with semantics. She's hoarse and eats hamburgers. She knows exactly whose hand to shake. Not to mention the more obvious parallel. When the blue dress hits the news, Andrea's heart goes out to Hillary and Chelsea, but mostly she thrills at Clinton's impropriety—the power differential does a little something for her as well. Later, after the impeachment hearings, Andrea watches Barbara Walters interview Monica, her fat flushed cheeks, her anime eyes. Barbara Walters looks incredulous but feigns sympathy. Of course Monica cries. The thing that most disturbs Andrea: clearly Monica is still in love.

A good year into Jordan's second term, Andrea's pacing the apartment, willing herself to do something constructive: take up knitting or at least sit down. Instead, she finds her step quickening, as if by walking as fast as she's thinking, her brain and her body will reach equilibrium. This works sometimes when she's running, not so much when picking her way through piles of books, empty Altoid tins, coins, and other nameless debris.

"I miss my living room floor," she tells Roslyn's voice mail, talking as she walks. "Just when I think she might be one of those people who keeps used Saran Wrap and newspapers from 1973, she goes on a spree and cleans everything up. Of course the first thing she does once it's clean is throw the box from a TV dinner into the sink. Okay. Call me."

Jordan's cat swipes at Andrea's leg as she passes. Andrea barely pauses. Busy not looking at the clock on the microwave, she's waiting for Jordan to return from the dry cleaners. It's just up the block, but Jordan's been gone for forty-five minutes. Andrea fights hard not to believe this means she's having an affair.

Hardly the hot issue, she tells herself, *just easier to conceptualize.*

She glances out the front window, sees empty sidewalk partially obscured by roof. Across the street, a lesbian neighbor packs sleeping bags and a cooler into her black Subaru. Watching, Andrea wishes she were Subaru Dyke's girlfriend. She seems normal, wholesome. Andrea witnesses her nine-to-five comings and goings, so at minimum, she knows Subaru Dyke can hold down a job. She imagines a life with her neighbor: summer camping trips, weekly jaunts to Target, grocery cart filled with toilet paper and detergent, how they'd alternate family Thanksgivings every year. Since Easter, Andrea's parents have not once mentioned Jordan. Then again, all the family approval in the world seems inconsequential when she pictures Jordan's hands.

The letter, she thinks. Over two months and she still can't take it in.

Why am I here?

It isn't just Jordan's physical presence that commands her, Andrea thinks, watching Subaru Dyke pull away. It's how deeply familiar she is, how instinctively they respond to each other, how Jordan seems in charge of what's genuine about Andrea. An automatic authority, she's the person Andrea turns to in stupid desperation, needing herself explained.

What She's Worth to Jordan:

Someone who accidentally shares Jordan's sexual ethos

A young, blank page, unjustifiably naive

As close to Jordan's thirteen-year-old rejecter as Jordan can legally get—Some sort of second chance?

Jordan's full of tales about women with whom she's passed time. According to Jordan, she never shared her heart. Except with Andrea. Of course she says that. Surely she says the same to every woman. But Andrea's the only one she comes back for, which has to mean something, but what?

Jordan's been gone at least an hour now, but Andrea refuses to check up on her. She can't abide the thought of finding Jordan prowling an alley laughing, hand furtively cupping her phone. In the pantry, Andrea reaches for the half-empty box of Grape-Nuts where she keeps her social security card and two rarely used credit cards. Few things about Jordan are certain, but Andrea can't imagine her ever pouring herself a bowl. From underneath the wax paper bag she takes Patricia's letter, and listening for Jordan's keys, she unfolds it.

Dear Andrea,
If you're anything like me, you won't believe what I have to say.
I'm hoping you're not. I'm hoping you're more self-protective. I'm
hoping you have more sense.

During their initial involvement, discussion of Jordan's past dalliances is one of Andrea's favorite things.

I've never been a savvy business owner. I focus on what I'm good
at—finding art, cultivating artists, and courting buyers.

Both educational and titillating, the stories make Andrea feel privy to the inner-recesses of Jordan's brain.

It's a sort of tunnel vision; generally, I let the money part take care
of itself.

She requests a particular anecdote like it's a bedtime story: in her late twenties, the Criminal Mastermind has a run-in with a closeted celebrity, a woman who plays the quirky sister on a '90s sitcom, later appears on the *L Word*, her queerness contextualized, brash where once restrained.

Jordan may have told you she did my books when we were together, a system I wish I could say I questioned at the time.

Jordan's riding her motorcycle down Sunset and sees the celebrity at a table in front of The Coffee Bean and Tea Leaf, laughing with her friends. When Jordan's bike stalls at a red-light, she pulls over and kick starts it. The celebrity approaches, asks Jordan for a ride home. The punch line: when Jordan asks where home is, the woman smiles. "I meant *your* home," she says.

Instead, I felt relieved of a burden. Despite her issues with infidelity, I assumed that financially she had my best interests in mind. More tunnel vision.

Compelling when Andrea exists peripherally, the story no longer stimulates her now that she's ostensibly primary in Jordan's life. Still, Andrea churns it over regularly, her mind's insistent current wearing the edges down. Where once it gave her a queasy rush of jealous lust, there's nothing rollicking about the queasiness now. She's gone from carnival-queasy to something like morning sick. She hates to think of Jordan's life before her, the life she still leads inside herself, where Andrea can't reach.

After she left, I went back to neglecting the gallery's finances, and if I hadn't been audited, I'm ashamed to say I might never have noticed the discrepancies.

Andrea jolts when she hears the front door slam, her pulse thumping wildly, a small insistent person pounding her fists against the walls of Andrea's veins. No time to return Patricia's letter to the cereal box, instead she tucks it into her back pocket before meeting Jordan at the front door.

"What took you so long?" Andrea asks, reluctantly joining the paper doll parade of women who find hotel matchbooks, wait up to ask accusing questions, have their worst suspicions confirmed. At least she's in good company. Probably Ellen DeGeneres right before Anne Heche left her, Billie Holiday every day since she was born.

"That effing dry cleaner!" Jordan's face is the exact shade of crimson it turns when she can't convince someone to counter company policy or cut some illicit deal. "Would you believe he sold my coat?"

"What?" This has so little to do with what Andrea expected, she's not sure what it actually means.

"According to him, if a customer leaves an item for over six months, he has the right to sell it! You'd think he'd have the decency to contact us first!"

"You left your coat at the dry cleaners for six months?"

"We should sue that asshole. He came all the way here from Korea just to rip off people like us."

"So you weren't on the phone?" Andrea asks, still somehow fixated on an imagined affair.

"What? No, my phone's right here on the counter." Jordan hooks her fingers through Andrea's belt loops, a gesture which never fails to render Andrea weak.

"Oh," she says, shivering as Jordan's fingertips trace her low back.

"You're so insecure," Jordan says, like she's paying a compliment. "It's cute."

~

ANDREA THINKS JORDAN holds inside a healthy version of herself. Sometimes she's certain she sees Healthy Jordan, the top of her head, her ragged fingernails, or just the whites of her eyes. Like looking at blueprints crisscrossed and layered, Andrea can briefly discern who Jordan, minus defining events, might have

become. This fleeting clarity breeds moments of such tenderness, Andrea grits her teeth to get through. Afterwards she wonders about her discomfort, a sloppy jumble of revulsion and love.
Amidst it she feels undeserving, thinks a better person, older
maybe, or more nurturing, would embrace Jordan's vulnerability,
unlike Andrea, who never knows what to do with her hands.
Still, Andrea mostly believes she's waiting for Healthy Jordan to
emerge, that this is the version she truly wants. When she tracks
items keeping her with Jordan, these split-second glimpses make
her top five.

Other Reasons to Stay (In Order):

1. SEX (Obviously)

2. Nothing Andrea does shocks Jordan. This feels
like unconditional love. (Twelve and babysitting,
Andrea changes a charge's diaper, lets her fingers brush the baby's vagina, mostly because she's
stunned at its size. Girls must grow into them, she
thinks, but if she enquires she'll have to admit she
looked, more shameful, touched, so she never says
a word. But when Jordan asks, "What's the most evil
thing you've ever done?" Andrea gladly tells her.
Jordan: "I used to play this game where I'd hold a
match to my dad's college ring, then get the kids
on my block to take off their pants and lay across
my lap so I could brand them. I think that's probably worse.")

3. Possibilities collect around Jordan; she talks
like everything from a midstream career change to
lunch with Bono is attainable. For her it often is.

4. The fantasy person Jordan believes Andrea is.
("How'd I get so lucky?" Jordan asks sometimes, and
Andrea freezes, thinking of the multitudes that have
found her resistible. But with Jordan, Andrea feels
like a sought after leading lady, Cyd Charisse, long
legs flashing, or Ann Margret in her *Bye Bye Birdie*

days. She even starts to notice men casting her ap-
proving glances on the street. This feels new, but
Andrea doesn't know for sure. Maybe it's been happening forever, or maybe it's not happening at all.
Anyway, Jordan acts like the rules governing her own
life apply to Andrea, like Andrea too could have any
man or woman she wants. She's grateful for Jordan's
assumption, but more than likely it's a lie.)

"I love Winnie the Pooh," Jordan says, spotting the battered book
on Andrea's shelf in Westwood.

"Did your mom read it to you?" Andrea has yet to understand
Jordan's mother is one of several topics only Jordan can bring up.

Other Verboten Topics:
Cocaine

Whether or not Jordan's ass sags (It does.)

"My mom doesn't read."

"Not ever?"

"*TV Guide* sometimes." Jordan slides the book from its place.

"My mom read to me till I was fourteen. I was totally conflicted
because I liked it, but I thought I was too old."

"Tough life." Jordan plops the book on Andrea's coffee table
and takes a sip of her Diet Coke.

"What did you like to do when you were fourteen?" Andrea
perches on the couch's arm.

"I played softball. Sometimes I'd babysit. I babysat for my coach
a couple times."

"I can't picture you babysitting."

"I was a great babysitter. I'd have done it more, but the coach's
wife found out we were messing around." Jordan's voice is dead-
pan. Andrea can't tell if she's kidding.

"What do you mean?"

"What I said." Jordan encircles her knees with her arms, a gesture remote from her standard repertoire.

"You were sleeping together?" Andrea already knows pressing Jordan is dicey, but Jordan's never answered so many consecutive questions. Andrea may not get this chance again.

"Mostly he just touched me."

"Did you want him to?"

"Not at first, but then I liked how it felt." Jordan peeks at Andrea. "It wasn't his fault. I was a really sexual kid." The way Jordan says it tells Andrea she's repeating something she was told.

"But he was a grown man."

"So?"

"So, he molested you." Andrea slides onto the couch next to Jordan, lays a hand lightly on her back.

"I never thought of it that way." Jordan shrugs like its nothing, but after a moment she rests her head in Andrea's lap.

Andrea thinks of Jordan's school portrait, faded and stashed in Jordan's money clip. In it, Jordan looks like the perfect 1970s poster child: pointy collar, short shaggy hair, her only peculiarity the flatness of her gaze. Andrea hesitates, embarrassed by her impulse, then, swallowing self-consciousness, she picks up *Winnie the Pooh* and begins to read aloud.

⌒

THE FIRST TIME they're together, Jordan is an on-again, off-again vegetarian. She seems quintessentially carnivorous, so it's hard for Andrea to remember this the second time around.

"I don't know what to tell you," Jordan says. "Out of the blue I just wanted a steak. This priest I was friends with goes, 'You know what it means when a lesbian craves red meat, right?'"

"What kind of priest talks like that?" Andrea knows whom

Jordan's referencing, some charming young guy Andrea is certain Jordan's fucked at least once. She has no idea what he looks like, but she pictures him compact yet burly like the guys she sees Jordan eyeing at the gym. Jordan claims to be studying their musculature, but Andrea suspects there's more to it than that.

"Todd's great. I wonder whatever happened to him."

"You didn't stay in touch?" Andrea's sarcasm is lost on Jordan, who doesn't know a thing about friendship, can't figure what's in it for her. Andrea's totally clear on this shortcoming. She knows when they inevitably part again just how little value she'll hold.

"We went our separate ways," Jordan says.

Jordan's Over-Used Catchphrases:

-We went our separate ways. (Said of each friend she mentions, her parents, all the girlfriends she's had.)

-That hits the spot. (In reference to sex, food, the arrival of the Victoria's Secret catalogue.)

-Ho Di Doh. (From her favorite joke:

Q. What has four legs and goes Ho Di Doh?

A. Two black men running for an elevator.

Andrea dreads waiting for elevators with Jordan, always prays no African Americans will arrive.)

-I love you.

She lets the last slip on a surreptitious phone call before they even sleep together, Andrea, hugging her knees in her desk chair, clutching the phone to her ear. The call itself is unexpected; Jordan's away with Patricia on a church retreat.

"I'm on the beach," Jordan announces when Andrea picks up the phone. "It's beautiful here; the stars are reflected in the water and the fog is rolling in."

Fog and stars? Andrea thinks. Not at the same time.

Later she'll play a game: what would happen if she'd called Jordan on the incongruity, if each time Jordan gussied up reality to suit herself, Andrea pointed to her lie? Bad things, probably. Jordan's tiny deceits hint at her larger ones. If Andrea starts tugging at stitches, Jordan's liable to unravel, and what will Andrea do then?

Only in retrospect will Andrea consider this. In the moment, and without thinking, she makes a move that becomes easier over time. She swaps in Jordan's truth for her own observations, folding reality like tissue paper, matching corner to corner, when really it ought to lie flat. Just a fold, she can undo it. Besides, what's so important about instincts if they stand between her and where she wants to be?

"Where's Patricia?" Andrea asks.

"She's meditating, which of course I should be too. Andrea?"

"Yes?" Andrea jolts at the sound of her name.

"I love you. I'm not sure what that means for us, but I wanted you to know."

Andrea stares at her gold filigreed drinking glass, stolen from her church's kitchen at age twelve. Its theft never makes her feel guilty. On the contrary, the acquisition feels like the righting of some terrible wrong. An eyelash hangs suspended in the day-old water, its weight forcing the surface to ripple and bow. Jordan's words so close to her ear make her feel like she's falling, the furniture in her apartment rushing upward as she soars down.

Jordan says "I love you" a hundred thousand times after that, and Andrea waits, neck craned, a fox before a tree heavy with low-hanging fruit. Above her the words spin on their branch, plump and sunripened. No matter Andrea's lightning quick reflexes, by the time the words hit the ground, their sweetness speaks of decay.

When Jordan starts talking about getting back into vegetarianism, Andrea feels strangely unsettled by her resolution. In the same way she is privately, guiltily glad Jordan's lost faith in religion, Andrea appreciates Jordan's adjustment from vegetarian to non. She guesses she resents anything Jordan gives herself over to. Between the two of them, Andrea's the one giving ever over; Jordan's impenetrable. She'll never allow Andrea that close. Andrea doesn't discriminate, Jesus or tofu, she's jealous of both. Still, that isn't exactly what bothers Andrea. It's tangled around it, but isn't the thing itself.

"IF YOU'RE LOOKING at Christ as competition, there's probably something wrong."

Roslyn is in Chicago for the weekend visiting her older brother whose wife has just given birth. She looks spindly and elegant in white bug's eye sunglasses and wide-legged jeans when Andrea meets her at The Chicago Diner, one of Jordan's favorite places to eat.

"Chicagoans are obsessed with patios." Andrea changes the subject. After mentioning her feelings on Jordan's former vegetarianism, she finds she could have predicted Roslyn's response. "It's not such a big deal in LA, probably because they have access all year."

Roslyn smirks at the occupants of the rickety picnic-style table to her right, two teenage blondes taking digital pictures of themselves.

"What is that woman eating?" Roslyn asks, pointing toward a different table. She hasn't removed her sunglasses despite the gray sky.

"Fake chicken and buckwheat biscuits, I think."

"Jesus, Andrea."

"It's really not that bad if you give it a chance."

"A rousing endorsement." Roslyn scans the tall menu.

"Their guacamole is great. That's what I'm going to have." Andrea checks her cell phone. Jordan's an hour late. Who knows if she'll even show.

"Did you try calling her?" Of course Roslyn picks up on Andrea's thoughts.

"She's not answering. Something probably came up."

"Between the cats and the Internet she's got a lot on her plate."

"Can we not talk about it?" Andrea slaps on a smile as their server approaches.

"Looks like she came straight from a yoga class," Roslyn says later, after the server returns with their food. For a moment Andrea thinks she means Jordan. She looks toward the back garden entrance, set to make cheerful introductions, put her mounting anxiety aside.

"Who, the waitress?"

Roslyn nods.

"She reminds me of Ned O'Donnell's older sister. Remember her?" Andrea fingers the letter in her back pocket. She's been transferring it from one pair of pants to another—risky, sure, but it's become a sort of talisman.

"The dancer?" Roslyn sniffs her seitan club sandwich.

"Yeah."

"You had such a crush on him in sixth grade."

"So embarrassing." Andrea dips a chip in guacamole. "Every time I talked to him I'd say the opposite of whatever I meant. Remember when we had to read a biography, and the kids who wrote the best book reports got to dress up as the person they'd read about and give a speech in front of the school?"

"Yeah, you were Diana Ross and you couldn't understand why Mrs. Jackson got mad when you came in with your face painted brown."

"I thought she'd appreciate it. So, Ned reads about Robin Williams. We're backstage waiting to go on and I'm all excited, cause for once he's talking to me. He says something about how great Robin Williams is, and keep in mind I loved Robin Williams."

I need to tell you something, she imagines herself saying. *I got this letter and . . .*

"Sure." Roslyn sips her coffee. "You were obsessed with that horrible movie, *Hook.* Whenever you slept over you brought the video box with you. Not the video, just the box."

"I hated sleepovers. Anyway, instead of saying, 'Me, too, I love Robin Williams,' I nod all enthusiastic, and say, 'I hate him.' So self-sabotaging. I have a theory about why I did it though, why I always said asinine things to boys I liked."

And what?

"Of course you do."

"Ned especially. I think I really liked his sister, but I couldn't admit it to myself, so I latched on to him, but I didn't really want him so I made sure to mess it up."

"Maybe. Or maybe you were just a dorky kid."

"God, remember I kept making you call his house? And remember how we used to follow the two of them home? Even then, the whole thing seemed so distasteful, but no way could I stop."

Have I confronted her? No. That would require willpower, courage—farfetched, impossible things.

Roslyn rubs her temples. "Do you have any Advil?"

Immersed in her thoughts, Andrea doesn't answer. "Remember Jacob in fifth grade? That was mortifying too."

Just say something, she thinks, reaching for the letter.

"All this because some chick showed up for work in a leotard." Roslyn shakes her head. "You're like Proust with his fucking madeleines; everything reminds you of something else."

"I wanted to tell you something." Andrea says, looking over Roslyn's shoulder rather than at her, afraid she'll lose her nerve.

"Yes?"

"A disturbing thing happened, uh, recently."

Behind Roslyn, an attractive woman in a black motorcycle jacket approaches. Andrea watches her as she talks, thinking how she sort of looks like Adrienne, which means she's exactly Andrea's type. A few feet from their table, Jordan does a quick nod and parts her lips, and belatedly, Andrea recognizes her.

"Roslyn," Andrea stands, knocking her knees on the table.

"Jesus, what?" Roslyn reaches to steady her water glass.

"This is Jordan." Ridiculous, the words, like saying, "Roslyn, meet my Sasquatch." Andrea giggles like she's twelve. Despite everything, she surges with pride when she introduces Jordan.

Look at her, she thinks. *Mine.*

"Andrea," Jordan wraps her arms around Andrea and kisses her forehead.

"What am I, your ward?" Andrea says, confused by the use of her name, the fatherly kiss.

"Don't be silly." Jordan turns to Roslyn. "I've heard so many wonderful things about you," she says.

Silly? Wonderful things? Andrea is somehow whole strides behind.

"Same," Roslyn says.

"So, you two have been friends forever, right?" Jordan puts her hand over Roslyn's.

Bad move, Andrea thinks.

"Something like that." Roslyn shifts in her chair. If you didn't know her you'd have no clue how much she hates to be touched.

"Have I seen that jacket?" Andrea asks, hoping to distract Jordan so she'll release her grip.

"What's the first memory you have of Andrea?" Jordan reaches for Andrea's water glass and Roslyn's hands flee to her lap.

"Maybe when we were in kindergarten and a girl in our class had a sleepover."

"That's your first memory of me?" Andrea props an elbow on the table. "We've known each other since we were three."

"My first clear one."

"What happened?" Jordan looks from Roslyn to Andrea. Andrea wishes she could see Jordan's eyes.

"I had to pee but I was too shy to ask where the bathroom was, so I took off my shoes and peed in them." Roslyn laughs, remembering. "Then I started crying because I didn't know what I'd tell my dad when he came to pick me up."

Roslyn's description surprises Andrea. Not the words, but how freely she speaks them. Is she making an out of character effort, or has she fallen under Jordan's spell?

"Where does Andrea come in?" Jordan leans back in her chair, smiling wide, but underneath the table, Andrea feels her knee jiggling.

"She gave me her shoes."

"I was always losing things," Andrea says. "My parents were used to it."

"That's my girl." Jordan's fingers graze Andrea's cheek. In private or the company of strangers, the words, the gesture might melt Andrea. With Roslyn watching, Jordan seems paternalistic.

"Roslyn is here visiting her new nephew," Andrea says, angling her face subtly away.

"Congratulations." Jordan's eyes on Andrea's are purposeful. She wants Andrea to know she's noticed. "You must be so excited," turning to Roslyn, Jordan touches her again.

"Thanks." Roslyn's expression reveals little, but Andrea sees the muscles in her arm tense. "How do you like Chicago so far?"

"It's no LA." Jordan sips Andrea's water.

"Ah, so you like it?" Roslyn says.

"Funny." Jordan turns to Andrea, "You ordered without me."

"I'm sorry," Andrea says.

"You're almost two hours late." Roslyn seems more amused than aggressive.

"You Midwesterners." Jordan shakes her head.

"I'll get you a menu." Andrea stands, jostling the table again.

"Sit, babe. I know what I want." Jordan hails the waitress. "Grilled cheese," she says. "Thanks, honey."

"What *about* us?" Roslyn asks.

"So anal about time. In LA, we get there when we get there. We all run on Colored People Time."

"What did you say?" Cool to begin with, Roslyn's voice turns instantly to ice.

"Jordan, Roslyn's here visiting her . . . " Andrea stops, realizing she's repeating herself. "Do either of you want some guacamole? There's plenty left."

Please, she thinks hard at Roslyn, *please just let it go.*

"So, Jordan, what do you do for a living?" Roslyn asks after pausing so long Andrea's stomach starts to ache.

"This and that." Jordan dunks a chip.

"Meaning what?" Roslyn says. She's steepling her fingers, never a good sign.

"In LA, I was a parish administrator. Right now I'm taking some classes at DePaul. I'm close to an MBA, but we'll see how it goes."

Andrea opens her mouth then goes for her water, takes a long swallow to make sure she doesn't talk. Roslyn's eyes meet Andrea's as Jordan continues, "Gotta support this one in style, you know." She waits for Roslyn to laugh or agree. Jordan does this a lot, Andrea realizes, talks above and past Andrea, as if she's a child.

"What do you do?" Jordan asks, when it's clear Roslyn won't play.

"I'm a lawyer," Roslyn says, still looking at Andrea. She knows Jordan's dawdling through college; an MBA years down some remote, unpaved road.

"Andrea said you were smart."

"Andrea's pretty smart herself." Roslyn adjusts her sunglasses, and Andrea realizes she's the only one whose eyes are exposed.

"Sure she is." Jordan gives Andrea's knee a quick squeeze, then grabs for her sandwich almost before the server has set down her plate.

"Did you just buy that?" Andrea indicates the jacket, not sure why she keeps bringing it up.

"Yeah, the Alley was having a sale. Tough, right? I had one just like it when I was a kid."

"It's nice." Glistening and supple, the jacket squeaks against the back of Jordan's chair.

"You don't like it?"

"I didn't say that." When Andrea smiles at Roslyn, her face hurts. "She has great taste. Lots of high quality coats."

"You think I have too many coats?" Jordan's still holding her sandwich; she has yet to bring it to her mouth.

"You can't have too many coats." Inane, but who cares? What with all the subtext, it hardly matters what Andrea says.

"This is ice cold." Jordan drops the triangle of bread and imitation cheese to her plate.

"Tell the waitress." Andrea says.

"It's not worth it." Jordan pushes her chair back.

"Where are you going?"

"If you hate the jacket so much, I'll return it."

"What, now?"

Jordan shrugs, walking away. Andrea's expected to follow, of course, and she would, if Roslyn weren't there.

"Cute." Roslyn says, arms folded across her chest.

"What do you mean?" Queasy, Andrea presses her fingers to her solar plexus.

"She couldn't charm me, so she decided to throw a fit."

"It's not that simple."

"Andrea," Roslyn takes her hand, an unexpected move, "simple is exactly what it is."

"What, you think she's stupid?"

"Not stupid, no." Roslyn settles her sunglasses on top of her head.

"She's sensitive; don't judge her."

"She's not worth judging. I'm judging you."

"Don't do that either." Andrea stands.

"Where are you going?"

"I have to find her." Jordan must be halfway down the block by now.

"Andrea, when is enough enough?"

"You don't understand. I can't let her walk away angry—who

knows what she'll do?" Voice rising, Andrea pulls cash from her pocket.

"You know what? I can't do this." On her feet, Roslyn throws money on the table.

"What is that, a threat?" Andrea swallows, certain she's going to be sick.

"I feel like a goddamn enabler."

"You can't leave me alone in this." Panicked, Andrea waves her arms crazily, her gesture taking in the diner, absent Jordan, everything empty inside.

"Look how scared you are. That isn't a normal way to feel!"

"What the fuck do you know about feelings?" Andrea says. The lines she's crossing—each becomes tardily apparent. "You live your life according to some spreadsheet! I'd rather die than be like you."

Roslyn nods once, and Andrea glances at the surrounding tables. Incredibly, no one seems to have noticed a thing.

"I didn't mean that." Andrea feels herself shivering. Cold sweat bathes her skin.

"There's a difference between not having feelings, and letting your feelings run you." Roslyn tosses her trench coat over one arm.

"I know. Please." Andrea reaches for Roslyn, thinking to take her hand.

"You can call me when you get your shit together; until then, please don't."

"How will I know when that is?" Around them, patrons clink their silverware, raise and lower their glasses. Andrea wants to go from table to table, shaking them. She's never felt more alone. "Fine, fuck you then, whatever happens is your fault." She sits down hard, dropping her head into her hands.

"You need to get some therapy."

"You don't believe in therapy!" Andrea says.

"I'm making an exception," Roslyn turns, nearly colliding with Jordan.

"Hey now," Jordan says. "Nobody tells Andrea what to do."
Nobody puts baby in the corner, Andrea thinks and almost laughs.
"I hope someday that's actually true." Roslyn pauses.

```
"I'm sorry. I didn't mean it, not a word. I'm here for
you, Andrea. I could never leave you to fend for your-
self." Roslyn puts a hand on Andrea's shoulder.
     "You gave me the strength," Andrea will say later. "I
could never have done it without you."
     "Jordan," Andrea stands, arms folded, "I know where
you get your money."
```

"I see you," Roslyn says, brushing past Jordan. "Andrea may not, but I do." She makes leaving look easy. Andrea watches her stride away.

"Someone oughtta keep that one on a leash." Jordan says, shaking her head.

"Why did you come back?" Andrea's hand goes momentarily to her back pocket.

"Forgot my phone and my keys. That was pretty rough, huh?" Jordan sits, fingering her discarded sandwich. After a moment, she takes a tiny bite. "Try some, babe, it's actually pretty good cold."

Andrea doesn't answer. She's watching the Camera Blondes at the next table. They delete their photos as fast as they snap them. The pose each girl takes is always the same.

⌒

I'M INTO INCEST." Jordan says this casually one day in LA when they're discussing sexual fantasies.

Now we're talking, Andrea thinks, contrasting Jordan's disclosure with "That's private," Linda's standard response to all sexual inquiries. She'll take depravation over priggishness any day of the week.

"Pheromones," Roslyn used to say, whenever Andrea defended her relationship by appealing to sex. "Useless in modern society. It's better to have someone who wants what you want. Someone trustworthy."

But why, Andrea wonders, *should shared goals or integrity hold more weight than endlessly revelatory sex?*

In theory, Andrea has no patience for role-playing. Her standard assessment: just a last ditch attempt to salvage a floundering sex life. Not so with Jordan. Whatever relationship Jordan assigns them, in the moment, Andrea buys.

"You're white and I'm black," Jordan tells her. "I'm a Nazi and you're Jewish." "You're my mother and you walk in on me."

Reluctant at first, Andrea quickly finds herself calling Jordan "Sir," making Jordan choke on her fat cock, begging Jordan to fuck her rather than send her to the showers, all without a speck of unease.

True, sometimes Andrea wonders about the correlation between Jordan's elastic relationship to the truth and her ability to make any liaison seem authentic. But mostly she plain doesn't care. How could she explain that in sex, Jordan proves herself trustworthy? They're like trapeze artists; fully present and committed, anticipating each other's every move.

Anything is worth this, Andrea thinks each time they have sex. *I could never get here with anyone else.*

⁓

IN LINE, ANDREA and Jordan swap Cry Wolf anecdotes, a dependable way to pass the time. Today in Green Bay, Jordan's befriended Becky, a woman whose ripped army pants and bristly upper lip belie her perky name.

"I shot pool with Adrienne once in Racine," Becky says, and Andrea drops her gaze to the cement. If she looks Jordan's way, she'll laugh.

"Sweet." Jordan nods as if she buys the story. Maybe she does; she's never been to Racine.

"She wasn't as good as you'd think." Becky spits chaw into her Sprite can, runs her tongue over her teeth. Butch posturing, Andrea's certain. She's seen Adrienne play pool too, after a show in Madison, and as far as she can tell, Adrienne's great.

Across from Linda at a tall corner table, Andrea bites her cuticle bloody when she spots Adrienne near the bar. She's laughing with three Frat-ish lesbians, all tequila shots and madras shorts. One Andrea recognizes as a roadie, the others are probably local friends.

"I told you, she comes here when she's in town." Andrea stares at Adrienne's shoulders, broad beneath her beater. Offstage she's aggressively lean; her bones fairly stab through her skin.

"Great." Linda sips her water.

"Can you tell what she's drinking?" From beneath lowered lids, Andrea watches Adrienne stride to the pool table, friends in tow.

"How long do we have to stay?"

Andrea doesn't answer. Watching Adrienne chalk up a cue takes her right back to middle school. Adrienne might be Jacob, Ned, or any of the boys on whom Andrea focused, trying to get through each day.

"God Andrea, I'm sitting right here." Linda crosses her arms over her chest. "How about some self-control?"

"This is a big deal for me," Andrea says. "She was like this turning point in my life."

"You've made that clear."

Obviously Andrea should apologize, but as Adrienne breaks, an out of body sense of elsewhere overwhelms Andrea. Adrienne's bare throat laugh, her sinewy arms, the hint of tan skin that peeks between her shirt and her belt—Andrea's not so much attracted as she is calmed; her precarious state of absorption superseding everything restless inside.

Tuning back into Becky's voice, Andrea remembers the last thing Linda says before stalking to the car: *"Of all the people in here, you think she'd actually choose you?"*

"I asked her where Peter was and she said he was back at the hotel." Becky says, preparing to spit.

"He's shy." A tiny brunette with blue plastic glasses runs a hand over her frizzy curls. "That's what he says in all the interviews. He'd rather be alone writing than out at some bar."

"You've talked to him, haven't you?" Andrea asks Jordan. She wants to one up the brunette.

"Sure." Jordan stretches her legs in front of her. "Before they got big."

"What was he like?" The brunette hunches forward, squeezing her knees to her chest. Her breath smells milky, like that kid at birthday parties you try to avoid. Andrea takes the top from her Starbucks cup, inhales the steam.

"He's a good guy." Jordan nods, sage-like. She's only missing a cloak and a lonely hill. "Quiet, like you said."

The brunette smiles and Andrea feels Jordan's somehow taken her side.

"He told me he got into music after his girlfriend dumped him for a jock in high school."

"He used to run cross country though, right?" The brunette nods rapidly, willing Jordan to agree.

"Right, right," Jordan says. "But he said he figured guitar players get all the girls."

"This was at that club in Venice?" Andrea asks, a familiar uneasiness awakening in her chest.

"Yeah, back in '86." Jordan pauses like she's got more to say.

"Was his hair darker then? In pictures it looks darker," the brunette says.

"Adrienne's hair was great in the eighties," Becky tells Andrea. "Short in front and long in back. I don't know why she stopped wearing it like that."

"It was about the same color," Jordan says, her voice dropping so the brunette has to lean close. "And he wore this tiny gold cross all the time. He said it was his grandmother's."

"You mean a mullet?" Andrea asks, knowing that's exactly what Becky means. She tries to catch Jordan's eye.

"Wow," the brunette whispers. "I know how much he loved her, but I didn't know he wore her cross."

"He's got her name tattooed on his inner thigh," Jordan says. "He said he tries to honor her every day."

"He showed you?" Andrea asks, quiet, just as the brunette squeals, "God, what else did he say?"

"It was so long ago. I don't remember much more." Jordan shrugs.

"Anyone want a slice?" Becky stands slowly. Andrea hears her knees pop. "Best pizza place in town is right up the street."

"I'll come." The brunette takes a ragged blue wallet from her backpack. Held together with duct tape, it looks like a tiny tent. Andrea's certain there's Velcro involved.

Watching Becky's expansive rolling walk, Andrea tells herself not to ask. Of course she disobeys.

"You didn't," she starts. "Did you sleep with him?"

Jordan shuffles through her pocket, dropping coins, receipts, and business cards in a heap.

"If you'd asked me in front of Butchy, I'd have had to lie." She rips through the cellophane surrounding a toothpick and clamps it between her teeth. "When they get back, I'm going to tell the little one Peter likes girls with curly hair. It'll make her night."

⌒

THE CRIMINAL MASTERMIND appreciates Andrea's sexual compliance, but occasionally she demands Andrea delve into her past; she suspects a history of abuse.

"Don't get me wrong, I'm happy to benefit," she says at four o'clock one morning, "but something must have happened to make you this way."

Andrea easily recalls each item in her closet at age seven. She can recite word for word a dream Roslyn described having in ninth grade. If there's anything Andrea can do it's remember, but Andrea indignant is no match for Jordan on a roll.

"I'm just saying, you're too innocent to come up with this shit on your own." Jordan shifts her weight on top of Andrea, pinning Andrea with her eyes.

"I think I'd know if I'd been molested." Andrea says. She tries to sound confident, but her exhaustion and Jordan's natural authority force her inflection up at the end.

"Here, let's try something." Jordan sits up, tugging her T-shirt over her knees. "Naughty," she says, then sits forward. "Well?"

"What are you doing?" Andrea gropes the bedside table for the Advil, palms two, and swallows them dry.

"We're free associating. Just say the first thing that comes to mind."

"Uh, naughty? That song from *Crazy for You*, 'Embraceable You'?"

"Why?"

"There's that line, 'Don't be a naughty baby . . . '?"

"You're thinking too much. What's the first sexual experience you remember?"

Only three hours till she'll pile on several layers of hard-winter clothing, stand on the corner waiting for her first bus to work, but obediently, Andrea thumbs through childhood memories. She's half convinced she'll suddenly recall some sordid scenario, an uncle flashing his penis behind the woodshed, a babysitter's hands in Andrea's swimsuit at the pool. Discomfited to understand some part of her that *wants* to remember, Andrea blames her exhaustion, tells herself it's only that she's desperate for relief. In truth, if it would guarantee Jordan's sustained interest, she'd turn up a past fraught as Sybil's.

"First sexual experience," Andrea repeats, searching, but the best she can come up with is something just short of nothing that happens at the church daycare one day in spring.

Five years old, and lining up for recess, Andrea sees Roslyn is absent, a rarity. She attends school five days a week, while Andrea goes only on Tuesdays and Thursdays, the days her mother sees patients. It occurs to Andrea that even though she and Roslyn are best friends, three days a week Roslyn plays with someone else. Three days a week Roslyn makes it through without her just fine. This seems a betrayal but also incredibly brave.

Andrea scans the line and spots Emily's long, perfectly straight blonde hair. Andrea half believes that all blonde girls are part unicorn, plus Emily is a full head taller than Andrea and almost a year older, so Andrea is shy around Emily.

"Andrea, come stand with me," Emily says.

Andrea lets James, Karen, and Reed, the biracial boy she pretends to be in love with, pass her and falls into line next to Emily.

"Jay says he likes me!" Emily whispers loud in Andrea's face. Her breath smells like apple juice and vegetables, and Andrea misses Roslyn, who dips broccoli in her juice at snack time, calls the florets little trees.

"He told you that?" Andrea asks.

They file outside and Andrea blinks her eyes in the sun's glare.

"Let's play on the slide," Emily says and runs toward it, her sea-green skirt skimming her knees.

Andrea is glad Emily's forgotten about Jay. He's tall and mean, the pastor's only child. He comes to the church daycare after his school day is over even though he's too old to be enrolled. She'd much rather play alone with Emily who is not, Andrea has decided, the misty hills variety of unicorn. She's the My

Little Pony version. She's pink with sweet-smelling rubber skin and rainbow-colored ribbons for hair. Emily whizzes down the slide a couple of times, then sneaks in behind Andrea, twines her legs around her, and they take a turn together, their combined weight slowing them down. Later, Andrea stands behind Emily, waiting her turn when she notices Jay and two other boys surrounding the slide's base.

"If you slide down, your skirt will go up and your underwear will go down!" The boys chant.

Emily giggles, waits till all eyes are on her, then slithers down the slide.

"Come on Andrea!" she says. Andrea considers. She is wearing purple corduroy pants because her mother thinks skirts are bad for girls. Something about how much money women earn and a thing called the patriarchy. Since she's not wearing a skirt, Andrea figures it's safe to slide down.

She hits the ground, her sneakers kicking up small clouds of dust, and sees Emily and the boys are already halfway across the playground, standing near the gymnasium windows, hidden behind a clump of trees.

"Show it, Emily," Jay says as Andrea approaches.

Emily puts a hand on her hip, cocks her head to the side.

"Hmm," she says. "I just don't know."

"Come on."

"You go first."

"No way," Jay folds his arms over his chest. "You went down the slide even though we said what would happen! You have to show us. You don't have a choice."

By now one of Jay's friends has wandered away and the other looks nervous. Jay is still grinning and confident though, and Emily's not going anywhere either. Andrea can tell this is the sort of thing she lives for: a laughing boy and an audience, herself the star of the show. Andrea can't see an alternative, so she does what she'll spend all of high school and some of college doing, stands quietly next to a pretty girl, watching her flirt with a boy.

There's more to this memory, though. The image never makes sense when it appears to Andrea. She's unclear on her motive, the heights don't seem to work out, and Emily would have required three hands. These inconsistencies are irrelevant however; the memory has truth's hue.

Andrea sees it through her six-year-old eyes. Sees herself standing close enough to Emily to feel her long hair tickle her face. She leans her head into Emily's skinny back and peers from beneath Emily's crooked elbow, the scene like a picture in a triangular frame. She watches Jay and his friend, she thinks the boy's name is Robert, watches them giggle and point as Emily wriggles out of her panties. She hears Robert yell, "Gross!" Watches him flee toward the slide. This is where things get muddled, because how could she have peered between Emily's arm and hip when Emily's hands were both occupied? Andrea can perfectly picture the right one lifting her dress, the left carefully separating the lips of her neat vagina. But how could she have seen what Jay, awed and silent, saw when she stood behind Emily, when she didn't face her head-on?

"That's it?" Jordan asks when Andrea finishes.

"That's all I can think of." Andrea has never shared this particular memory; it's actually something of which she's imprecisely ashamed.

"Think some more," Jordan says, punching a pillow, "maybe think about your father. I'm sure there's something there."

⌒

ANDREA'S HAD THE letter five months now, but still she focuses on sex. She studies Jordan's types like the fine print on an insurance policy, certain that understanding them will protect her this time around.

Types to Whom the Criminal Mastermind is Attracted:
Tall equine blondes (Patricia obviously)

Anyone Italian or Jewish (Andrea and half of New York City. Small comfort, that's not where they live.)

Angel from *Buffy the Vampire Slayer* (Jordan's gaze doesn't hunger, it appraises. Monitoring it, Andrea thinks Jordan wants to be—not have— Angel, so she isn't threatened. The fact that he's a fictional vampire also helps.)

Chunky freckled girl-next-door types (Andrea finds a picture of Jordan and the intern tucked inside Jordan's copy of *Left Behind*. In the photo the intern resembles a Midwestern pioneer girl. Arm hooked possessively around her shoulder, Jordan, all hooded eyes and precipitous cheekbones, looks like the Indian chief who's captured her covered wagon, made her his wife.)

Jennifer Beals (The first time Jordan leaves, Andrea focuses on the fact that she'll never again have to sit through the scene in *Flashdance* where Jennifer's ass smacks slow-motion onto the wet, polished tiles. This probably speeds her recovery time by at least a month and a half.)

⌇

"THINGS WERE EASIER before the Internet, not in the sense of being, like, easy, but . . . " This is all Andrea says before she decides seeing a therapist is a mistake. Nothing against Cathy, she's an unfussy shade of blonde, navy-clad and energetic, exactly what a therapist should be. Earlier, in the waiting room, Andrea panics when a blousy redhead with turquoise cowboy boots, a matching

chunky necklace, and one of those long sweatshirty-skirts calls
her name.

"Follow me," she says, "Cathy's running a few minutes late."

"You're not Cathy?" Andrea's fingers are poised on her phone's
keypad; "I bet she has a batik print couch," the message she's typed.

"I do couples' counseling." The redhead hands Andrea a business card on which, inexplicably, two grinning wedges of cheese
hold hands.

In Cathy's office—no tribal patterns; the sunlit space is
streamlined and sparse—Andrea suppresses another urge to text
Roslyn. Odd to feel so adrift without a person she sees less than
three times a year. Roslyn's always just a phone call away, though.
Even when she doesn't pick up, Andrea finds solace in her familiar voice: "I'm Roslyn, and I like messages." When will Andrea
hear it again?

Cathy is sincere, painless to talk to, and after the requisite intro-
ductory questions, Andrea decides to begin with Cry Wolf. It's
part of her life, she reasons, a constant shame-tinged pleasure, and
in some sense, the only long-term romance she boasts. Besides,
to start off talking about Jordan seems inconceivable. How will
this put-together blonde ever understand? She'll bring Jordan up
eventually, Andrea thinks, if things with Cathy work out. For now,
when Cathy asks if she's in a relationship, it seems simplest just to
tell her no.

"What do you mean about the Internet?" Cathy asks, head
to one side. Andrea is thinking how as a nineteen-year-old fan,
she assumed herself exceptional, didn't realize how many others
shared her vice. Now, friends with a handful of fans on Facebook, Andrea scans other people's updates, confronted daily with
funhouse images of herself. She recognizes every person who
clicks to "like" each update—their faces, not their names. Each
is someone she's met in line. Reading, Andrea wonders why she's
the only one recoiling from updates so blindly self-indulgent, so
eerily close to home.

Hannah

is at McDonald's, super psyched to hear "Swimmer" on the radio!

Like · Comments · 4 minutes ago

8 people like this comment

 Matilda Kennedy: Lucky, I *never* hear it!

 Annette Mcdonald: Swoon!

 Kestra Patel: Which McDonalds? I'm on my way lol!

Annie Shultz

Got God, got my family, got Puss n' Boots and Adrienne. No mountain too high, right? ;)

Like · Comments · 5 minutes ago

20 people like this comment

 Kelsey Rosenblatt: Give that kitty a squeeze for me.

 Bertha Dean-Prusko: lol Kels, you're dirty.

 Kelsey Rosenblatt: ??

 Justine Heimmer: When I had problems with baby Genie I thought about how strong Adrienne and Peter are. The whole time I was on bed rest, I thought of them, and even though Genie was born early, I knew she'd be ok. Two years later, she's just like every other baby her age. Be strong!

 Kelsey Rosenblatt: Oh, I get it lmao

"It's a way for fans to connect with other fans, but I've never really wanted that." Andrea spots a picture of a yellow Labrador on Cathy's desk. Bright eyed and smiling, the dog looks like Cathy herself.

"Some kind of Groucho Marx thing?" Cathy asks, impressing Andrea with the half-articulated reference. Cathy isn't pedantic at all.

"Not exactly."

After her watershed concert experience, the one she describes to Jordan (which, in the two years they're apart, Jordan commemorates by sending a card without a return address, yearly, on the concert's date), Andrea attends a show with a group of other Women's Studies majors. Prior to this, Andrea arrived for concerts when the doors opened, never realizing some people waited hours to get in first. The performance is in Milwaukee, and luckily one of Andrea's classmates has a car, a geezer of a Volvo. Andrea skips class to attend, something she's never done. She's smashed in the wide backseat with three girls; two others ricochet around in the rear.

"At least we have seatbelts," says Linda, at the time a casual friend.

"No chance I'd sit back there," Andrea agrees.

In the front seat, a girl named Amber chatters about Adrienne, raising her voice over the Cry Wolf tape the driver, Kim, plays nonstop.

"It wasn't so hard," Amber says. "When the guard wasn't looking, I just slipped backstage."

"No way." Andrea's shocked by Amber's boldness. A guard, inattentive or not, means "stay back."

"Way. That time I got a hug." Amber turns, playing with the leather strap encircling her throat.

"From Adrienne?"

"Yep."

"She wasn't mad you were back there?"

"Are you kidding? They want us back there. Just sometimes the venue isn't that hip." Amber's eyes surprise Andrea. Wide-set and welcoming, they're somehow intelligent, more so than her words.

"What did she smell like?" Andrea asks, her peripheral vision picking up Linda's scornful expression

"Um, amazing." Amber's sitting backward in her seat now. Arms wrapped around the headrest, she's inches away from Andrea. She smells pretty good herself. "I love that you asked that," Amber says. "I always wonder how people will smell."

"Speaking of," Andrea says, "what are you wearing, patchouli?" Am I flirting? She wonders.

"It's my signature, you gotta have one. What about you?"

"Me? Nothing."

Pretty, Andrea thinks, but is she even my type?

Next to Andrea, Linda sighs loudly and curls toward the window.

"Really? I smell something." Amber leans closer.

"I don't know, shampoo?" Too pretty, maybe.

"Well, you smell great." Amber smiles.

"So, how many times have you met her?" Andrea asks, ready to move on.

"About a dozen. You?"

"Just a couple," Andrea lies, understanding for the first time that she could meet Adrienne if she chose to.

Cathy makes a note on her yellow pad. "Why aren't you interested in meeting other fans, then?"

"It's . . . uncomfortable."

"How so?"

"Part of me wants to one up them by going to more concerts, getting closer to Adrienne, being more obsessed, but that's wasteful. All that time and focus—I don't want to be forty years old, sitting in some camping chair, proud 'cause Adrienne caught my eye."

"You want more for yourself."

"At least I want to want more."

In Milwaukee, lined up in front of the Rave, Andrea sticks close to Linda, who seems the sanest one there.

"I only went cause you were going," Linda tells her later. "I'm not even much of a fan."

Behind them in line, a fey boy strums a stout acoustic guitar. People gather around him to sing "Jack Rabbit," one of Cry Wolf's oldest songs. Third in line, Amber fidgets with her ring, a yellow oblong stone.

"I always try to wear amber," she says when another line-waiter compliments her. "It makes me feel empowered."

"Calm down," Andrea hears Kim tell Amber later. "Third in line's as good as first; we'll still get to pick where we stand."

"You should've driven faster." Amber says.

After the concert, Andrea will forget her discomfort when the doors opened and Amber made a panicked dash for the stage. She'll forget the quick slap of shame she felt afterwards when Amber took her hand and they raced around back to the stage door, just in time to intercept Adrienne before she reached the bus. She'll remember only the hot flare of purpose that warmed her for days after, as if she was constantly gulping wine.

After the session ends, Andrea texts Roslyn.

"I went to a therapist. Will you talk to me now?"

When there's no reply after forty-five minutes, she leaves a message on Cathy's voice mail, canceling their next appointment.

Small Hard Truths:

1. Dramatic events aren't necessarily important, just memorable.

2. If Andrea fell into a coma, everyone would discover her pesky chin hair issue.

3. Generosity has little to do with it. Tip jars work because people hate coins.

4. You can't sit on a curb forever. At some point, you have to stand up.

OBLIVIOUS, JORDAN MANAGES to ignore Andrea's fall. She's smiling at Gioco's host, a young Italian woman with chemically straightened hair, an elegant mole beneath one brow. Eyes on the host, she pushes open the plate glass door.

Standing takes Andrea's remaining strength, handily depleting her last reserves. Confronting Jordan will be like dropping a penny from the Sears Tower; Andrea could shift life's course just by loosening her grip. The same is true for less loaded inquiries; rather than distinguish between offensive and innocuous, Jordan finds insult wherever she wants. Impossible to live a spontaneous life with someone like that, Andrea is worn out from monitoring her thoughts, editing and excising before each turns to word.

She touches Jordan's arm. "I don't want to be here. Can we please go home?"

"That's where we're headed, aren't we?" Jordan digs her hands deep in her pockets and ambles toward the bus stop. "Would you look at those stars? You may not have Disneyland, but you've got stars."

In Andrea's bag, her cell phone vibrates. The idea of talking to Scott seems outlandish, exhausting. Where she is now, no satellite beam should reach. It should take a wax-sealed letter delivered by a guy on a camel to access her. And on the way, the camel might die.

"You miss LA?" Andrea asks, because while Jordan's answer may sting, it won't obligate her to make any life-altering choices. She hits ignore, sending the call to voice mail. Just like always she thinks, *next time I'll pick up.*

"I did last winter. I still can't believe I made it through. Really can't believe we're heading into another. Shouldn't one January per lifetime be enough?"

"If you hate it so much, why did you come?" Still not the right question, certainly not prudent.

"Who says I hate it? I just need to get myself one of those red padded suits the kids wear when they sled."

"A snowsuit."

"Zip myself in come November, take it off in May." Jordan rubs up against the bus stop sign, a characteristic gesture Andrea has come to hate. Jordan's always leaning back into things, expecting them to support her weight.

"I know where you get your money." As soon as she says it, Andrea realizes she's made an irrevocable error, so of course she repeats herself, louder, more insistently.

"Pardon me?" Jordan's face remains expressionless, her voice pleasant.

Andrea chews her thumbnail miserably. She's reneged on their tacit covenant; it's her job to exist in the slim, abstract hall-way between ignorance and confrontation, doling out accep-tance and setting boundaries in accordance with a formula she's been lucky enough to approximate, now realizes she will never understand.

"You're unemployed and it's not like you're independently wealthy, but you live like you are."

Jordan stands silent. Down the street a car door slams.

"You've been here a while now, over two years."

More silence, Jordan lets Andrea work with what she has.

"And you don't have any savings."

"How do you know?"

"You told me you lived paycheck to paycheck." *Get to the point*, Andrea instructs herself.

"If I'd known you'd use it against me, I probably wouldn't have."

"I'm not using it against you; am I not supposed to remember the things you say?"

"What exactly are you accusing me of?" Jordan unbuttons the sleeve of her fleece-lined jacket, folds the fabric over, baring her lower arm.

"You gonna fight me?" Joking Jordan out of her anger is a move Andrea normally wouldn't attempt, but at this point she figures, What the hell?

"So now I'm a drug pusher and an abuser?"

"I only meant—"

"Or maybe you just wish I was." Jordan raises an eyebrow, a "so there" expression overtaking her face.

"What are you talking about?"

"I'm too *dang*erous," Jordan hits the first syllable with mocking force, "for you to love me, but not dangerous enough to keep you entertained." She steps into the empty street, scanning for the bus. "Except when we're fucking," she adds, looking north.

"Jordan, no one's talking about—"

Jordan pivots to face Andrea. "I sure as shit satisfy you then."

"You always satisfy me." Andrea says, struggling. She has no idea how they got here, or even where here is.

Jordan laughs, a small hiss.

"Tell me what you think you know." Skin flushed and eyes glistening, Jordan seems to have doubled in size.

"I don't *think* I know anything," Andrea says.

For just a moment, Jordan looks worried, which Andrea finds she likes. Slowly, she removes her gloves and stuffs them in her jacket pockets. Slipping the letter from her back pocket, she pauses, hesitant to let the worn paper go.

"What's that?" Jordan folds her arms over her chest.

"Here."

Andrea watches Jordan open the letter. Not an instant of guilt or recognition; Poker is definitely Jordan's game.

"You went through my things?" Looking up from the letter, Jordan steps toward Andrea.

"I was looking for a recipe."

"For one of your famous meals?" Another step.

"Scott asked me to . . . " Andrea peters off.

"How long have you had this?" Inches away from Andrea, Jordan carefully enunciates each word.

"A few months."

"How many? Look at me," Jordan demands, grabbing Andrea's face.

"Maybe five or six."

"You kept this from me for almost a year?" One hand gripping Andrea's chin, Jordan uses the other to pin her to the bus stop sign.

"Not a year—" Andrea's spine hurts. Certainly, she'll have another bruise. "Jordan, stop, this is backwards, you're the one who kept it from me!"

As Andrea watches, Jordan's face seems to fold inward. *There goes the vein,* Andrea thinks, and like clockwork, the one above Jordan's right eyebrow trembles as Jordan's eyes grow moist.

"You went through my stuff and found something that scared you, and now you're taking it out on me." Releasing Andrea, Jordan covers her eyes with her hands. "Why don't you trust me?" A lone tear straggles down Jordan's cheek.

"Just tell me if it's true."

"This is so fucking offensive, Andrea." Jordan moans into her hands.

"Please."

"Please, please," Jordan mocks, "Please what?"

"Tell me the truth!"

"I am!" Turning swiftly, Jordan flails her clenched fist into the stop sign. "Fuck!"

"Are you okay?" Instinctively, Andrea reaches for Jordan.

"Don't touch me." Clutching her injured hand to her chest, Jordan makes a show of catching her breath.

"Never mind, okay?" Andrea whispers. "I believe you."

"No," Jordan says, "ask me your questions. Let's finish this."

"I don't have any—"

"Yes you do, so ask." Tears staunched, Jordan begins to pace.

"Just, why would Patricia say all that if it isn't true?" Andrea keeps her voice quiet as if low volume will mitigate her words.

"Patricia is very used to getting her way."

"I don't understand."

"It's funny, in some ways you're such a grown-up, but in others, you're totally naive." Almost smiling, Jordan moves closer to Andrea.

"What do you mean?" Andrea puts her gloves back on, her hands suddenly unbelievably cold.

"Relationships are complicated."

"I know that."

"Do you?" Jordan's eyes feel like search beams. Andrea struggles to hold her gaze. "The account is Patricia's clever little way of keeping me under her thumb."

"But you left her."

"For you."

"No, for Wendy." This at least Andrea knows.

"Forget about Wendy, I was confused. I came here, I'm about a hundred years old and I uprooted everything. I did that for you."

"But the money."

"Patricia gave it to me, and now she regrets it."

"Why would she do that?"

"She loves me, and when you love someone, you accept them for who they are."

"I don't understand."

"That's not surprising. Unconditional love isn't one of your strengths," Jordan says, like the statement is her sad responsibility to make.

"That's not fair."

"It is what it is."

"But . . ." Dizzy, Andrea tries to focus. "Patricia told me exactly what you did."

"Which was?"

"She said you set up a savings account for the gallery." Andrea stops.

"Go on."

"She said you auto-transferred a percentage into savings each month." Andrea pauses, seeing Patricia's words in her mind. "Then you moved a smaller percentage from that account to your own."

"Sure."

"You admit it?"

"Admit it? Am I on trial? You think that's the first letter she's ever sent?"

"To me?"

"She wants me back." Jordan spreads her hands. "I told her 'No, I'm with Andrea.' Then she said—and I'm quoting, 'We'll see about that.'"

"In a letter?"

"On the phone. Don't act surprised; I've seen you snooping through my cell. Bet you've got my history memorized."

"I don't!"

Jordan's Phone History:

```
Andrea
Thai Avenue
JB Alberto's
Patricia
Andrea
213-842-4887 (Wendy?)

Vivo
213-859-3727 (?)

Noodle Zone
310-443-2121 (Who does she know in Beverly Hills?)
```

"I couldn't let her get between us."

"She wrote me to break us up?" Andrea bites her cuticle.

"Seems like."

"What about the money?" *It's like the end of* Murder She Wrote, Andrea thinks, *too easy, but everything's explained.*

"Look, Andrea, your lack of trust really hurt me, but I'm not angry anymore. I'm trying to put myself in your shoes. I stopped accepting the money months ago. You believe me?"

It's not that Andrea believes Jordan exactly; she's just unimaginably tired.

"Babe, if she thought I was stealing, why didn't she call the cops?"

"I don't know."

"Because if she did, she couldn't hold this over me. She's always known about my account. She's the one who set it up. Next time you think you have a big secret, will you come to me first?"

I give up, Andrea thinks, nodding. "Do you still love me?" she asks, hating herself.

"Come here."

Jordan's arm around her back, her hand in Andrea's hair—both feel so perfect that Andrea starts to cry.

"You're okay, you big baby." Jordan says, releasing her. "Let's grab a cab; this bus ain't gonna come."

Striding to the mouth of the deserted street, Jordan raises her hand to hail a distant cab. On the sidewalk at Andrea's feet, the letter twitches in the rising wind.

"C'mon, Babe," Jordan says as the cab pulls up, "shake a tail feather. You said this isn't where you want to be."

⌒

WHEN JORDAN AND Andrea stop having sex, they stop like everyone stops: imperceptibly but also on a dime. They stop like something on the weather channel, torrents and gusts and electric air segue into light steady patter, becomes scattered pinpricks, finally blows out across the lake. Notwithstanding her instincts and all she knows about Jordan's former girlfriends, Andrea can't believe it's happening to her. If there is one thing she has over the Criminal Mastermind, it's sex.

At first she tries to take initiative, finds herself rejected almost every time. Once at a cruisy Boystown Starbucks, Andrea seizes her courage and Jordan's hand.

"I'm," she pauses.

"What's that?" Absorbed in a *New York Times* headline, Jordan looks distractedly at Andreas's pale fingers against her bronzed skin.

Desire and dejection whack each other with bats inside Andrea. She swears she used to have more confidence. It must have been relative to Jordan's ardor; now she'll have to fake her way through.

"I'm uh, wet, I-want-you-so-bad."

Exhausted by her feeble attempt, she glances at Jordan. Unless she's into pathetic androids, chances are she's not aroused.

"Oh yeah?' Jordan folds her arms, her eyes unreadable behind her sunglasses.

Andrea nods, "Uh, yeah."

Jordan exhales, "Okay," she says and leads Andrea into the bathroom where she sets her Americano carefully in the sink before fucking Andrea with quick efficient thrusts until someone knocks at the door.

AROUND THE SAME time, Jordan decides she wants to exchange tattoos. She says it would mean everything to her, seeing her name blazing (she says this, blazing) across Andrea's skin. As for her own tattoo, she's already chosen a place for Andrea's name. Andrea watches Jordan's face as she describes what she pictures: "ANDREA," ferocious and tiny, crawling the inside of Jordan's arm.

"Whenever couples exchange tattoos it's a death knell," Jordan says. "We're different though, don't you think?"

Andrea imagines Jordan's name tattooed across her chest or spiraling low on her back. It appeals to the part of her that wants to be owned; her more sensible aspects (and they sound a lot like Roslyn) would prefer she not become a cliché.

"I'm not sure I can afford it," Andrea hedges.

"Don't worry babe, I'll pay. One condition though." Jordan rubs her palms together, "I want my name right here." Startled, Andrea blushes as Jordan smacks her ass.

Things Jordan Convinces Andrea (Against Her Better Judgment) to Do:

1. Bankroll a class in Gourmet Cooking. (Jordan thinks she might want to open a restaurant, but the class conflicts with *The Biggest Loser*, so she never actually attends.)

2. Ride Space Mountain. (A few weeks after their trip to Ventura, they go to Disneyland for Jordan's birthday.

"I've done it every year since I quit drugs," Jordan says.

Jordan rides the coaster herself, then begs Andrea to try. Andrea watches Jordan hop from one foot to another, her hands clasped to her chest. "You'll love it," she says, moving Andrea toward the line, "it's just like sex!"

"In what possible way?" Andrea asks, but less afraid of Space Mountain than she is to say no, Andrea lets herself be towed.)

3. Help Jordan talk a Quiznos worker into making them a meatball sub five minutes after close. (Andrea takes no issue with the free food but she balks when Jordan turns to her, eyes brimming, and says, "I don't know

what we would have done without him, do you?" The
pot-bellied teenager looks from Jordan to Andrea un-
certainly, "Your mama having bad day?" he asks Andrea
when Jordan goes to find a napkin to wipe her eyes.)

Andrea tries, but she can't justify adding "Tattoo Jordan's name on my
ass" to the list. On the other hand, the idea of her own name, forever etched on Jordan's arm, fills her with fizzy satisfaction. The tattoo
won't stop Jordan from leaving, but for the rest of Jordan's life, no matter who she sleeps with, Andrea's name will be the first thing they see.

Luckily Jordan's key feature is her inability to follow through.
Normally, the transition from enthusiasm to forgetfulness infuri-
ates Andrea; it's like watching a slow-motion mudslide down an
inestimable slope. For once she's counting on it; she won't directly
oppose anything Jordan thinks she wants, but once Jordan moves
on to the next idea, she'll be off the hook. Strangely, this time
Jordan's slow to forget.

"I have an idea," she says weeks later, "you'll wear red lipstick, kiss
right next to your name. We'll have the guy tattoo your lip print too."

Andrea wakes a few nights later to find Jordan online researching tattoo artists.

"Kim Saigh," she says the next morning, "Rumor is she did one
of Kanye's, but she won't confirm. Classy, right? She's not accepting new clients, but her receptionist was born in Alta Dena too. I
talked her into squeezing us in next Monday at six."

On Monday at five thirty, Andrea's leaving the gym when Jordan calls.

"I just heard about a Mexican place on Halsted that has bur-
ritos as big as your head! Grab a cab and meet me. Afterwards we
can hit the Apollo. There's an improv show I want to see."

Andrea's been where she is too long to distinguish: relief, disappointment, they've begun to feel the same.

Ahead, she sees the number 22 bus pulling up at the corner. If she runs she can make it.

"See you there," she says.

Say Andrea's Relationship with Jordan Is an Olympic
Event, Which One Would It Be?

ANDREA IS PASSING time waiting for Jordan to quit hiding in the bathroom, finish what she started, or better, put equal energy into fixing what earlier this afternoon she seemed intent on breaking apart.

Andrea wants to think Javelin, but only because she
likes the way the word sounds.

Perhaps downhill skiing, each team member hurtling
downward, present due to a mutual agreement, now dependent on her own skills.

Maybe a figure skating competition in which one
partner skates away at the last minute after encouraging
the other to leap spectacularly into his arms.

Most likely a marathon: just when you're nearly
vomiting with exhaustion you realize you're only halfway there.

The arguing is new and makes Andrea feel nauseated, not liberated, unanchored and out of control. When she looks back, she'll fault the letter, or rather, her reaction to it. If she'd left when she found it, things might have ended, if not peacefully, at least without the slow unraveling that will keep her for years immobile, terrified to let go again. Instead, she retreats to denial, the exact state for which she judges Jordan's exes. Justifiably unnerved, still angry about the letter, she fights with Jordan over everything else.

```
Topics Argued Over:

Jordan's flirting

Diet Coke cans in the sink

Jordan's tardiness

Andrea's nagging (Unfair—she wouldn't nag if Jor-
dan followed through)

Kittens

Jordan's mysterious habit of tossing her tampon
applicators behind the bookcase
```

Really, subject matter seems beside the point. Powerless to demarcate the arcs and loops of their fights, Andrea loses herself in their intricacy; maybe that's part of their draw. She's heard walking a labyrinth embodies meditation at its most intense. She wants to call Roslyn, say her battles with Jordan remind her of a labyrinth.

"Because of their blurred complexity," Andrea would say.

"Not 'cause they're like that last scene in *The Shining?*" Roslyn might reply.

When it comes to shameful psychosexual secrets, Andrea guesses she has to add to her file. She learns about this one slowly. Bit by bit it reveals itself as her romance with Jordan falls in shards at her feet. It seems explosive fights are the carob version of sex with Jordan.

```
[Carob is to explosive fights as chocolate is to sex.]
```

In terms of release, they work almost as well. As what's sexual between them fogs with hurt feelings, the pull of escalating slights becomes relationship glue. Like a favorite TV show or a love of antiquing, their arguments create a new kind of intimacy. At this point it's all they have left. But unlike antiquing, arguing offers Andrea the mounting tension, the crescendo of climax, the swooping slide back to peace, all of which she'd prefer to get from sex, but has come to understand she'll accept from Jordan in any heightened form.

Sometimes she touches herself when they're fighting, a thing which, despite her compulsion for confession, she'll never tell a soul. Words don't approach why she does it. Compelled by a primal ache, she has no choice. The first couple of times she doesn't think Jordan notices—they usually fight in dark rooms. But a Criminal Mastermind is a Criminal Mastermind; no matter they live together now, eat breakfast at the same table, share a bathroom and split rent. It's easy to forget this, waking up beside Jordan, whose morning face, Andrea finally realizes, she will never grow to love. Jordan looks like a carp when she's sleeping, but she's still preternaturally attuned to Andrea, so when Jordan calls her on her furtive self-pleasuring, Andrea isn't surprised. True to form, Jordan doesn't so much call Andrea on it, as obliquely employ it to justify her own dubious behavior, laying blame squarely in Andrea's twitching lap.

"You wanted me to do it," she says the first time she hits Andrea, outside of their sex life, in the middle of a heated debate. "I don't want to say you're asking for it, but the thing is, you kind of are."

"Yeah, that was Ike Turner's excuse." Andrea leaps from the bed on which they're piled like puppies, Jordan's slap having reduced Andrea to relieved tears.

"You get so worked up, I have no other choice."

"That's . . . "

"Or were you planning to take the edge off some other way? Hmm?" Jordan's amused condescension should incense Andrea, but God help her, even now it still turns her on.

The last time Jordan grabs Andrea's hair, forces her to her knees then her back, pins Andrea's arms to her sides by sitting on her chest, Andrea closes her eyes for a moment then says quietly, "You need to get off."

Jordan obeys, her expression saying something along the lines of, "You promised me a bicycle for my birthday and all I got was a pair of socks."

Since then, when Jordan gets angry she retires to the bathroom with a knife or scissors, the attitude of a child taunting an animal, holding something indispensable just out of reach. Andrea can always tell when Jordan's cut herself—not so much cut as aggressively scratched. Jordan's habitually rolled-up sleeves droop over her fingertips. Her expression is hangdog but pacified. Jordan says Andrea pushes all her buttons; she has to do something to match the pain. That a woman in her forties would engage in such high school behavior makes Andrea fear for the species, makes her feel guilty for not feeling guiltier, worse, makes her wonder why mere scratches are sufficient to combat the emotional pain Andrea supposedly inflicts.

"I'm calm now." Jordan opens the bathroom door. "Ready to slog on."

Andrea does a sleeve check. Jordan's cuffs hang to her knuckles.

"That's great that you're calm. Do you also need a tourniquet?"

"I have to do something with my feelings." Jordan perches on the edge of the kitchen table.

"You have to hurt yourself?"

"Better me than you."

This statement is classic Jordan, irreproachable on the surface, teeming with maggots underneath.

"I'm sorry I forgot you introduced me to Ani." Soothed by her bloodletting, Jordan is ready to throw Andrea a bone.

"That's not the point."

"It sure seemed like the point when you ambushed me about it this afternoon."

Andrea glances through the window where sunset's pink remnants throw black tree limbs into bold relief. She hadn't felt the afternoon slip away.

"I didn't ambush you. You don't care who gave you what."

"What the hell does that mean?"

"I remember things that happen between us because you matter to me."

"You think you don't matter to me?"

"I was washing dishes in my Westwood apartment, I remember because the radio was on the windowsill above the sink. Ani DiFranco came on; it was back when 'Little Plastic Castles' was actually getting play. You asked me what I was listening to, and I said, 'Ani DiFranco. You'd love her; she's one of my favorites.' And you said, 'if you love her then I'll love her. Which CD should I buy?'"

"We're talking about a thirty-second exchange that happened more than five years ago! I'm sure there are things you've forgotten too."

"I never forget anything," Andrea mumbles, almost certain it's true.

"Well, so what?"

"I just think it's indicative of how little I mean to you."

"Really? Which one of us started dating some little blonde girl when we'd been together almost two years?"

"That's a relative term, don't you think? Weren't you married to Patricia at the time?"

"Andrea." Jordan's voice is low, exhausted. "You're the one who's always mattered. My God, do you want me to sing it for you? You think I'd put up with this shit from anyone else?" Jordan locks her hands behind her head, arches her back, stretching.

"Everything you promise comes to nothing." Now Andrea's just lobbing random disparagements, her actions too lawless to qualify as sport. "Like that thing at the concert with Jan. You make everything in the world seem possible then disappear when it all falls apart."

"Wow, Andrea. It sounds like you really hate me."

Andrea can summon no acceptable response.

"And who the heck is Jan anyway?"

When Andrea thinks back on the fight, she's not sure how it ends. Odds are Jordan winds up back in the bathroom or one of them starts to sob. Certainly without sex or a square slap from Jordan to connect them, they continue to drift.

Here's why Andrea tells herself she stops Jordan's physical aggression: despite the true complexity of their unspoken negotiations, Andrea can't live with the fact that on paper, what's happening between them just looks like abuse.

Here's the real reason she does it: violence is the Clark Kent/ Superman of their relationship—as it bleeds into their everyday interactions, it seeps from their sex life. It's never been spotted in two places at once [Figure 7].

Questions Andrea Must Ponder Single-Handedly:

How much do abused women ask for?
How much do they secretly want?

She'd be burned at the stake if she asked these questions aloud.

~

ONE DAY, SCOTT dies. By now he's little more than a colleague, someone Andrea jokes with at staff meetings, never sees outside of work. Still, when the department secretary, a woman Jordan, having met her once at a holiday party, refers to as "the troll," snags Andrea's arm to deliver the news, Andrea feels she's swallowed something ancient like marble, unimaginably heavy and cold.

"Heart attack," the troll says.

"He wasn't even forty, was he?" Andrea tries to breathe around the marble.

"Thirty-nine." The troll leans so close, Andrea can smell coffee and toothpaste, see something tan stuck between the woman's front teeth. "It's not uncommon for black men," she adds. "I've known a couple who died that way, and young."

"His poor parents," Andrea says, realizing she has no idea if Scott's parents are alive. She thinks he's mentioned his mother; she's a bank teller or she runs a greenhouse.

"It's the fiancée I feel bad for. I'm circulating a card for her. I'll leave it in your mailbox.

"Fiancée?" Andrea repeats.

"Weren't you two friends?"

"I started this other job and . . . " Rather than finish, Andrea lets the sentence wander off.

"Make sure you find Tom, he's collecting money for a wreath."

"Of course. Tom teaches ESL, right?"

"Art history." The troll shakes her head.

"That's what I meant."

At the funeral Andrea stares at Scott's casket, a deep glossy brown. Wood grain and morning light merge; the casket seems comprised of flame. She's been to other funerals—her uncle, her grand-mother, her mom's childhood best friend—but their deaths seem natural, explicable. Scott isn't the sort of person who dies, not a person Andrea knows well enough to mourn fully—someone she figured would always be around.

I could have known him better.

Andrea watches his fiancée, a fragile redhead not more than twenty-five. Pressing a linen handkerchief to her eyes, she clutches an older woman's arm.

After the service, at Scott's parent's small Southside home, Andrea stands next to the dining room table, watching her col-leagues and Scott's family mingle and chew. The food on the table looks like an aerial view of a landscape, minute and false. Scott's the person she talks to at events like this. Without him she's an outcast.

Walking to the den, clean and precise like a room in a doll-house, she remembers Linda's response when Andrea's grand-mother died.

"I don't do death," she says, and spends the day of the service studying for her Sociology exam.

In Los Angeles, Andrea describes her grandmother's funeral to Jordan.

Jordan cries and says how death is a reckoning, but for the living not the dead. For days, she asks questions about Andrea's grandmother: What was her favorite flower? What was her mid-dle name? Answering, Andrea feels gratified. She thinks how wonderful it will be to experience life with a true partner, someone who isn't afraid to feel. It doesn't occur to her that Jordan's merely skipping stones on the surface of someone else's tragedy, playing house inside Andrea's grief.

Through Scott's family's living room window, Andrea sees his fiancée. Wearing a bright red pea coat, she's walking a low brick wall. Slim white ankles stark in the fading light, she lifts delicate feet in black Chinese slippers, step by careful step. Only hip high, still she treats the wall like a tightrope; her arms stretched wide to form a stiff 'T.'

"She was like a character in a Victorian novel," Andrea tells Jor-dan, beside Andrea, playing with her cell.

"Except for the part where she's marrying a black guy." Jordan closes her phone.

Scott was more than a black guy. Like the star of an after school special, Andrea pictures herself saying, *He was my friend.* Not worth the hassle—if she says it Jordan will get suspicious. She thinks all black men are predators; she doesn't believe women and men can be friends.

"I keep thinking, who was Scott that this girl, she was like something Mercer Mayer might draw, pre-Raphaelite, who was he that she'd choose him?"

"Why didn't you want me at the funeral?" Jordan asks as Andrea sets her alarm clock.

"You've got so much going on at work."

Jordan has tweaked old job titles, made friends with the right people, and set her sights on a new goal. She's talked her way into an assistant manager position at Starbucks. Working sixty-hour weeks now, she's rarely around.

"Or maybe you're ashamed of me." Jordan says. "Maybe you don't want me near your friends."

What friends? Andrea pictures Roslyn. Without her, Andrea's bones are hollow as a bird's.

"I'm not ashamed of you." Andrea says. "That's not it at all."

"Why then?" Jordan asks.

Clicking off her lamp so she won't have to see Jordan's expression, Andrea thinks of Scott's fiancée. Her long rippling hair, the way she pursed her lips as she negotiated the wall.

"You'd have made it about yourself," she says.

"IT'S THE BLONDE barista, isn't it?" Andrea asks three weeks after the last time they have sex.

"Babe." Jordan rolls her eyes. As a morale booster, most of the partners at her store are going bowling, an outing Jordan came up with and is now late to attend.

"She's a lesbian, right?"

"Sad to say, not every lesbian is automatically attracted to me." Jordan runs gel-coated fingers through her recently cut hair. She's stopped wearing it slicked back in a ponytail. It's short and carelessly layered like Adrienne's now, a change Andrea encouraged.

"But things between us are different lately," Andrea says, stepping back to let Jordan through to the bedroom. Jordan slides on jeans still creased from the iron. She leaves the top button open, stands in her lacy front-closure bra vigorously ironing her shirt.

"I still can't believe you iron your jeans," Andrea sits on the bed.

"I know we haven't had much time together." Jordan tucks her shirt flawlessly, buttons her jeans. "But that doesn't mean I'm sleeping with someone else."

"You can't go two days without sex," Andrea says. "It's been almost a month. You must be getting it somewhere."

Jordan's dressed now; she's sliding her delicate feet sockless into her brown Vans.

"I'm perfectly capable of abstaining from sex without losing my mind," she says, rolling a wad of cash into her back pocket. "Perhaps you're confusing me with yourself."

"But we're the same." Andrea trails Jordan to the door, feeling wretched, fighting the instinct to throw her arms around Jordan's legs. "That's what you told me."

"I don't remember saying that," Jordan says.

Hours later, Andrea is tangled in sheets, sweaty and exhausted from rolling and tossing, trying to hurl herself in sleep's path. She's thinking of the confrontation at Gioco, how every day since she and Jordan continue to back warily away. A few nights afterward, she startles from a murky sleep fought for hours, desperate to keep pace with Jordan, on her fifth crossword of the night.

"The money's not all Patricia's." Jordan leans over, gently prodding Andrea awake.

"What?"

"It's from the hair salon. I did the books for Wendy, skimmed a little off the top."

Everything comes abruptly into focus. Andrea couldn't be more alert.

Things could go very badly from here, she thinks. Any real vulnerability Jordan offers, any single step toward Andrea usually results in incalculable strides away.

"I see," Andrea aims for blandness.

"I'm not that person anymore." The acidic scent of red wine skims the surface of Jordan's claim. "I want to be better. I want to do that for you."

Wordlessly, Andrea leans forward and kisses Jordan, feeling Jordan's body tense then almost imperceptibly release.

Drunken sex is something Andrea prefers to leave rather than take, but she's never once said no to Jordan. Also she is frantic to find a way back in. When she's drunk, Jordan's more likely to let Andrea penetrate her, something she rarely otherwise does.

Rare Occasions:

When drunk or premenstrual

After watching *Alias*

On days Jordan feels really bad about herself

The list flickers behind Andrea's closed eyelids as Jordan squeezes one of Andrea's thighs between her own. Andrea's incensed at the words for finding her. Here with Jordan she's supposed to be safe. Jordan grabs the back of her head, stares into Andrea's eyes. Down the hall the bathroom faucet leaks dawdling drops of water.

"Fuck me," Jordan says, voice hushed.

Andrea does as she's told, pulling out Jordan's tampon, feeling Jordan tighten around her fingers.

"I need to get closer."

Not sure whether she's thought the words or said them, Andrea finds Jordan's legs drop effortlessly open under her hands. Unaccustomed to surrender, Andrea takes advantage. She doesn't stop till Jordan's come twice and Andrea's tongue aches dully at its base.

Now she lies awake considering a walk or warm milk when Jordan unlocks the front door.

"Babe," Jordan sheds her pants and slides in beside Andrea, "I didn't mean it; of course we're the same."

Andrea's throat goes thick and her eyes fill. In the dark she curls her knees to her chest, "Why don't you want me?" she asks.

"I want you," Jordan forces Andrea onto her back, soothes Andrea's hair away from her face.

"Not enough for sex," Andrea says. "Not the way you wanted me before."

"Two people can't live forever the way we did," Jordan says seriously. "I have to prove myself at work right now if I'm going to get a store of my own."

Of course what Jordan says is reasonable, healthy even, and if Jordan were anyone but the Criminal Mastermind, if she were Linda, for example, some regular girlfriend, Andrea would support her. This is what Andrea tells herself, secretly wondering if it's true. The problem is, this is the Criminal Mastermind, the woman she's with because of fate and passion and because she can't live without the sex. That Jordan would develop healthy goals and priorities, that she would pursue something innocuous and other than Andrea wasn't part of the plan. Andrea always figured she was in it till Jordan was arrested or more likely till some other woman caught her eye. Then Andrea would be wounded, but righteous and free. Now it looks like the other woman is a green mermaid icon. Maybe it's Jordan herself.

"I wonder if we should even be together," Andrea says, not because she means it, though she might, but to jar Jordan.

"Don't say that," Jordan says fiercely. "I see who you are and I want all of you. You think you're going to find that with anyone else?" She's quiet for a moment, stroking Andrea's hair. "I love you," she says, arranging Andrea in the crook of her arm.

"I love you too," Andrea whispers even though she's never been certain.

Doing an easy downhill cruise into sleep, the way she only ever can with Jordan beside her, Andrea hears Roslyn's voice in her head.

"You don't even like her. You're just hanging around waiting for what she does next."

Three Versions of the Same Idea:

1. Andrea must either hate or have sex with someone; love alone doesn't give her enough to do.

2. When Andrea loves someone she needs a sexual outlet for her passion. In the absence of sex her love turns to hate.

3. For Andrea passion equals hatred or lust; she doesn't know a thing about love.

⌒

AN EPISODE ANDREA would prefer to forget: they've been arguing for hours and somehow the fight culminates in Andrea removing her clothes. Maybe she does it remembering: when they're first together and fighting, the air between them thickens—beach house humidity before a summer storm. Rare, the arguments, their topics inconsequential, the energy brewing supersedes whatever they think the fight is about. Andrea would need a magic pocket knife, a wooden headboard the length of the great wall of China to tick off the number of conflicts that end this way: Andrea spread eagle and sighing, Jordan flushed and furious, fucking her way to calm.

It's also possible Andrea has watched too much *Oprah*. She thinks, like a restored amnesia victim, Jordan will quake back to life at the sight of Andrea's nude body, grateful to reacquire what she didn't know she lost. Oprah may be a by-and-large infallible cultural engine, but every once in a while she's off base.

Evidence:

James Frey

Her tendency to talk with her mouth full

Rhapsodizing editorials in *O Magazine* compelling readers to make time each day for their sacred yoga practice (She probably has no clue what milk costs or how many jobs most of her fans hold.)

"What are you doing?" Jordan's eyes narrow then widen as Andrea unbuttons her shirt.

"Don't you remember?" This might be sarcasm. Andrea's not being facetious though, at least she doesn't think that's her intent.

"Remember?" Jordan's hands are up like she's a target, like Andrea's gun is cocked, her trigger finger slippery with sweat.

"If you just tried to remember." Inside her head, Andrea's voice is level, but it skids and cracks when it hits the air.

"Andrea." Her name in Jordan's mouth slows Andrea for a second. It sounds magnifying glass–close, way too familiar; she'd begun to think "babe" was her real name.

"Just look." Andrea's on to her skirt now. Unzipped, it falls next to her shirt on the floor.

"You need to stop."

"Why?" Andrea unclasps her bra.

"This isn't something you'll want to have done."

Jordan might be right. Andrea's making one of those dramatic gestures no one really needs to make. Despite this, she slowly wells with a strange sense of stillness. She's calm like she hasn't been for ages. Jordan's reaction fascinates her. She's never seen Jordan so floored.

She steps out of her underwear and walks toward Jordan, pauses when the tap of her footfalls remind her she's still wearing heeled boots. It's the boots that do it. She has a brief sense of herself as ridiculous, a drunken starlet flashing the paparazzi as she exits her car, enough to stall her for a moment, not enough for her to call the whole thing off. She reaches for a boot and Jordan freezes like Andrea's some horror movie creature.

"Please," Jordan says, absurdly, "please don't take off your shoes."

Shoeless, Andrea continues forward. The pitch of Jordan's fear equals her former arousal, the change striking, significant although Andrea's not sure of what. When she reaches Jordan, a process that takes years longer than it ought considering Jordan's just a few feet away and frozen where she fell when she backed into the bed, Andrea sees Jordan is subtly trembling. *Not my responsibility,* she decides.

"Andrea, please." Jordan recoils as Andrea crawls toward her.

"Touch me," Andrea says. "Maybe that's all you need to do." She reaches for Jordan's hands, attempts to bring them to her chest.

"No!" Jordan throws her body on top of Andrea as if smothering a fire. "This isn't how you want me to remember you."

Andrea doesn't hesitate. Suddenly it's easy not to care.

Standing, she pulls on jeans and a T-shirt, slides her feet into an old pair of Jordan's shoes.

"I'll go to a hotel," she says.

Of course this isn't what happens. Instead, Jordan begs Andrea not to leave, and when she relents, Jordan loses interest and Andrea wishes she'd gone.

⁓

WHEN JORDAN BECOMES a store manager, an unheard of leap for someone who's been with the company for just eight months, she tells Andrea to stop teaching.

"I'll take care of you," she pledges, unbuttoning the blouse she's borrowed to wear to her interview.

On the theory that to get the job she needs to look femme, a day ear-lier, Jordan demands Andrea lend her a raw silk blouse which she insists on calling a button-down.

"The word blouse reminds me of someone's mom," she says.

Andrea matches the blouse to a pair of blue pinstripe trousers Jordan already owns, lends her faux diamond earrings, applies navy liner to the outside corners of Jordan's eyes.

Watching Jordan model her outfit the night before her interview, Andrea isn't sure Jordan's mission has been exactly accomplished. She's lost the home court advantage of wearing clothes that align with her temperament, garments the effect of which she is familiar enough to predict. On the plus side, due to her delicate build and sharp features, she's avoided the cross-dressing man syndrome that afflicts most butches when they stray from their cargo pants comfort zone. On the other hand, Jordan hates restrictive material, so the outfit, all baggy folds and rolled up sleeves, makes her look small and slightly baffled, more rodent than femme.

"She could for sure find work storing nuts for the winter." On the back porch, Andrea struggles to light a cigarette. "Beyond that, I'm not so sure." She's talking to Roslyn's voice mail. Even though Roslyn never returns her calls, Andrea's taken to leaving messages once or twice a day. The cigarettes are something new. If anyone asked, she'd explain that everyone in Chicago smokes—she held out as long as she could.

"Babe," Jordan knocks on the glass. "Can you hurry up? I need help deciding what to do with my hair."

"I gotta go." Disconnecting the call, Andrea opens the screen door.

"Do they still use scrunchies?" Jordan asks, a plaid one wound around her wrist.

"Absolutely not," Andrea says, aware her voice has gone pointy with embarrassment. Jordan out of her element is alarming to witness. Andrea can't think why it upsets her so much.

She fingers the pack of cigarettes jammed in her pocket. She's had it two weeks now, and has only managed to smoke three.

Why Andrea Smokes:

Jordan hates cigarettes

Without sex Andrea has nothing

She wants to taint herself in some minor way

The next day she checks her phone ten times during the first hour of her eight AM class, even though Jordan's interview won't start until eight forty-five. She reminds herself that Jordan gets anything she sets her mind to, and like all shape-shifters, her appearance in one moment has no consistent relation to how she looks in the next. No doubt at the interview Jordan will tap into her charisma, smooth as Lance Armstrong clicking his racing shoes into the pedals of his bike. Besides, no one but Andrea knows the discrediting truth: as usual Jordan has refused to wear underwear. Also her shoes are stuffed with tissue paper; unclear on women's sizes, she bought them one too large.

"You'll take care of me?" Interview over, Andrea watches Jordan step out of her dress pants.

"Of course I will! I can't believe they called me back day of. You can do whatever you want now. Quit that crappy job; really do something with your life!"

"She's managing a coffee house; I'm educating America's youth!" Andrea tells an imaginary Roslyn.

"It's not like I work at McDonalds," she says, censuring. "Teaching's supposed to be an honorable profession."

"Yeah, but is it what you really want to do?" Without waiting for an answer, Jordan flings the blouse in a corner and wanders off to find her board shorts, absently scratching her ass.

TWO WEEKS LATER Jordan moves out, leaving behind two blow dryers, a braided leather belt, some jumper cables, and her cat.

"I won't be unfaithful to you, Andrea. I've changed. And besides, you're too good for that," Jordan says when Andrea finds her, literally one foot out the door.

Wiping her nose on her sleeve, Andrea doesn't speak. Instead, she looks. Purple backpack square on her shoulders, Jordan balances an overflowing garbage bag of clothes. She's wearing beige Vans and sunglasses. As usual, her jeans creep down her hips. A thermal shirt traces her biceps, still taut beneath her softening skin. Aside from her choppy new cut, Jordan's hair, russet laced with silver, appears the same. Untrue. Sometimes when Jordan sleeps, she twirls hanks around her fingers. Andrea has seen the underside. Only she knows about the hidden, encroaching gray.

"Aren't you going to ask why I'm home?" Andrea's messenger bag cuts into her shoulder. She lifts it over her head, still watching Jordan who looks almost like she did that day at the Troubadour. If she tries, Andrea can believe they met only hours before.

"I know this is hard." Jordan sets the garbage bag at her feet.

"I'm home because I have a fever. One hundred and one if you care." Andrea doesn't so much choose to sit as allow her knees to suddenly bend.

"We'll have to put you to bed." Jordan eases her backpack from her shoulders and sits beside Andrea on the steps.

"We?" Andrea giggles. "You always say we, but that's never what you mean."

How do I feel? She wonders. *Like someone in an inner tube carried by waves.* Whether the root is relief or fever, Andrea can't be sure.

"You should lie down." Jordan pulls her phone from her pocket, maybe checking the time.

"Were you even going to wait till I got home?" Andrea thinks of the Troubadour. Jordan said something important about Cry Wolf that day, but each time Andrea feels on the verge of remembering, the sentence slips like salt through open hands.

"Of course. I just had to be ready. I knew after I told you, you wouldn't want me around."

"That's my hat." Andrea points at a brown newsboy cap peeking from the garbage bag.

Something about obsession, Andrea muses. *She said something that made it seem okay.*

"I'm doing this for both of us." Jordan says. "You just can't see it now."

"Is it because I stopped letting you hit me?"

Nothing to lose by asking now, Andrea thinks.

"I don't know what you're talking about." Jordan stands and shoulders her backpack.

"You said you uprooted everything for me." Looking up makes Andrea woozy, so she concentrates on her knees.

"I'm sorry." Jordan takes the cap from her bag and sets it lightly on Andrea's head. "I thought I was ready for how much I love you, but I guess I'm still not."

Around then, Andrea begins to pretend the scene is a movie—easy, given what happens next. A car slows in front of her apartment, as if at a director's cue.

"There's my ride." Jordan gestures toward the car.

"You're wrong," Andrea says. "I *can* see it. It's what we both need."

She tips her head back, knowing how dizzy it will make her feel. Jordan is watching her, maybe even hesitating, though Andrea's never known Jordan to second-guess a plan. Andrea laughs, remembering, "You said, 'This isn't obsession. This is what makes us who we are.'" She wants to look into Jordan's eyes as she says it, but the sun is behind Jordan, and reflected in her sunglasses, Andrea sees only herself.

The first time Andrea meets Adrienne Anderson, is very like the second, the third. Andrea remembers a concert hall or bar, a bottle of Corona, beads of moisture stippling the neck. Onstage, Adrienne's songs animate her, graffiti scrawling her body's clean page. Offstage: smooth skin, clear eyes, hair falling across her brow, Adrienne stands within inches, but her polite nods are roadside markers—really she's miles away. Inscrutable, her expression; Andrea isn't prepared for that.

She's hiding, Andrea thinks, or remembers thinking, waiting her turn in line.

Behind Andrea, three Frat-ish lesbians, all canned soft drinks and madras shorts, laugh and wait their turn. Ahead, fans pass Adrienne black Sharpies, hand her promo pictures and album jackets; some want Adrienne to sign their skin.

. . . waiting her turn for the bathroom . . . running to the back of The Rave . . . shoulder blades pressing the brick wall in front of the Post Office . . . on a camping cot in Ventura . . . lined up outside the stage door . . .

Andrea imagines what she and Adrienne will say to each other; best- and worst-case scenarios fight for the upper hand.

"Of course I recognize you, you're always first in line."

"Of all the people in here, you think I'd actually choose you?"

Adrienne might say both or neither. Andrea will remember what she wants.

WHAT SHE'S WORTH

■ ■ ■

■ ■ ■

During her time in Chicago, a time both BC and AD, Andrea adds a new move to her sexual repertoire: she finds herself crying as she comes. A trick picked up from the Criminal Mastermind, it makes her lovers feel essential, involved. The truth is, like the engine that powers a rocket, they propel her upward, then fall away as she leaves the earth behind. She hopes she's learned, finally, her lesson. Sex may be impossible without a partner, but the place sex takes her—she vows to go there alone.

■ ■ ■

THE FIRST TIME Jordan leaves, Andrea does too. Finished with school, there's little to keep her in LA. She hopes her return to the Midwest will reunite her with internal purpose—something she blames the Criminal Mastermind for stripping away. Andrea envisions herself practicing yoga, spurred by a newfound inner peace. She hopes to find fulfillment teaching community college kids, anticipates their pay-your-own-way gratitude, how she'll woo them one by one. She imagines returning to her spiritual roots, or expanding on them. Finding a church open-minded enough to accept queers is no problem, but she may be hard-pressed to explain her involuntary distrust of God.

Three hours early for her flight to Chicago, she wanders through LAX, which, she texts Roslyn, looks to her like the consequence of a one night stand between San Quentin and a tropical resort. Jordan asked Andrea to meet here once to watch the airplanes, an innocently romantic gesture, Andrea thought at the time. When Jordan let slip she'd come to the airport to drop off Patricia, Andrea managed to cling to the romance angle. Even now she can't muster bitterness; what she feels is closer to awe. She marvels at the way the Criminal Mastermind overlaps girlfriends, fills her days with movies and baseball games, listens to the radio, watches television and falls asleep all at once. Right now Jordan's snug in Echo Park with Wendy, at the salon, watching her snip glossy celebrity hair, or sprawled on Wendy's couch learning to play guitar.

Andrea tells herself she would have fled Los Angeles regardless of the Criminal Mastermind. LA's the sort of place you live temporarily; hang out more than a few years and it starts to leech away your soul. The truth is, everything about the scattered city suggests Jordan. She's written her name in the front of it, cracked the binding, spilled coffee on most of chapter ten. Even before Andrea runs into Patricia at Joan's on Third, Andrea knows her time is just about up.

"ANDREA," PATRICIA SAYS when she sees her, breaking away from a group of monochromatic women, placing a hand on Andrea's arm.

Andrea stands shocked and silent, clutching a white paper take-out bag in her hand.

"We're better off, both of us." Like a therapist, Patricia cocks her head to one side. "I always felt sorry for you," she adds when Andrea fails to respond.

Andrea looks down at her shredded black Converse, then over at Patricia's chestnut suede boots.

"See you later then." Patricia moves to walk away.

"How did you recognize me?" Andrea asks. "How did you know who I am at all?"

"You came to my Christmas party." Patricia turns, her face unreadable.

"You knew?"

"I kept myself from knowing. She told me you were friends." Patricia presses her lips together.

Andrea remembers a Psych 101 factoid: a person who does that wants to say more. Patricia steps closer, lowers her voice. Once she speaks, Andrea wonders if she will ever stop.

"The way she talked about you, not Wendy, just you. After the fact it dawned on me—I've been through it with her before so I don't know why I didn't see it at the time. I figured I could weather them all, I guess. She talked like you were her salvation, though, if one read between the lines. She didn't give me a lot of information when she left," Patricia laughs, "so I assumed you were the one she was with. She came back for her fucking CD collection, excuse me. I followed her to the hair salon. My best friend Gretchen gets her brows waxed there! Not anymore." Pausing, Patricia eyes Andrea, backed against a wall lined with cozy jars of jelly, plastic tubs of gourmet gumdrops, and fruit favored wine.

"She probably bowled you right over. She does that at first. She half-convinced me I'd be a world-renowned painter when the truth is I can barely hold a brush. I don't blame you. You hardly look a day over nineteen."

"I'm twenty-five." Andrea says, so quietly she's not sure she's spoken aloud.

"I thought for sure she'd choose you. But I guess she never really chooses anyone, does she?" Patricia's gone low and breathy now, a quivery smile tickling her lips.

"I'm sorry." Andrea says, hating Patricia, her ash blonde hair, her flawlessly made-up face. This woman had a piece of Jordan. Who knows what intimacies they shared?

"This used to be our place." Patricia stares past Andrea at the cheese display. "I guess that's why I still come."

AT A FUN-SIZE airport Barnes and Noble, Andrea skims through at least ten articles about Brad Pitt and Angelina Jolie. If she were Brad she'd never have left Jennifer, who reminds her of every kid's favorite babysitter. Angelina looks like she bites. Though she isn't certain she wants any of it, Andrea buys a bottle of water, Orbit mint mojito gum, a book on Ashtanga yoga, and Eckhart Tolle's *The Power of Now*.

IN CHICAGO, MOVING into the apartment she's subletting from Roslyn, starting her teaching job, lakeside jogs and late-night grocery runs all feel like a slideshow she's watching, chin in hand, trying hard not to nod off. Even the small friendship she cultivates with Scott, a colleague who whispers wryly to Andrea throughout their first staff meeting, although a buoyant distraction, seems like it's happening to someone else. Andrea lurks, ghostlike, pacing the long hallways of a body she hardly considers hers, certainly doesn't think of as her*self.* This isn't mind/body dualism. This is something worse. One night as she's showering after a run, she glances down suddenly, doesn't recognize her knees. She blames her disassociation on the Criminal Mastermind's nimble thievery, easier than admitting her suspicion: internal purpose, a strong sense of identity, neither are things she's ever had in spades.

ANDREA'S IN CHICAGO three weeks when Cry Wolf comes through. If she were the sort of fan she hasn't been since her early twenties, the sort with Cry Wolfs' faces tattooed across her torso, she would think nothing of relating the two occurrences. As a college senior attending a concert in Indiana, she actually meets a woman like that. She remembers the look on Adrienne's face when the fan, waiting at the venue's back door, lifts her shirt without preface to reveal the portrait. Adrienne's lips part as if by pulley system, her mouth gathering into a gracious smile.

The distance between Andrea and the tattooed woman narrows in times of stress though, and she allows herself to see the opportune tour date as a sign.

She attends the show with her Buddhist yoga instructor, a woman who responds to Andrea's pre-show excitement by telling her to relax and take a few deep, rejuvenating breaths.

SARAH TEREZ ROSENBLUM 195

An hour before the doors open, the Buddhist arrives to meet her, sipping ginger tea from a purple thermos.

"Won't the people who've been here longer be angry?" she asks, fitting herself limb by double-jointed limb into line beside Andrea.

"Fuck 'em," says Andrea, noting the faded mermaid sticker on the Buddhist's thermos. She knows exactly what sex with this woman will be like.

"I don't think I agree with the concept of rows," the Buddhist says, and once inside the theater, she spends the concert shifting from side to side, trying not to block anyone's view.

THE DAY AFTER Cry Wolf's Chicago date, Andrea heads to Madison to catch the next show. She's the eighth person in line—good enough, considering she drove three and a half hours to get here, waking early after last night's concert. Much as Andrea loves to stand within spitting distance, she won't arrive at dawn for the privilege. That's Jordan's job, but then, so was chatting up other line-waiters. Andrea always found Jordan's compulsion to charm distasteful; more than that she never saw the point. Lately though, Andrea has picked up Jordan's facility for quick affiliations. She finds herself putting the best parts of her personality forward, mimicking inflections and gestures, giving people what she can tell they need. Never mind she makes few substantial connections in Chicago; post office clerks love her, baristas throw her coffee for free.

Within minutes Andrea's got the wild-eyed girl in front of her leaking her life story. Seems she quit her secretarial job when her bassist girlfriend got a gig opening for Sleater-Kinney. She worked the merch booth till they hit Nebraska and her girlfriend's ex showed up at a show.

"That's the last time I saw her," the girl says, stroking her long purple hair like a stole. "I guess her ex is selling T-shirts for her now. Since then I mostly clean houses, but I'm thinking about enrolling in an online university. I'm almost ready to get my life back on track."

Andrea tsks and smiles and admires the girl's tattoo, a tear-streaked dog face, ears perked, nose robust.

"You're easy to talk to," says the girl. "I can tell we have a lot in common."

When the tour bus pulls up, the girl rummages through her embroidered bag for a Sharpie, goes careening off to meet the performers as they file from the bus.

Tour bus run-ins are a thing about which Andrea has mixed feelings. The feelings are shame and embarrassment, so really it's one feeling that comes in two shades. She worries what Cry Wolf thinks of them, all these ardent women fiercely guarding their spots, eating fast food and comparing war stories, two out of three with heavy guts and limp hair.

"That one has done-lap disease," Jordan would say, pointing. "Her belly done lap over her belt!"

By now, Andrea's been to enough concerts that Adrienne recognizes her. Because of in-store signings and ill-advised stage door stakeouts they were even on a first name basis for a while. But over the years, Andrea's willingness to grovel for an autograph or a picture shriveled. Now she's happier to nod her hellos from the front row or a safe distance in line, which is what she's doing when the purple-haired girl returns, smoothing her too-short cut-offs, her neck flushed a mottled red.

"They signed my copy of *Treaty*," she whispers, dropping to her knees, pressing the CD firmly to her heart. Andrea barely hears her. A few feet back in line, a broad-shouldered woman squats to talk to a younger brunette in tortoise-rimmed glasses. They lean towards each other, smiling. As Adrienne and Peter stride past waving, the brunette removes her glasses; the older woman takes her hand.

After the show, Andrea goes home with the girl in cut-offs. Turns out she's a screamer, which gives Andrea an excuse to press her hand to the girl's mouth.

ANDREA ISN'T SURE what possesses her, but the next morning driving down South Park, rather than continue toward 90 East, she turns right onto Ridgewood Way. Who knows what she expects, but she's startled to find Linda's house hasn't changed.

"What do you want?"

An all-around good question, Andrea thinks as she eyes Linda through the screen door.

"Can I come in?"

Linda's jaw does the quick right/left shift Andrea recognizes from fights about Andrea's lackadaisical approach to housework. *"I clean for myself,"* Linda says. *"I want to feel proud of my home."*

Linda's Strong Points:
```
Organized

Adult

Owns a tool box

Nice bone structure

Only two cats
```

As she waits for Linda to answer, Andrea thinks how, set against Linda, she's the messy, capricious one. Working since she was twelve, Linda's credit is immaculate. She takes care of her plants, keeps Kleenex tucked in her sleeve. With Jordan, it's Andrea who's conventional, a reliable old sheep dog, nipping at fickle Jordan's heels. Is she constantly in flux, Andrea wonders, dependant for identity on whomever she's with?

Linda steps back and Andrea enters, just like she used to every day of the week. Locking the door, Linda adjusts a tiny crocheted throw rug with her foot. If there's one thing Andrea doesn't miss about her life with Linda, it's throw rugs. The front door opens directly onto the kitchen, a house quirk Andrea remembers Linda thinks uncouth. Smelling faintly of garlic and coffee, the room has grown more like itself in Andrea's absence, years of baked bread and crock-pot dinners melding to achieve some platonic kitchen ideal.

"So, to what do I owe?" Linda brushes past Andrea to stand in the tight angle where two Formica countertops meet. Formerly about ten pounds heavier than Andrea, she's maybe fifteen lighter now, pinched and librarian thin.

"Fuck hip bones," Jordan says about skinny girls. "Nothing to get a grip on, and you end up black and blue."

"I probably should have called." Andrea slides into a hard kitchen chair. "Among other things."

"Right."

Once she leaves Jordan in her Westwood apartment to run to the grocery store and returns to find her online watching a man with thick muttonchops fucking a skeletal woman on a glistening tile floor.

"Skinny," Jordan says, hearing Andrea's key, "but here, let me rewind, she can touch her toes to the back of her head."

"Did you want some tea?" Hospitality a reflex, Linda waits for Andrea to respond.

"When it comes to tea, I'd rather be a fag," Jordan says. "They drink it when they're sick maybe, or at their mother's. Twigs and ferns in water. No thanks."

"Sure." Andrea ticks her nails against the tabletop. "Grandma's Tummy Mint?"

Linda nods and opens a cupboard door. Glancing around the kitchen, Andrea recognizes her aunt's hulking toaster oven, vaguely remembers leaving it behind. Next to it three cans of cat food, a bag of English muffins, and a bunch of green bananas spill from a taupe canvas bag.

"I just got groceries." Setting a squat copper kettle on a burner, Linda notes Andrea's gaze. "It's usually neater."

"I know."

"Really Andrea, what's the deal?" Linda smoothes her jeans, brand new by the looks of them, but two years out of style.

"Nothing more important than a good pair of jeans," Jordan tells Andrea, zipping a dark pair of Diesels. From Andrea's perspective on the floor of the dressing room, Jordan looks like the hero in a Marvel comic, chin jutted, hands on hips.

"Like 'em?" Jordan turns to check out her ass.

"Three ninety-nine?"

"Worth every penny." Jordan stares into the mirror, gently lifting the translucent skin beneath her eyes.

"I'm sorry things got weird when I moved to LA." Andrea says, tucking her hands beneath her thighs so she won't be tempted to chew her finger, a habit Linda hates.

"I'm still at the bookstore." Linda silences the kettle, pours careful streams of boiling water into fat blue mugs. "Must seem boring."

"Not at all." Andrea sinks her tea bag with a spoon.

"I do all the ordering. I'm in charge of the reading groups, poetry slam night too."

"Sounds great."

"That's how I met my girlfriend, Marnie—well ex, we're taking a break. She's in Thailand on a grant and I told her I just couldn't do long distance, not after what I've been through." Linda throws Andrea a meaningful look.

"Of course not," Andrea says. "I'm teaching in Chicago now."

"Not Madison?" Linda's expression stalls somewhere between disappointment and relief.

"No, I'm just here to see Cry Wolf. They played the Orpheum last night."

"Isn't it a little late in the day for that? You're what, twenty-five?" Linda sets her tea bag on a saucer, blue and white, exactly like one Jordan owns.

"I'll be front row Adrienne side till I'm eighty," Jordan says. "I don't give a damn what people think."

"You know me." Andrea singsongs, trying to sound harmless, an eccentric family friend.

"I used to." Linda stares at her hands, folded in her lap. Break ups generate triteness, Andrea reminds herself. Still, she really wants to roll her eyes.

"I don't think we should rehash—"

"I trusted you." Linda crosses her arms over her bony chest.

Here we go, Andrea thinks. "I know."

"I thought fine, you're interested in some woman; as a couple, we can survive this."

"You told me to do what I had to." Andrea sets her mug on the table, splashing tea over the rim.

"I meant you should get it out of your system so we could get back to normal. You were supposed to come home."

"Things got complicated." Some childish part of Andrea wants to laugh in Linda's face. *You thought I could fuck her and then come back to you?*

"Complicated, yeah. Did she ever leave her girlfriend?"

"No." Andrea fights irritation, tries to look chagrined. One tenth of Jordan is better than all of anyone. For one night with Jordan, she'd leave Linda again and again.

"I knew it." Linda stares into her mug.

In the silence Andrea hears what she couldn't in Los Angeles or Chicago: a train in the distance, chugging through and past. She's forgotten Madison's quiet, how only on game weekends is it ever hard to sleep. Now she wears earplugs on a nightly basis, but living with Linda, three times a day she would hear the train roll through. Nights, headlights and summer leaves traced intricate patterns across the bedroom ceiling. Linda tranquil beside her, Andrea would try to predict what shapes she might see.

"Serves me right, huh?"

"Yeah." Linda takes a napkin from the blond wooden holder, a present from Andrea's mother, if Andrea remembers right. "You two are through?" She lifts Andrea's mug and sops up the tea.

"As we'll ever be." Not sure why she does it, Andrea puts a hand on Linda's thigh.

The first time Jordan cups Andrea's knee they're stuck in traffic on Wilshire. Three weeks after the Cry Wolf show at the Troubadour, they're still playing nice, acting like friends.

"You're going to love Sweet Lady Jane," Jordan says, her fingers light. "Best desserts in the world."

Andrea watches Jordan's hand creep higher.

"Oops," says Jordan, "forgot I had a girlfriend." She winks and withdraws her hand.

Linda laces her fingers through Andrea's. Long and cold, they don't feel a thing like Jordan's.

"Hang on, I have to kick the cats off the bed," Linda says.

Andrea nods as Linda heads to the bedroom. She can see Linda would take her back if she wanted. Maybe like the Criminal Mastermind, Andrea's a little bit irresistible herself. More relieved than aroused, she follows Linda down the long narrow hall.

⌒

WHEN ANDREA CAN'T sleep, she thinks about Adrienne. There's always something more to think. That Jordan never ruined Adrienne, Andrea considers testament to Adrienne's inherent primacy. She's genuine, solid and dependable where the Criminal Mastermind is pretty much a sham. Of course, over time Adrienne has become less crush, more savior, a false idol imbued with power to rescue Andrea from any number of threats. Her fantasies, although sexual, rest more on Adrienne swooping and swaddling, lifting Andrea out of whatever snake pit or raging ocean, wrapping her in expensive sheets and setting her in front of a fire to recover or dry. In one of her favorites, there's a gravel road and a stalled car, a rape attempted or actual. Back at Adrienne's cabin, she tends to Andrea, and at the same time falls desperately in love. Where Adrienne would find a cabin in Venice Beach is problematic, but according to fan gossip Adrienne has family money, probably she owns a summer home.

Most frequent fantasies:

Andrea's done something, written a book or become an expert on a meaningful topic. Looking out at the audience, she sees Adrienne in the front row.

The zombies/terrorists/ice age is coming. Adrienne and Andrea are all each other has left.

Adrienne's entire fist inside her, Andrea feels whole.

Though better than melatonin, Andrea's nighttime fantasies aren't enough to sustain her. She needs something more immediate, some distraction to carry her through the daylight hours. She thinks what she needs is probably sex.

Her feet haven't been on Midwestern soil three days when Andrea embarks on an odyssey. She works from a long list of types and interactions. She tells herself it's composed of people she'll want to have been with, things she'll want to have done. Somewhere inside she knows she's out to discover what drew her to Jordan, exactly what makes Jordan impossible to refuse. For Andrea's purposes, Internet dating is fastest and easiest, websites like OkCupid a panoply of succinctly labeled sex partners, bullet point intentions, a catalogue of flesh. She pours nightly over profiles. Which one will look best with her coffee table? She'll take one of these and one of those. She also meets women the old-fashioned way, drunk and out of control, them not her. At a bar on Southport she almost goes home with a Tom Cruise look-alike, at the last minute decides not to add men to her list.

Doing a clerkship in Minnesota, Roslyn calls Andrea's years of frenetic dating her Tour De Lesbian Stereotypes. As they talk, Roslyn lights cigarettes and absorbs details. She refuses Andrea's offer to mail her *The Power of Now*.

Once Andrea remembers to say, "I don't mean to be self-centered. What's new with you?"

Roslyn sips something or maybe just swallows. "By 'now' does he mean right now, or five minutes?" she asks.

No one Andrea dates intuits her history; no one asks probing questions or really tries to get to know her at all. At least that's how Andrea sees it. She's probably wrong. She finds herself furious at women for being nothing like Jordan, pleased when they embody her worst characteristics. She comes to acknowledge an attraction to those who overlap Jordan—more than an attraction, a sense that everything has fallen into place.

Traits that Interest Andrea:

1. A dismissal of health food

God forbid anything refined or chemical-laden enter Andrea's body, but Andrea falls briefly for a produce-eschewing UPS driver. She bought her metabolism at the same store as Jordan, or maybe it's all those stairs and heavy lifting, the calories she expends fucking secretaries on their lunch breaks. She takes Andrea to diners where Andrea watches her pound fried chicken, gravy-drenched mashed potatoes, biscuits, and beer. The driver grins, "My favorite food group is brown," she says.

Andrea blinks, startled. She's years deep inside herself, on her Westwood apartment's tiny patio, offering Jordan a segment of orange. Jordan yawns and pulls at her tank top.

"That isn't breakfast, that's garnish," Jordan says.

The UPS Driver overlaps the Drag King by one evening. When the Drag King pushes through a crowd of high-pitched admirers to meet Andrea, the driver turns to the woman on her left and buys her a drink.

2. Excessive tipping

Although they sleep together that night, an experience Andrea efficiently checks off her list, she doesn't stay over till two weeks later. The next morning they stop for coffee before the Drag King drives her home. Andrea is muzzy from waking up next to a near-stranger, an awful cotton-swaddled feeling she'd associate with a hangover if she drank, which she doesn't, so she relates it to not drinking her usual ten glasses of water, a number she arrived at because, since eight is sufficient for the average person, she figures she needs more.

At the condiment bar adding Splenda to her small half-decaf coffee, she notices the Drag King, still at the register. She folds a five dollar bill carelessly in half, plants it in the tip jar, her hands firm, her sunglasses opaque. Andrea doesn't fight it: comforted by the familiar, she swells with desire.

3. Alcoholism

Andrea can't be sure that what Jordan has qualifies as a problem, but on their San Francisco road trip, she drags Andrea to Wal-Mart at three AM to buy a corkscrew, replacement for the one she's forgotten. Back at the hotel when Andrea notes she's also neglected to bring her toothbrush, Jordan shrugs. "No big deal," she says.

There are other signs, all of which Andrea chooses to ignore, or rather, ignores by self-protective instinct, concentrating instead on more concrete forms of treachery, the specter of infidelity one such.

No doubt about the Alcoholic Trust Fund Baby though. Early on, the chemicals of novelty still alive in her bloodstream, Andrea arrives at the Alcoholic's apartment, two lattes in hand.

"Thanks," the Alcoholic's voice is all black sand and gravel. She shuffles to the kitchen, does something that makes a glubbing sound. "You and Kahlua and coffee," she says, returning. "I'd wake up to that shit every day."

Andrea tells herself she doesn't mind dating a drinker. She won't be tempted to get serious, and with the Alcoholic in her constant fumey daze, nothing Andrea does really counts.

When she considers her conquests, lines them up in a row in her head, here's what Andrea hopes: that she was born genetically inclined to covet evasive broad-shouldered women, women intent on invisible battles, who don't know a thing about impulse control. She hopes her tendencies are innate, Jordan their coincidental recipient. She hates the idea of spending the rest of her life caught in Jordan's orbit, intergalactic space trash, discarded but retained. She wants to believe it could have been anyone. A better liar might be able to get there. Jordan, for example, has persuasive powers that let her choose her own reality, a kid with one of those books. "I'm like this because my parents were alcoholics," Jordan might say one day, then, "I'm like this because I choose to be," then, "I'm not like this at all." It's a freedom Andrea craves, which might be why she needs Jordan. Andrea's a tourist in the land of self-delusion, buying tiny seashell replicas, posing smiling in front.

The most accurate truth seems to be that Jordan shows up when Andrea is inexperienced, suggestible. Just like those ducklings, Andrea imprints on the first live thing to cross her path. If not, Andrea might want someone totally different, for instance, the young vegan gym teacher who refuses to go down on Andrea when she's bleeding.

"Are you sure you're not straight?" Andrea taunts.

At this point it probably doesn't matter. Andrea is who she is. She guesses it's harmless to covet Jordan's innocuous traits, but she worries about her attraction to the darker parts of Jordan, her own scarf-a-bag-of-Oreo-cookies-tendency to privilege the worst.

```
The Alcoholic sometimes cuts herself.

The Drag King battled a cocaine habit.

The UPS Driver owns up to cheating on every girl-
friend she's had.
```

Like Jordan, the gym teacher wears Vans and rides a 1974 Honda CB450, but although Andrea finds herself attracted, she dismisses the teacher instinctively. She gardens and has dimples. Jordan could never be that nice.

~

ALONE IN CHICAGO, Andrea's phone rings sometimes in the middle of the night. Caller ID tells her nothing, and the first time it happens, rather than answer, she slips directly back into an uneasy sleep. In the morning she checks her voice mail, hears static mostly, then flares of music in vengeful foghorn blasts. Finally she makes out the tune, Adrienne and Peter singing Jordan's favorite, "Time Past Gone." Mournful and evocative, the song's a note in a bottle, but what was Jordan thinking when she set it afloat? Andrea goes online to check Cry Wolf's tour schedule. Sure enough, they spent last night in Anaheim. After that when she gets a late night call from anonymous, she knows exactly what to expect.

The calls themselves are not strange; Andrea makes concert-calls herself. She keeps in sporadic touch with a vet tech named Jessica, perhaps the only normal fan Cry Wolf can claim. Andrea considers her tiny friendship with Jessica victory snatched from the Criminal Mastermind's jaws. She actually tells Jordan Jessica's off limits; brave, when Jordan requires access to everything Andrea owns.

"Don't turn her into something messy; I could use an actual friend."

"Why so interested?" Jordan's doing her careful crawl off the 405. License-less, she's wary at off-ramps, any other place a police officer might lurk.

"I can't explain it." The moment Andrea sees Jessica in her gypsy skirt and frayed olive tank top, she's sure they're meant to be friends.

"Her sister's name is Roslyn," Andrea says finally, watching Jordan parallel park. "It kind of seems like a sign."

"It's not that you want her to fuck you?" Lights snuffed, Jordan stares straight ahead.

"What? God, no." Whenever Jordan accuses her, Andrea feels immediately culpable, her excuses ringing false in her ears.

"You sure? I saw how she looked at you. Like she couldn't wait to get you on your back."

"Me?"

"You'd let her, wouldn't you? That's what you're good for is letting. I can't be the only one." Jordan grabs the front of Andrea's shirt and twists, pulling her closer as Andrea's collar tightens around her throat.

Andrea loves Jordan's sexual gravity, a thing Linda very much lacks. With Jordan there's no giggling at bodily noises; it's serious business when they fall off the bed. The downside: Andrea can't tell when to be turned on, and when, just maybe, she ought to feel afraid.

"It's only you, of course it is," Andrea whispers, conscious of the fabric at her neck.

"No talking." Jordan hoists Andrea's skirt. "Touch yourself."

"But—"

"No talking." Jordan watches as Andrea slides her hand into her panties. Andrea keeps her eyes on Jordan as the white cotton rises and twists. Jordan's gaze climbs from Andrea's fingers to her face. Expressionless, she places a hand over Andrea's nose and mouth.

"What are you doing?"

"That sounds like talking." Graceful despite the small space, Jordan throws a leg over Andrea.

"Keep touching yourself," Jordan says, pressing Andrea's head against the passenger window's glass.

"But what if—"

"Coming's all you care about. You don't need to breathe." Jordan pinches Andrea's nostrils precisely, her other hand covers Andrea's mouth.

Some strange version of drowsy, Andrea lets her fingers accelerate. Each time her vision narrows, Jordan allows her one quick breath. Somewhere inside herself Andrea wonders why when everything under the sun ramps up her anxiety, the threat of suffocation allows her to relax. She feels the electric heat beginning just as the image of Jordan above her contracts to a pinpoint. She struggles instinctively, distantly dismayed by her body's will to live.

"You're right there." Jordan's words are mild. "Come on now. For me."

The voice is all she needs. Andrea's up and over, Jordan's arms wrapped around her, panting and on the other side.

Upstairs Jordan chugs a bottle of Gatorade, says, "How about a game of Uno before bed?"

"You're staying?"

"I'll say I crashed at a hotel in Long Beach, tell Patricia I was too tired to drive back."

"Okay." Andrea says. "Let me take a shower first." In the shadowy hall she turns. "I don't have a lot of friends here. I just think Jessica seems nice."

"Whatever makes you happy." Jordan's skimming an article in *The New Yorker*, her indifference feigned or bona fide, Andrea can't guess.

ANDREA'S ASLEEP NEXT to the Vegan one night when her phone startles her awake.

Hey there, anonymous, she thinks, hitting reject. In the morning she sees online that Cry Wolf did a special set last night at the Amoeba Records on Sunset.

After the first call, she tries several times to force Jordan to speak to her, snatching up the phone and yelling, "Hello?" into the concert hall void. In answer Andrea hears only Adrienne.

"Got a ticket to travel if only I knew / where to find you / can't have you / I'll always be true."

This casual torture to which Jordan would never admit ices Andrea's organs, makes her sob like a kid forgotten after school. She starts letting the calls go to voice mail, listens to them when they'll do the least possible damage, say between ten AM and two PM, and only on sunny days.

"Couldn't it be Jessica?" Roslyn asks when Andrea first mentions the calls.

"She and her husband moved back to New Jersey like four

months after we met. The calls are from concerts on the West Coast."

"You could change your number." Roslyn's voice betrays resignation. She knows that's something Andrea will never do. Jordan alters her contact info constantly. Even in the future, when they live together, sometimes Andrea's e-mails bounce back. Right now, all Andrea knows is Jordan's somewhere in the Echo Park area. One of them has to stay visible, consistent enough to someday be found.

The day preceding the Amoeba call, the Vegan suggests they go for a bike ride in the suburbs, cruise along a trail she used to take as a kid. In a field she leans her bike against a tree and reaches for Andrea, her sun-warmed hair like baby grass under Andrea's hands. That night, the Vegan makes her dinner, puts her fork down to kiss Andrea three times during the meal. She lets the Vegan stay over, something she hasn't done before. Lying beside her, Andrea visualizes her heart like a bear trap, easing open inch by inch.

"What's that?" The Vegan mumbles when the phone rings.

"Listen," says Andrea, "I'm going to need you to leave."

SOMETIME DURING THE Criminal Mastermind's two-year hiatus, Andrea starts wearing her perfume. It amuses her to think that the women with whom she sleeps associate her with a scent she wears in homage, that isn't really hers. She doesn't consciously set out to emulate Jordan, but one day at Whole Foods, drawn to the cosmetic section, she sniffs a vial of China Rain, decides to mix it with ginger—Jordan's signature laced with something of her own.

"You smell like a stranger," Linda says, the one time they sleep together, and for a breath Andrea feels guilty, but their encounter seems to finalize something for Linda. After that they're cordial. Linda even invites her to spend Thanksgiving with Marnie, home from Thailand, and some of their friends.

The Alcoholic open-mouth-inhales the night she meets Andrea, says, "You smell amazing. Do you smell that way inside?"

The Drag King calls her scent beguiling; the tall marathon-running lawyer tells Andrea she wants to swallow her whole.

After making an honest attempt with the Vegan, Andrea has to acknowledge she couldn't care less about any of them. She fucks them for numbers and to replicate what Jordan lent her temporarily, what she cannot live without.

The big joke is that sex doesn't do it for her, not even when tinged with violence. Maybe she really loved the Criminal Mastermind. She always thought she was in it for the sex.

IN BED IN Chicago, Andrea lies on her back, composing fragmented lists.

> One Possible Explanation for the Strength of Their
> Sexual Connection: Jordan wades in the same dark
> water as Andrea; sex distracts them both.
>
> Movies from which Andrea flees weeping between the
> ages of five and ten:
>
> *Bambi* (Mother deer shot, Bambi crying helplessly
> for her. There are easier ways for a cartoon fawn
> to come of age. Why not let him win the forest
> spelling bee or be the first in his grove to get
> an after school job?)
>
> *Fantasia* (It isn't even "Night on Bald Mountain"
> that gets her; it's all of those mops and pails,
> their defiance of logic, the way they multiply.)
>
> *Pinocchio, Dumbo* (Why are Disney's young innocents
> always alone and caged?)

Andrea happens on a cartoon at age seven, a hallucinogenic quest: Scooby-Doo races up a staircase that crumbles behind him, shifting and separating until Scoobs and the gang hop from stair to drifting stair like frogs over lily pads. Terrifying already, what happens next blows Andrea's seven-year-old mind. The scene expands to reveal a star-swollen galaxy, the room in which they started, a facade. Seems reality is only a set piece; what's genuine is this borderless night. Bleak and existential, the cartoon sticks stubbornly with Andrea, seeming to underlie even the most innocuous daily activities. Brushing her teeth or doing dishes, reality frays around her. She finds herself scrabbling at the edge of the abyss.

It must be like this for others, she thinks, picturing prostrate rows of people in their late twenties, shivering under army blankets, all gone PTSS from waking up early one Saturday morning, eating soggy cornflakes in front of *Scooby-Doo*.

Then again, she's pretty sure she recalls Roslyn watching the cartoon with her. She remembers the show's closing credits, a kitchen chair scrap, the sound of the freezer door, then Roslyn standing over her sucking a grape Popsicle, Andrea hiding her face in the couch cushions, ashamed of her tears.

Was I just born sensitive? Andrea wonders, listening to the distant sound of the El. She's been lying here so long she can almost hear the dragging sweep of minutes, chains scraping the floor. How many times has Jordan said it: something must have happened to make you this way?

Andrea shifts to her back, propping a pillow beneath her knees. *So much for going to bed early,* she thinks.

She'd been asleep for probably thirty minutes before a dream shocked her awake. Elephants, she thinks, or wooly mammoths, a deep sucking swamp and a lightning torn sky. She's a month from the Criminal Mastermind's return, her second chance at what she thinks she wants, and she doesn't know it.

The first year in Chicago, she thinks about Jordan daily. The second her ruminations diminish: once a week, twice a month, one time every three. Lately, without explanation, thoughts of Jordan fortify, renew their assault, her past howls nightly in her ears. It may be her relationship with the Alcoholic that does it, makes her wistful for Jordan in a way she hoped she was beyond.

A few weeks back, ensconced in a bar on Clark Street, the Alcoholic buys Andrea drink after drink. She doesn't seem to notice Andrea's still on her first gin and tonic; she's barely taken three sips. They're surrounded by Andrea's acquaintances: Scott, another straight colleague, the colleague's pre-med boyfriend, and a lesbian couple, the taller of whom lives on Andrea's block. With the exception of Scott, all people they chanced to run into, all of whom Andrea can do without.

The shorter lesbian complains about her salad, it isn't what she expected; the chunks of chicken are covered in rosemary, also much too large. The taller lesbian rolls her eyes at the Alcoholic but leans in to comfort her girlfriend, offering her part of her burger. Outside two shrill gay men toss insults like filmy scarves, across the table the med student checks his watch. The taller lesbian watches her girlfriend walk to the bathroom.

"Trouble," she says, "but take a look at that ass."

"Her too," says the Alcoholic. She inclines her head toward Andrea who feels not one bit owned or known.

"Your girlfriend's worse than a dude," Scott says the next day in the teacher's lounge.

"She's just someone I'm fucking," Andrea replies.

"Let's go home," the Alcoholic's hot breath hushes against Andrea's ear.

"Fine." Andrea reaches for her jacket.

"I just gotta hit the john first," the Alcoholic says.

"I'll wait outside."

"I thought it was supposed to be August; feels more like November tonight." The tall lesbian joins Andrea in front of the bar. She's struggling to light a cigarette.

"I was just thinking that." Andrea says. She'd been thinking about the word "home."

"You two serious?" The tall lesbian asks.

"This is terrible," says Andrea, "but I don't remember your name."

"Jess." The tall lesbian sucks at her cigarette, a gust of wind herding her ashen exhale down the street.

The Alcoholic falls laughing through the door. "Come on," she says, hailing a cab and throwing a heavy arm around Andrea.

"What?" Andrea asks as they pass Jess.

"You're not trouble," Jess repeats, louder. "I think you might be lost."

In the cab, the Alcoholic pleads, "Can we fuck when we get home?"

"When we get to my apartment, you mean?"

"S'what I said."

"Fine." Andrea replies, "As long as I don't have to do anything."

"Just lie there and take it." The Alcoholic winks at the cab driver, who averts his eyes.

Another Possible Explanation (for the Strength of Their Sexual Connection):
There is no sexual connection. It's all one-sided. Despite assurances to the contrary, Jordan only pretends to feel what Andrea does.

The streetlight outside Andrea's window perfectly illuminates the overlapping layers of paint on her ceiling. Like finding nursery rhyme pictures in the clouds, she lets the chipped paint images transform: crow in an oak tree; a scowling old man; mother and child, hands clasped, arms entwined.

When they get to Andrea's apartment, she asks the Alcoholic to hit her. The Alcoholic grunts above, says all the right, belittling things. The sound of her open hand on Andrea's skin is satisfying, and Andrea feels a first warm rush. She waits, skin smarting, her chest like the Tin Man's. Obdurately physical, the sensation refuses to cross over. The Alcoholic's clammy gut slaps against her; nothing transcendent occurs. In the unit above, she hears her neighbor's dog thud to the floor. She saw him in the yard that morning, elbows patchy from years of contented hardwood-floor collapses, blissfully stretching his nose toward the sun.

Once Jordan pins Andrea's arms above her head, whispers "I could snap these like dry wood," sticks her tongue in Andrea's ears, in her nose.

Once Jordan's hand slips when she hits her, Andrea's vision bursts with amber stars, she rolls reflexively to one side, hand cupped over her eye.

Once Jordan tells Andrea she wants to feel what Andrea feels when Jordan slaps her. Andrea forces Jordan's head between her legs, tells her she has no choice, smacks her lightly, then flips Jordan on her back, with her fingers inside tells Jordan to touch herself, strikes and ridicules her while she obeys. When she's finished Jordan turns wide eyes on her, "You hit hard," she whispers, and Andrea wells with benevolent scorn.

It's three in the morning when Andrea finally falls asleep.

WHEN THEY FIRST meet, Jordan tells Andrea more is never enough, also that she would beg borrow or steal to feed her Cry Wolf habit, admissions Andrea mistakes for hyperbole. For Jordan a sublime week looks like seven concerts in seven days, but Andrea usually overloads after day four. Before Jordan, Andrea never attended more than two consecutive Cry Wolf shows, but Jordan insists they hit every venue within a few hundred miles.

Striving to be first in line, watching the tour bus pull up, Adrienne sightings at nearby restaurants, the security pat-down precluding the race to the stage, sunstroke, rain-drenched clothes, sneaking cameras past security, talking to Adrienne after shows, all thrill and overwhelm Andrea. What depress her are the fans, each one certain of her singularity. At every show Andrea attends, someone has a song she wrote for Adrienne, a personal letter to Peter, someone's just out of rehab or recovering from a car accident, without Cry Wolf she'd never have made it through. One fan, Tina, so slim her veins seem to hover above her pale skin, comes to every show on the West Coast and cries through each one.

"She works at Boston Market," Jordan tells Andrea. "I've seen the inside of her apartment. Even the bathroom is covered with pictures of the band."

"When did you see her apartment?" Andrea asks. Her long-sleeved shirt sticks to her body but she's afraid if she takes it off she'll burn.

"I've got swamp ass," Jordan says, pulling at her jeans. "It's gotta be a hundred degrees."

"At least it's not freezing. If we were in the Midwest it'd be worse."

"Yeah, good old San Bernardino or wherever the heck we are."

Andrea drops her head into her hands; she can barely focus her eyes.

"Try and sleep, babe, we've got a long night ahead." Jordan pats her lap and Andrea rests her head on Jordan's thigh, throws an arm over her face.

General admission shows are Cry Wolf's bread and butter, a bonus for fans willing to put in the time. Andrea wishes just once they'd play a seated venue. Jordan has ins with various scalpers—they'd still end up in the front row.

Next to Andrea a woman plays solitaire. Her hair is so dirty Andrea can smell it. Beyond her two fourteen-year-olds paint each fingernail a different shade of pink. These are Andrea's compatriots, these people she'd cross the street to avoid.

AFTER MOVING TO Chicago, Andrea finds it impossible to return to her pre-Jordan, two-show maximum. She starts a tour reasonably, with tickets to concerts in Milwaukee and Chicago, finds herself adding Champaign and Green Bay, sometimes Minneapolis and Cleveland too. She buys ticket upon ticket, cancels too many classes, extends her car rental for another week. The self-loathing she feels mixes with exhilaration; she buys concert T-shirts in every color and style.

In her apartment after a Midwest run, Cry Wolf heading to Pittsburgh and Jordan still stubbornly gone, Andrea wants out of her skin. She swears she can feel it decomposing around her as each moment lumbers slowly past. Just out of the shower, she pauses in front of the foggy mirror. Her body isn't something she spends much time examining, not since she switched from starving to running, but for a moment she lets herself look. What do pale flesh, hazel eyes, and square calves add up to? What could Jordan possibly have seen?

```
A Text Exchange (After Jordan Leaves, Before Andrea
Moves):

Andrea: But it can't be as good as us.
Jordan: It's . . . different.
```

```
Andrea: How?
Jordan: She has sex like a lesbian. You fuck like
a straight girl.
Andrea: ?
Jordan: Or a man.
```

Dressed, her hair soaking her shirt back, Andrea flicks on her iPod, immediately turns it off, opens her phone to dial Roslyn, throws it on a chair. Innocent possessions crowd her, strangers packed together on a train. In her living room she smells the mingling scents of her neighbors cooking, oregano from downstairs, curry from next door. She stares at a stack of her summer school students' midterms abandoned on her coffee table at the start of the tour. The light in the pantry is burnt out; in the kitchen her faucet drips. The limits of her life, its circumscribed shabbiness, all is laid violently bare.

Opening her front door, she runs down the creaking stairs. On her porch, she forces deep breaths, tries to picture her diaphragm expanding. If only she were Tina, she could give in to the emptiness, fill it with bootlegs and autographed posters. Instead she sees too clearly how misdirected her passions are, how foolish and needy she'll never cease to be.

A Journal Entry Andrea Will Never Revisit (She knows this, so she folds and glues the page.):

```
I had sex just how you trained me, slowly, over time.
You only let me touch you through your jeans or I
couldn't penetrate you unless I played a man, or you
pretended you were gay and I ass-fucked you, or you
told me about your neighbor touching you through your
shorts when you were ten and then I could do that,
but only the one time, and you stopped me whenever
I tried to touch your breasts because you said it
made you nauseated but once you touched them first
```

and then I knew I could, and if you didn't shower
we couldn't have sex unless you'd had two glasses of
wine, and you told me I made you feel like a hero
when I begged, but later, when I said I couldn't
wait for you to fuck me you told me I put too much
pressure on you and you were the one who introduced
me to porn, you said you felt accepted, thrilled to
share rather than hide, but then you walked in on
me watching and you sneered and left and I saw you
through the window shaking your head as you stomped
down the street without a coat even though it was
below fifty which to you was freezing, and the first
time we had sex you acted like it was great but later
you told me you were thinking, boy she has a lot to
learn, which would have been crushing except that
you had just said I was the best fuck of your life,
and once you'd been distant for days and then you
went down on me and afterwards you said, that always
makes me feel so close to you and I knew you were
lying and I told you and you were delighted and came
back from wherever you'd been but only temporarily
and another time you got mad because it hurt too
much when you fisted me and you never did it again
no matter I apologized and pleaded and I ~~don't know
myself~~ BECAME WHO YOU WANTED, so how can what I am
be wrong?

⌒

ANDREA'S BEEN IN Chicago nearly two years when Roslyn phones
and asks her to visit. Washing dishes, Ani DiFranco pumping
through delicate white earbuds, Andrea almost misses the call.

"You need a vacation from your women," Roslyn says, "and I need
to talk to someone who doesn't care what 'Habeas Corpus' means."

"I don't know." Andrea's afraid for Roslyn to see her though she
doesn't know why.

"This is the best offer you're gonna get all year."

"Have you heard of Ani DiFranco?" Andrea asks, twirling her sponge around the perimeter of a large white bowl.

"Is this some Lilith Fair reject?"

"You'd love her. She's one of my favorites." She plunks the bowl in the dish rack, begins to wipe down the grout bordering the sink.

"Come on Andrea," Roslyn's voice is uncharacteristically gentle. Andrea is quiet, thinking. "Just for a couple of days."

"Good." There's a sound like squirrels and shuffling papers. "I'm getting a pencil," says Roslyn. "Which CD should I buy?"

THE NIGHT BEFORE she leaves to visit Roslyn, Andrea dreams she and Adrienne are riding the enormous Ferris wheel at the Santa Monica pier.

"Don't look at the Atlantic," Adrienne whispers, laughing and putting a hand over Andrea's mouth.

Below them she sees Roslyn packing important items into what Andrea understands is a briefcase even though it looks like a JanSport backpack. She's arguing with someone, a woman, Andrea thinks, although she can only see her hands. Strange rings adorn every finger, extending like glass stir sticks, yellow butterflies quivering at their tips. As she watches the women, the Ferris wheel begins to shake. Andrea wants to ask what's happening, but Adrienne's hand is still pressed to her mouth.

On the ground, tiny and intent as an ant, Roslyn unloads the purple backpack into the ocean. It's not just the Ferris wheel that's shaking, Andrea realizes, as the woman with the rings loses her balance and slips from the pier.

"We're having an earthquake," she tells Adrienne using only her eyes. Adrienne doesn't seem to notice, or if she does she isn't afraid. She's slipped on a pair of gold-rimmed aviator sunglasses, and despite the fact that it's night, she is trying to tan.

In the distance, Andrea sees Roslyn, now wearing midnight blue jogging shorts, racing across the desert.

"It's the Pacific!" Andrea shouts, startling herself awake.

WHENEVER AN INTERESTING group of people board a train, Andrea assumes imminent disaster so makes certain her cell phone is charged. Cinematic convention dictates that if there's a tell-it-like-it-is black woman, a wise conductor, and an older couple traveling with a child, in less than two hours she'll be calling her loved ones to whisper tearful good-byes.

On the train to Minnesota, Andrea is only one day out of a four-month entanglement with the Alcoholic, and already it feels like an embarrassing mistake she made in her teens. She'll be glad to temporarily unzip from her life, leave her Chicago self at home on a hanger, see what sort of person she is on Roslyn's turf. She understands from Roslyn's insistence that she's concerned about Andrea, but she's known Roslyn long enough to suspect it's more then that. Roslyn rarely asks anything of Andrea. She prides herself on her independence, but every so often she'll request Andrea's presence. When she does, Andrea complies.

Andrea scans the landscape outside the train's wide window, sees a sandy-haired boy and girl strolling a gravel road, a backyard where Big Wheels and swing sets bloom like flowers. The land seems strewn with identical Olive Gardens and Outback Steakhouses; over half an hour she counts ten of each.

The summer has been slow and wet and the grass and the trees are lush, Crayola green. In California this year it's just the opposite; wildfires stutter through parched fields, bright spots of sienna dotting the hills. Mudslides are general in the Echo Park area. On the national news, a house built on stilts slides into a canyon; Andrea watches someone else's calamity, hoping to catch a chance glimpse of the Criminal Mastermind, not necessarily hoping the house is hers.

At a station in Normal, Illinois, Andrea watches a thirty-something woman disembark. A small boy with a scrunched up face clings to her hand. The woman bends low to talk to him, and Andrea can't help it, her breath quickens at the sight of the part in the woman's dark hair. She may as well have scalped the Criminal Mastermind, Jordan's zigzagging, broad part is right there on this stranger's head. As the train pulls away, Andrea deliberately slows her breathing. As always her body's betrayal unnerves her. Seems like every day she sees someone who could be Jordan if Jordan were richer or shorter or straight or surgically enhanced. You'd think she'd be used to it by now.

Roslyn picks Andrea up at the station, thinner than Andrea remembers, although Roslyn's always been slim.

"I want to get a tattoo," Andrea tells her, which of course she doesn't. She wants to do something deliberate though, something irrevocable that's only her own.

They have a greasy dinner at the CC Club and because Roslyn is worn out from fourteen hour days at her firm, by ten they are lying foot to head, they way they always lie together in bed.

"Is lawyer stuff everything you hoped?" Andrea asks, thinking maybe just this once Roslyn will let Andrea be the one to dispense advice.

"Sure." Roslyn sets her wine glass on the floor.

"Ever wonder how you got here?"

"Minnesota?"

"No."

"Nah."

"We start out one thing and each experience takes us farther away from that thing. Or maybe brings us closer. I can't decide which, but one thing leads to another."

"Wasn't that a song by The Fixx?"

In the room's dark stillness Andrea exposes herself to Roslyn the way she's always done, because she feels compelled, but also because she knows it's her function. With Andrea's vulnerability as backdrop, Roslyn gets to feel strong.

"I really miss her," Andrea says.

"Jesus."

"I can't help it, I do."

"What about yourself?"

"What?"

"You lost it when you were with her. Did you miss yourself then?"

Of course what Andrea misses is herself when she's missing, that particular way Jordan frees her from the white walls of her mind. Since she can't say that to Roslyn, she settles for, "Right now I just miss her."

"She won't be back," Roslyn tells her and, maybe for the first time, Andrea believes her.

Two months later, Jordan returns.

AT HOME, ANDREA carries her suitcase up to her apartment. Cold spell over, August is up to its usual moist tricks. Inside it's sticky and humid; even her furniture is damp. Across the street, Jess mows her lawn. Through her window, Andrea watches Jess grip the mower, forcing it up the slope of her lawn. The grass's mellow fragrance seems actually to cool the air, and Andrea inhales deeply, as if the scent carries the antidote for whatever she's got.

Before leaving for Minnesota she made a date with a microbiologist, a pale-skinned blonde who replied to Andrea's e-mails so quickly, Andrea envisioned her perpetually sunk into a runners lunge, stop-watch in hand, waiting for the e-mail starting gun to go off. Now, she prepares for the date without much thought or enthusiasm, drawing on the low-necked red shirt that never fails her, a jeans skirt, and flip-flops, which may or may not be the ones she wore to that Dodgers game. When the microbiologist honks twice, Andrea counts to ten before locking her door, descending the stairs, stepping onto the porch. Her date walks toward her, hands in her pockets, a shy smile on her face. Andrea bats her eyes and smiles like she's thrilled when the microbiologist opens the passenger door for her, already certain whatever's special about this woman won't sustain Andrea for more than a month.

~

FORTY DEGREES AND gray; Chicago in March might be Los Angeles in Antarctica, that's how cold and bleak it is. Three weeks after Jordan's second departure, Andrea moves to a different apartment in her building—not strictly necessary, but she's more than an adjunct instructor now. With some extra cash in her pocket, she might as well get a better place. More than that, she wants to live somewhere that hasn't housed the Criminal Mastermind, could not possibly be holding out for her return. South facing, her new apartment gives the impression of being constantly sunlit, as if the sun rents storage space there, even on rainy days.

Linda says she's pulling a geographic; Marnie is a dry alcoholic, and Linda's picked up all kinds of AA terminology. When Andrea tells Linda she's moving, Linda says, "Wherever you go, there you are," and right then Andrea misses Roslyn so much she has to close her eyes and force herself to breathe. She's not ready to call her, though. She needs to make sure Jordan's absence sticks.

Packing, Andrea pictures herself stoic as a fur tree, blanketed by a chilly sense of calm. In reality, she ricochets from composure to breathless hysteria, then slingshots into relief. She wants to view the relief part as healthy—progress made toward containing within herself all she needs to move on. Problem with that: most often the feeling is preceded by a crying jag so epic it leaves her gasping and stunned. On the floor and spent, her feelings cannonballing marvelously away from her, she finds respite, and for a moment, Andrea feels fine. This seems less like personal growth than just more proof: she's addicted to the sensation of build up and release.

Still, taping and stacking boxes, Andrea experiences the moment she inhabits as deliberate, a well-placed comma in a sentence that runs incoherently on. How long could she and Jordan have plowed forward, really? Everything about them smacked of impermanence. She should count herself lucky; now's her chance to have an actual life, a thing she swears she wants. Problem is, after years waiting for Jordan (and here Andrea includes their time together), a post-Jordan life seems a waste.

Certain Wastes of Time:

Milk Duds (Too much chewing.)

Sex Columns (Sexperts are likely more clueless than their readers.)

Cats (Whatever personality an owner ascribes to her cat, she's wrong.)

Reality TV (Please.)

"The real waste was the time you spent with her." Andrea wants Roslyn to tell her this. Phone in hand, she almost makes the call.

Jordan's cat won't come out from behind the refrigerator. Andrea would very much like to beat him with a stick, this creature Jordan loved and coddled, thought nothing of tossing aside. She could deliver him headless to Jordan's new front door, along with a printout of their cell phone bill, the blonde's phone number highlighted in red. She could hand over Jordan's crosswords, her book on the Kabala; throw in an annotated list of everything Jordan lacks. The gesture would mean less than nothing to Jordan. Andrea pictures her staring blankly. "Who are you?" she'd ask. "What does any of this have to do with me?"

DAYS LATER ANDREA'S on the El, the cat growling and vomiting, crammed into a cardboard box between her feet. Andrea feels suddenly certain Jordan owns a cat carrier and has taken it with her, confused as always about which things to value and which to discard. The cat moans like he's desperate and she steals herself against pity; Jordan's second retreat may have made her a supporting player in Jordan's story, but she'll be damned if she'll be the kindhearted woman who learns to love by raising Jordan's cat.

At the "no kill" shelter, Andrea fills out a sheaf of unnecessarily detailed forms while the desk worker coos over the cat.

"What kind of person would let such a special kitty go, I wonder?" she says, never meeting Andrea's eye.

Andrea takes in the woman's wispy hair and neon pink leggings. On her shirt there's a picture of a dwarf with the caption "I'm grumpy cause you're dopey" printed above.

"We only lived together," she says. "He wasn't ever mine."

As she leaves, a male volunteer flashes her a peace sign—either that or he's showing her a paper cut, because he's wearing a palm tree-printed Band-Aid and mumbles "ouch." Something about him triggers a memory.

INT. ANDREA'S CHURCH—AFTERNOON

Andrea appears in the doorway, not positive why she's come.

                PASTOR GAIL
        Come on back to my office.

In her office, PASTOR GAIL motions for ANDREA to sit.

                   [CONT]
        It's always nice to see a
              young face.
The radiator clangs.

She's fourteen and school depresses her; nearly all of her focus falls on an out-of-reach boy in her class.

Andrea's quiet once they're seated, looking at Pastor's desk. Her screen-saver shows a tropical beach poised in the lean slip of time between day and night. Lavender becomes navy behind wild, wind-swept palms. Pastor Gail smiles encouragingly. The silent, stuffy room makes Andrea twitchy; she's startled when the radiator clangs.

[CONT]
Old buildings.
PASTOR GAIL uncrosses and crosses
her legs; her lined linen pants
shushing against her skin.

[CONT]
Is there something you wanted to
discuss?

Andrea looks at Pastor Gail, her
neat, wiry body, her messy brows
and long-lashed blue eyes. Pastor Gail seems part farmwife, and
part scholar. Andrea's had her
eye on Pastor since she arrived.

ANDREA
I thought maybe you could help
me.

Andrea stops, sifts her thoughts.
What exactly does she want to say?

PASTOR GAIL smiles and leans forward, rubbing her palms.

*There's a boy named Aaron. When
he walks toward me it's like I'm
bursting, but then he passes
right by, and I realize I'm a
husk.*

PASTOR GAIL
I'll do what I can.

ANDREA
I'm confused.

PASTOR GAIL
What are you confused about?

Andrea has a sudden image of the
pastor's arms around her, feels
a strange jolt at the thought.
More likely Pastor will say a few
words about Jesus and send Andrea
on her way. There's something
about Pastor Gail though, that
makes Andrea believe she might
understand, something wistful in
her sermons. She's curious and
contemplative, where her prede-
cessor was solid and smug.

ANDREA
I need guidance.

PASTOR GAIL
That's why I'm here.

Andrea studies the pastor's
hands, thick-knuckled but small.
She may be wearing clear nail
polish, Andrea can't tell.

She's getting closer to what she
wants to say.

ANDREA
I want to help out at church this
summer. I wondered if there were
any volunteer opportunities.

Pastor Gail smiles, and for a moment Andrea feels hopeful, then Pastor Gail glances at her watch.

PASTOR GAIL
You're always on top of things, aren't you?

Andrea looks at her feet.

ANDREA
Always.

PASTOR GAIL
You'll want to talk to Carl, but not till oh, maybe March. It's too early now for anything to be set in stone.

ANDREA
I'll do that, thank you.

PASTOR GAIL
Any time, Andrea. Thanks for stopping by.

EXT. ANDREA'S CHURCH — AFTERNOON

On the church steps, Andrea stares across the empty parking lot. Nearby, a plastic bag fills and deflates, startling her.

Only two hours till sunset.

Newspapers rasp along the pavement, spurred by the bitter wind.

Why is she always so far from home?

Andrea begins to walk.

On the train back from the shelter, Andrea wonders about her mind's capricious tendency to excise some memories but rattle the same dice-in-a-palm few back and forth for years. She tacks "New Pastor Visit" onto a half-hearted mental list.

Memories:

Mossy Lake's lily pad—speckled surface, slap of oars

Kentucky Fried Chicken at Maria Wallace's sixth grade slumber party

Reading *I Never Promised You a Rose Garden*, believing herself the narrator, also insane.

When the train stops at Loyola, a round black woman in a mustard colored sweatshirt takes a seat across the aisle from Andrea. One stop later, she begins to sob and murmur into her hands.

"Have you got a Kleenex?" she asks. "I got thrown out of my house," she adds when no one responds. Another black woman wearing delicate Lapis earrings hands her a tissue.

"Thank you, God bless you." The woman blows her nose and wipes her cheeks. "I got three children and lord knows he threw me out."

The other two women on the train, both artificially tan, simultaneously slouch into their seats and bring their cell phones to their faces, texting or just moving their thumbs. Lapis Woman pulls her purse into her lap and turns to the window, staring into the light rain.

Andrea sits frozen despite the need for action. This is, of course, nothing new.

When she disembarks she finds her neighborhood aberrantly vacant. Wet gusts of air rake her cheeks and she steps from the curb into a deep puddle, soaking her sneakers, also her socks.

A week before Jordan leaves, she lies on the couch watching The Bachelor. *Andrea walks to the bathroom, grimacing at the television as she passes.*
"This is who I am, you know," Jordan calls after her.
Closing the door behind her, Andrea pretends not to hear.

■ ■ ■

ALIVE IN ANDREA'S memory, the Criminal Mastermind spends eternity driving. Heedless, she covers miles without number, compelled to satisfy any craving she has.

In Westwood one night she rolls off Andrea and onto her back, hands like a farm boy pillowing her head. "What we need are chili cheese fries," she says.

"Good luck. "It's two AM." Andrea drops her arm over her eyes. By now she understands that for Jordan, the satiation of one appetite stimulates another. A need met is only a reminder of every other thing she lacks.

"Look who's not an LA native! That's what Tommy's is for." The Criminal Mastermind tugs on a T-shirt, a loose pair of cargo shorts.

"Tommy's?" Andrea repeats.

"The original. It's over on Rampart."

"Near downtown?" Andrea mentally writes off her morning class.

"Hurry up and put some clothes on." Jordan says.

Another time they stop at the La Brea tar pits on their way to a Jewish bakery.

"I have a yen for homentashen," Jordan says when she picks Andrea up.

"I thought you wanted to see *The Notebook*." To Andrea plans are firm things. She'll never get used to how little they really mean.

"We can catch the five twenty show. Maybe." Jordan flips through radio stations.

"How do you know about homentashen?" Andrea asks after a while. She's familiar with the Jewish dessert through Roslyn, all the holidays spent at her house.

"Jews are the chosen people," Jordan says seriously. "For a while, I thought about converting."

"What made you decide not to?" News to Andrea, Jordan's

statement hails from left field, source of everything Jordan has to say.

"Actually, I haven't fully made up my mind."

"How long have you been . . . ?" Andrea stops as Jordan pulls the car over, gestures for Andrea to get out. They cross a small stretch of grass.

Jordan points to a sad grouping of elephant statues, two adults and a child, as far as Andrea can tell. Their glistening black bodies the focal point of subtly indicated tragedy, they are drowning in what Andrea sees from a posted sign is simulated tar.

"Voila," says Jordan, adding, "as the Germans say." She notes Andrea's silence, "Well?"

"Why is this necessary?" Andrea asks.

The adult closest to the baby is frozen, mid-trumpet; the baby reaches its trunk imploringly toward her.

Jordan laughs. "It's terrible, isn't it?"

"The mother elephant is *drowning!*" Andrea's throat clutches, her eyes tear.

"It's the La Brea Tar Pits."

Andrea angles herself away from Jordan; if she tilts her head just right her tears will stay poised in her eyes.

"You crying, babe?" Jordan's voice betrays 50 percent surprise, 30 percent recrimination, 15 percent eagerness, 5 percent regret. Andrea wonders about the eagerness, a possible clue.

"Why did you show me this?"

"It's an historic part of LA. I thought it would be a hoot for you to see."

"It's a diorama from hell."

"I'm sorry." The percentages have shifted. Jordan's not sorry, she's insulted. "I had no idea you'd react this way."

"You didn't? Do you know me at all?"

Jordan doesn't answer. She's looking into some Jordan-specific distance over Andrea's right shoulder.

"Can we just go to the bakery or wherever?" Andrea suppresses an urge to glance behind her, see what Jordan sees. Instead she moves right, trying to intercept her gaze. Watching Jordan recoil almost imperceptibly—a rapid jaw clench, a half-closed eye, Andrea feels like a thud in the basement, surprising at first, but easily excused.

"If that's what you need." Jordan pats Andrea's shoulder half-heartedly as if she's afraid by acknowledging Andrea's distress, she'll accidentally give it her blessing. "When I first met you I thought you were Jewish." Back at the car, Jordan opens Andrea's door. She's cheerful and changing the subject rather than polishing her sulk, for some reason, generous this time.

"I get that a lot."

"Yeah, Jewish girls are hot."

"But I'm not."

"Of course you are. You're the hottest girl I know. Why do you think I nabbed you up?"

"Not Jewish, I mean."

"Your only flaw."

What's yours? Andrea doesn't ask. Instead, she constructs an equation, the kind the left-brained love to use as metaphor but actual mathematicians undoubtedly resent. She inputs the sorrow she intuits the elephants evoke in Jordan, Jordan's incongruous laughter, her watchful reaction to Andrea's response [Figure 8]. She thinks maybe her own ready-access to her emotions satiates Jordan's unpredictable appetites; her reactivity makes her the exact witness Jordan craves.

Andrea watches the road as she thinks this, presses her foot as if to brake seconds before Jordan, whose reaction time is never up to Andrea's standards. In the crosswalk in front of them, a group of Hassidic men amble across the street, heads lowered, hands folded behind their backs, pushing gently forward into whatever future they know God has arranged. Before the car stops safely within inches, a moment passes in which Jordan and Andrea merely coast.

■ ■ ■

ANDREA AWAKENS, BED bathed in sunlight. Fully clothed, she stares stupidly at her clock, registering the date, December twenty-second, the time, 7:37 am.

She's gone, Andrea thinks, same as every morning since Jordan left for the second time.

"I must have fallen asleep," like some useless fairy-tale heroine, she says the words alone in her room. Last thing she remembers, she was listening to Cry Wolf's new Christmas album, a fabulous misstep involving a brass section and gospel singers, Christianity run rampant throughout. Peter's always thrown in a psalm here or a prayer there but word online is he's started attending a Mega-church in Riverside. The album's final hidden track runs nine minutes. Unrelated to the Yuletide, it's called "God has an App for that." Andrea probably won't listen again.

She's pretty sure she fell asleep somewhere around "Little Drummer Boy" because a somber solo drumbeat and Adrienne singing, "Par-um pa-pum-pum," both echo low in her head. Icy under her bare feet, the floorboards creak as she walks to the window, open because her downstairs neighbors control the heat. With the radiators simmering from November to April, the outside air seems like a slow sip of water through a drinking straw, balm to her feverish lips. Strange, to awaken to sunlight though; drawing her drapes is a nightly custom she can't remember forgetting before.

Andrea's cell phone buzzes.

"Still on for coffee tomorrow? Home two days, already run into three people I hate."

Andrea hasn't seen Roslyn since the Chicago Diner episode, though they've talked on the phone a few times since March. An in-person conversation is something else altogether. Andrea catches herself wondering what in her life she'll need to conceal. Nothing, she realizes, feeling strangely lost.

"Driving in tomorrow, early," Andrea texts. "Meet you at three PM."

Through the window, Andrea sees her street is a morning sort of tranquil, quiet save for some faint car sounds, a brown and white dog on its daily walk. The week-old snow has hardened, beautiful but perilous; her front steps will be impassable. Still, Andrea feels something like contentment; the sky is blue like a robin's egg, and she can hear her next-door neighbor's daughter, bundled in a pink snowsuit, singing a song about lemons and ghosts.

"We don't want to be late." The girl's mother guides her to their car.

"The snow on the tree branches are like ghosts, mommy." The girl points with one hand, uses the other to tug at her scarf.

As they drive away, Andrea notices a woman in a purple down jacket stepping from her Subaru, kicking a tire. Belatedly, Andrea connects the almost imperceptible clicking sound she's heard to a dying battery, the Purple Parka Woman to Jess.

In the back hall, Andrea slides into boots and loops a scarf around her neck. She rummages in a brown cardboard box, sifting though blow dryers, a book of crossword puzzles, a black motorcycle jacket, until she finds what she needs. She isn't replacing one woman with another, she tells herself; she's just giving a neighbor a hand. Pulling on the motorcycle jacket, she hefts the jumper cables Jordan left behind.

Outside, Andrea's feet skid on the steps, but she's prepared. Placing one boot carefully in front of the other, she navigates safely down. Looking up, she sees Jess pluck her cell phone from her pocket, something, maybe a AAA card, in her other hand.

"Jess," Andrea calls, and her voice cracks as if she's finally entered puberty, as if this is the first word she's spoken aloud in years.

~~BONUS TRACKS~~
MINUTIAE
~~FIELD NOTES~~

Things Andrea Will Never Get Back:

Raw silk blouse

Faux diamond earrings

Sense of her sexual self (as distinct from Jordan)

Childhood photos Jordan snagged (Andrea reaching for
the camera with muddy fingers, clutching Brownie the
bear to her chest; Andrea, eyes caught in a blink,
pointing to a newly pierced ear)

Belief in the separation of church and sex

"Treaty" on vinyl (signed by only Peter so no big loss)

A neutral reaction to Altoids

The idea she might ever want a cat

Roslyn like she was before

A fresh limbic system

Deposit for that cooking class

Pristine credit

Linda's anklet

A taste for caprese salad

The Easter basket Jordan threw away

Best Cry Wolf Songs:

Ticket to Travel

Solace

Trinity

Drink it Down

Careless

Tell it Honest

Choke Hold

Shifting Tides

Time Past Gone

Kindred

Solemn

Swimmer

Noah Builds

One Time More

Can't Love You Now

Who's Walking Now?

Dead Tree Ground

Renewal

Kinfolk Secrets

Watch My Hands

Just Like Wine

Akin to All That

Laurel Canyon

Silverlake Kinda Girl

Born Right Here

Leave Me Now

Sandcastles in the Snow

Cold Light of Day

I Choose You

Baby Look This Way

Carve Me Up

Burns So Cold

Sounds Like Her

Handle Me

Warrant

Birds of Prey

Lay Me Down

Drifter

Hurts Like Hell

Rebel Howl

Love's Grammar

Lyric Street

Autumn's Bane

Killing Time

Bide Your Time

Daybreak

Just like New

Perfect Days:

First Milwaukee Cry Wolf concert

Roslyn sleepover (*Adventures in Babysitting*/pizza/
tiny cupcakes/phoned Ned three times)

Linda first date (lunch on State Street/resale
shops/browsing bookstores/walk along Lake Mendota/
coffee at the student union/Bascom Hill/brown La-
brador/impromptu dinner/walking each other home)

First time meeting Sejal

Jordan/Troubadour concert

Roslyn Venice Beach (Blue parrot dude, apple pie
at Fig Tree, stupid matching sunglasses, overcast
by the end)

Cry Wolf at The Fillmore/Jan (second night)

Cry Wolf Kalamazoo, 2008

Day before 2004 Ventura Cry Wolf concert (flowers from
Jordan, walk in Runyon, cleaned apartment, thought
about Jordan, dinner: Salade Niçoise, bed by ten)

Something with a picnic blanket and Roslyn and
mom. Baby carrots and Cheetos.

Last day of some family vacation (finally accustomed to tent/hot enough to swim/met that blonde
girl and pretended to fish till Mom and Dad packed
the car/drove home in swimsuit/stopped for dinner/
fell asleep in car

Nothing from high school

Worst Cry Wolf Songs:

For Better or for Best

Surf My Soul

Hold It All

Love's Last Laugh

Brown Leaves, Blue Water

Sacred Cows

River Flows North

Canvas and Burlap

Blue Jay Underground

Grass Roots Mama

Heart of Thorns

Mulberry Row

Ivory Dogs

Emma Ain't Home

Red Leather Boots

Molly Don't You Cry

I Will Not Forgive You

Can't Absolve You Now

Wet Like Rain

Big Texas Sky

Abundant Sea

Twisted Family

God Has an App For That

Good Old Che

ColdWater Canyon

Foods Jordan Hates:

Fish

Non-processed chicken

Dark chocolate

Radishes

Alfalfa sprouts

Arugula

Asparagus

Bean sprouts

Green beans

Snap peas

Bok choy

Broccoli

Brussels sprouts

Cabbage

Cauliflower

Celery

Endive

Fennel

Mushrooms (actually a fungus, not a plant)

Peppers

Spinach

Water chestnuts

Apricots

Bananas

Dates

Grapefruit

Kiwi fruit

Kumquats

Mangos (Who could hate a mango?)

Peaches

Raisins

Pickles

Tofu

Best Words:

Lackadaisical

Serendipity

Echelon

Attrition

Ludicrous

Convenience (From Latin, literally means to come together. Root: veni-to come, prefix: con-with/together)

Exegesis

Numinous

Semaphore

Worst Words:

Snot

Kelp

Scrumptious

Swarthy

Worst Physical Sensations (Not Pain):

Transition from running to standing

Transition from standing to running

Bra straps slipping under winter clothes

Wool on bare skin

Skirt riding up under backpack

Right before you sneeze

Unsatisfying yawn

Words/Phrases Students Commonly Misuse/Made-up Student Words:

Flustrated

Orientated

Inflammable

Irregardless

Literally

For all intensive purposes

Observative

Fast paste environment

Jordan's Overused Phrases (Unabridged):

A movie's just the thing

Starbucks fix

Hey, it's me

When we move in together

Keep that lesbian shit away from me

This is what I have to put up with

You never know when we might need a favor

When you get to be my age

When a woman says she's fine, she isn't

As serious as a heart attack

That's what she said

Why is this night different from all other nights

Sorry babe, I couldn't get away

It about broke my heart

You're so precious

Driving While Asian

Our new life

No man likes the person fucking his daughter

I live to serve

You're my little virgin

The hot ones are always crazy

I'll never leave you again

It's not that deep

We went our separate ways

That hits the spot

Ho Di Doh

I love you

You're attacking/ambushing me

You make me feel safe

You make me feel unsafe

Men and women can't be friends

That's a hoot

Let go and let God

Jordan's Select Women (No Order):

Tess

Two girls during Tess

English teacher (senior year high school)

Hanna/Tanner's BFF

Closeted lesbian celebrity

Personal chef (circa 1988)

Patricia

Wendy

Chrissie

Jackie

Julie

Jill

Kendra

Intern

Woman from Tide commercial

Jane Lynch

Dallas Cowboy's cheerleader

Bleachers girl

Karen S.

Karen L.

Candice from Wyoming

Literary agent (Lindsay? Lynn?)

Patricia's dog walker

Andrea

The redhead

The other redhead

The faux redhead

Front desk girl at The Sheraton

Martha and Julia (cousins)

Margaret

Hefty??

Crazy perfume girl

Lindsay Lohan look-alike (circa *Mean Girls*)

Stage tech

First girlfriend (age 13)

(Years later) first girlfriend's mother

That one who liked to eat during sex

Joan Spalding

Really tall, white eyelet dress, Peter's fan (maybe they just flirted?)

Jan (sort of)

Gelson's cashier

Karen J.

Radiology technician (Berkeley)

Religion Professor (UCLA)

The one who wrote a play about her

Blonde barista

Two-Term Presidents:

George Washington

Thomas Jefferson

James Madison

James Monroe

Andrew Jackson

Ulysses S. Grant

Grover Cleveland (Two full, non-consecutive terms)

Woodrow Wilson

Not Franklin D. Roosevelt (More than two, doesn't count)

Dwight Eisenhower

Ronald Reagan

Bill Clinton

George W. Bush

Andrea's Crushes (Preschool Through College):

Reed (invented or legitimate?)

Emily

Darrell Williams

Colby Sanchez

Ms. Stevenson

Andy Pullman

Ned O'Donnell

Ned's little sister

Jacob Goldman

David Hart

Chester Manheim

Sejal Gupta

Mrs. Orenstein

Chad Henry (two first names?)

Timothy Taylor

Jill Marlow

Dan Newcomer (three years running)

Jackie Mackenzie (first known lesbian: turquoise
ring, short, spiky hair)

Jennifer Coleman (Women's Studies 101 TA)

Amber Fitzpatrick

Kris Oberto

Ellie/Eliot

Linda

Tori/Tom

Anna Sinclair

Annabel Simmons

Carly Barizano

Andrea's Favorite Movies (Age Ten):

Tootsie

All of Me

Some Like it Hot

Auntie Mame

Jordan's Male Conquests (That Andrea Knows Of):

Softball coach

Doug from high school

That guy she slept with because Tess did

African American cocaine man (men?)

That actor

David (friend)

Things Stripped of Happiness (Unabridged):

Vanilla scented candles

Duck tolling retrievers

Sunny-side-up eggs

Mars bars

Everything funny about the word "troglodyte"

Cashews

Corn Flakes

LA Weekly movie reviews

Alan Ball

NY Times Sunday Style section

Aveda products

Mountain goats

Griffith Park

The Inn of the Seventh Ray

Summer Concerts at The Rose Bowl

Cinespia Cemetery Screenings

Indiana

Milwaukee

Green Bay

~~Madison~~ Berkeley

Ventura!

Pasadena

Coffee Bean and Tea Leaf in West Hollywood

Starbucks in West Hollywood

Starbucks in Boystown

Starbucks

Sweet Lady Jane (the song and the bakery)

The Rolling Stones (except Brian Jones)

Silver mustangs

Rumi (no loss there)

Ribbon-decked Christmas trees

That fucking "Apple Bottom Jeans" song

Russian nesting dolls

Caffeine

Spider monkeys

Midnight

Good Vibrations (Polk St, San Francisco)

Rough Trade (Sunset Blvd, LA)

Early to Bed (Sheridan Rd, Chicago)

E! True Hollywood Story

Yellow sheets

Mexican print blankets

Jack Kerouac

Will Smith

Ovaltine

Corona

Steve Martin

Orion's belt

Leather braided belts

Waffle knit anything

J. Crew red silk skirt

Newsboy cap

Bill Clinton

Jesus

Why Being Friends with Roslyn Is Hard:

She's goal-oriented

High school valedictorian

Bigger Barbie doll collection

Slightly more popular

"Y" in her name

Better at:

Hide and seek, dodgeball, four square, Red light/
Green light, hopscotch, softball, track, bas-
ketball, rowing

Looks: Audrey Hepburn meets Sarah Silverman*

*But no arm hair

Has a signature dish (spaghetti carbonara)
[Andrea's signature dish: canned minestrone]

Knows how to place an alcohol order

Never doubts herself

Accepted at more colleges

Taller

Law school

Isn't confused by shoes

Never seems to sweat

Scoffs at gym memberships

More interesting parents

Can whistle but never does

Thinks word origins are boring

Doesn't care about Facebook, for real

Eats sardines, bananas, hard-boiled eggs. In public. Without embarrassment.

Always has white wine chilling

Bird-boned

Hair products

All her bras and underwear match

Doesn't have to pretend to like green tea

No longer remembers any of the popular girls' names

Andrea's Sexual Conquests (Chronological Order):

Linda

Jordan

Screaming Cry Wolf Fan w/ Tattoo

Linda (again)

Buddhist Yoga Instructor

UPS Driver

Drag King

Marathon-Running Lawyer

Vegan Gym Teacher

Trust Fund Alcoholic

Microbiologist

Jordan (again)

(Subheading) Most Regrettable:

Jordan

Screaming Cry Wolf Fan w/ Tattoo

Microbiologist

Trust Fund Alcoholic (clammy gut)

(Subheading 2) Least Regrettable:

Jordan

Linda

Green Bikini (no sex but she counts here)

Vegan Gym Teacher

Drag King

(Subheading 3) Most (To Least) Conventionally Attractive:

Green Bikini

Buddhist Yoga Instructor

Screaming Cry Wolf Fan w/ Tattoo

Jordan

Linda

Microbiologist

Vegan Gym Teacher

Marathon-Running Lawyer

Trust Fund Alcoholic

Drag King

UPS Driver

Why Andrea's attractive:

Muscular calves

Doesn't wear glasses all the time

Full lips

Jordan says her ass is amazing

No above-elbow bulge when her arms are straight

Scott says her feet would be cute if she got a pedicure

Once in sixth grade someone made her a valentine
that said she had nice eyes

Looks thin next to fat people

Cry Wolf Concerts Attended

(to date):

July 1998
Madison, Wisconsin

October 1998
Milwaukee, Wisconsin

August 1999
Chicago, Illinois

August 1999
Ann Arbor, Michigan

June 2000
Indianapolis, Indiana

June 2000
Rosemont, Illinois

June 2000
Chicago, Illinois

June 2000
Milwaukee, Wisconsin

June 2000
St. Paul, Minnesota

September 2001
Whitewater, Wisconsin

September 2001
Madison, Wisconsin

September 2001
Milwaukee, Wisconsin

May 2002
Madison, Wisconsin

May 2002
Milwaukee, Wisconsin

May 2002
Chicago, Illinois

May 2002
Chicago, Illinois

May 2002
Detroit, Michigan

December 2003
Los Angeles, California

April 2004
Santa Monica, California

April 2004
San Diego, California

April 2004
Ventura, California

September 2004
Santa Rosa, California

September 2004
San Francisco, California

December 2004
Berkeley, California

January 2005
Los Angeles, California

January 2005
San Bernardino, California

January 2005
San Diego, California

January 2005
Las Vegas, Nevada

July 2005
Chicago, Illinois

July 2005
Madison, Wisconsin

August 2006
Chicago, Illinois

August 2006
Champaign, Illinois

August 2006
Madison, Wisconsin

August 2006
St. Paul, Minnesota

April 2007
Madison, Wisconsin

April 2007
Milwaukee, Wisconsin

April 2007
Minneapolis, Minnesota

April 2007
Chicago, Illinois

April 2007
Muncie, Indiana

July 2007
Champaign, Illinois

July 2007
Cleveland, Ohio

July 2007
Kent, Ohio

May 2008
Indianapolis, Indiana

May 2008
Kalamazoo, Michigan

Sept 2008
Green Bay, Wisconsin

Andrea's Biggest Fears:

Death

Snakes

Abandonment

God doesn't care

Jordan's Biggest fears:
Looking old

Not mattering

Stillness

Being the one who gets left

Why Jordan's Good at Sex:

Muscular

Intense

Stronger

Shrewd

Adrenaline junkie

Willing to invest money

Likes gadgets

Not overly dependent on gadgets

Charismatic

Tons of experience

Manipulative

May be a secret bottom (Knows what Andrea needs)

Believes her own lies

Adrienne's Best Clothes:

Army jacket

Black Bed Stu boots

On the Eighth Day God Created Harley Davidson

shirt (Ironically worn?)

Diesel watch (brown band)

Anything that shows her arms

Thin yellow T-shirt from Adrienne's actual summer camp

Blue Armani shirt she cut the sleeves off of on-stage (More the act than the shirt)

Mix CD (Made AD and BC. Never sent.)

"Time Past Gone"-Cry Wolf (Pertinent Lyric: "Call it love then, deep like forever / blink and you lose it / can't keep the wrong ones together.")

"Mercy of the Fallen"-Dar Williams

"Gravel"-Ani DiFranco

"Miss You"-The Rolling Stones

"Ticket to Travel"-Cry Wolf

"Swan Dive"-Ani DiFranco (Pertinent Lyric: "I'm going to go ahead boldly because a little bird told me / that jumping is easy, that falling is fun / right up until you hit the sidewalk, shivering, and stunned.")

"Want You"-Mariah Carey

"Choke Hold"-Cry Wolf

"The Same Boy You've Always Known"-The White Stripes

"Eternal Flame"-The Bangles

"Kindred"-Cry Wolf

"Right in Time"-Lucinda Williams (Pertinent Lyric: "Not a day goes by I don't think about you / You left your mark on me it's permanent a tattoo.")

"I Need This to be Love"-Maia Sharp

"Since U Been Gone"-Kelly Clarkson

"The Last Day of Our Acquaintance"-Sinead O'Connor

"Hands Clean"-Alanis Morissette

"One Time More"-Cry Wolf

"Why Can't I?"-Liz Phair

"Origin of Love"-John Cameron Mitchell

"Renewal"-Cry Wolf

"You Wreck Me"-Tom Petty

"Engineer Bill"-Eliza Gilkyson (Pertinent Lyric:
"Won't you carry me / Won't you try to save me.
/ Be my Sugar Daddy, be my honey baby. / Won't
you be my lover, be my loyal fan / Be my heavenly
mother, be my holy man.")

"Closer"-Nine Inch Nails

"Don't Think Twice"-Bob Dylan

"Oh!"—Sleater-Kinney

"My Skin"-Natalie Merchant

"So it Goes"-Chris Pureka (Pertinent Lyric "You're
trying to find a compromise / between remembering
and learning to forget / so now just pouring a
glass of water / is like trying to move boulders
with your breath.")

"Watch My Hands"-Cry Wolf

"California"-Eddi Reader

"Because the Night"-Patti Smith

"Save Yourself"-Stabbing Westward

"Sandcastles in the Snow"-Cry Wolf

"Breathe Me"-Sia

"Fever"-Sarah Vaughan

"Essence"-Lucinda Williams (Pertinent Lyric:
"Baby, sweet baby, whisper my name / Shoot your
love into my vein / Baby, sweet baby, kiss me hard
/ Make me wonder who's in charge.")

"Winter"-Tori Amos

"I Choose You"-Cry Wolf (Pertinent Lyric: "Can't you live up to / the figure I create for you / don't matter now / I choose you anyhow.")

"Every Little Bit"-Patty Griffin

"Hollywood"-Madonna

"Superstar" (as performed by Sonic Youth)

"Handle Me"-Cry Wolf

"Lovesick"-Bob Dylan

"Stay"-Shakespear's Sister

"Under Your Spell"-Once More With Feeling

"Northern Star"-Courtney Love

"Lyric Street"-Cry Wolf

"Goodbye"-Patty Griffin (Pertinent Lyric: "Occurred to me the other day / You've been gone now a couple years / well, I guess it takes a while for someone to really disappear.")

"Answer"-Sarah McLachlan

"Last Tears"-Emily Saliers (Pertinent Lyric: "You take things so much easier than I do / And you could live your life without me if you had to / And you believe that in the end it all works out right / And I might if not for you / And if you ask one which one lives just alone for love / I do.")

"You Never Get What You Want"-Patty Griffin

"We Used to be Friends"-The Dandy Warhols

"Girl from the North Country"-Dear Nora

"Killing Time"-Cry Wolf

"Sleeper"-Eliza Gilkyson

"Piece of My Heart"-Janis Joplin

"California Dreamin'" (Cry Wolf cover)

"Just like New"-Cry Wolf

"Useless Desires"-Patty Griffin (Pertinent Lyric: "I can't make you stay / I can't spend another ten years / Wishing you would anyway / How the sky turns to fire against a telephone wire / And even I'm getting tired of useless desires.")

"Bell, Book, and Candle"-Eddi Reader

"Ex-Girlfriend"-Gwen Stefani (Pertinent Lyric: "I kinda always knew I'd end up your ex-girlfriend.")

"Hallelujah" (as performed by Jeff Buckley)

Lists to Make:

Movies Never to See (*Armageddon*)

Favorite Religious Quotes

Best Tank Tops Owned

Places to Live

Expensive Running Clothes

Ways to have Prevented Scott's Death

Favorite Breakfast Foods

[Figure 1]

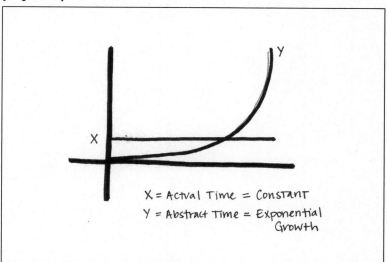

X = Actual Time = Constant
Y = Abstract Time = Exponential
Growth

[Figure 2]

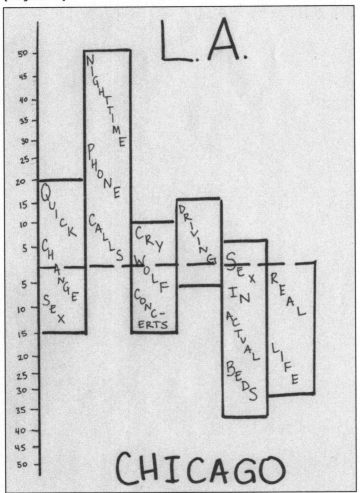

[Figure 3]

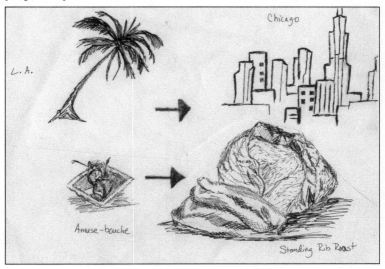

[Figure 4]

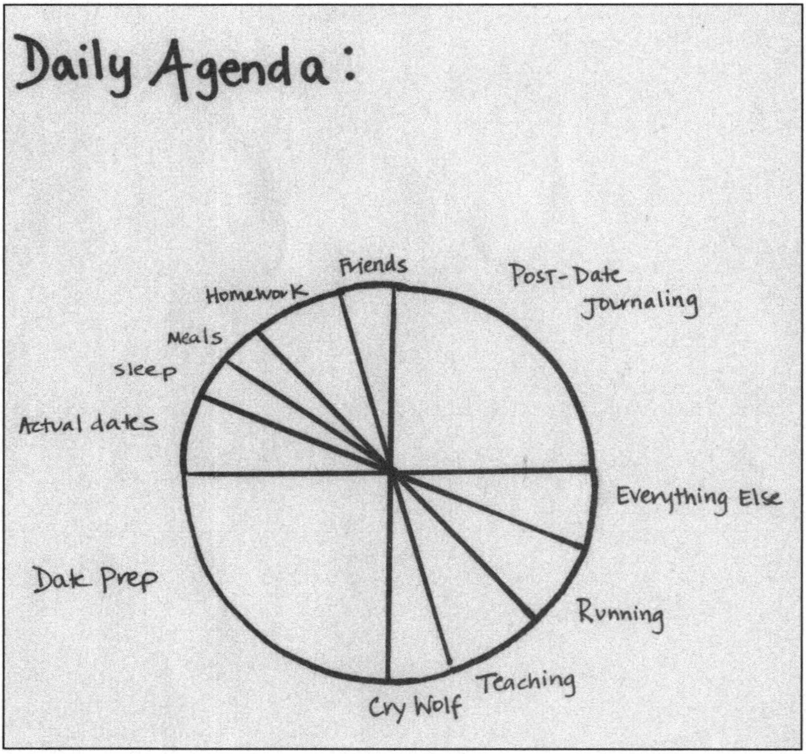

Daily Agenda:

Friends
Homework
Meals
sleep
Actual dates
Date Prep
Cry Wolf
Teaching
Running
Everything Else
Post-Date Journaling

[Figure 5]

...kissing Jordan

[Figure 6]

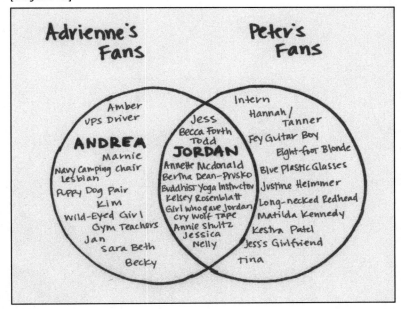

Adrienne's Fans

Peter's Fans

Amber
UPS Driver
ANDREA
Marnie
Navy Camping Chair
Lesbian
Puppy Dog Pair
Kim
Wild-Eyed Girl
Gym Teachers
Jan
Sara Beth
Becky

Jess
Becca Forth
Todd
JORDAN
Annette McDonald
Bertha Dean-Prusko
Buddhist Yoga Instructor
Kelsey Rosenblatt
Girl who gave Jordan
Cry Wolf Tape
Annie Shultz
Jessica
Nelly

Intern
Hannah /
Tanner
Fey Guitar Boy
Eight-foot Blonde
Blue Plastic Glasses
Justine Heimmer
Long-necked Redhead
Matilda Kennedy
Kestra Patel
Jess's Girlfriend
Tina

[Figure 7]

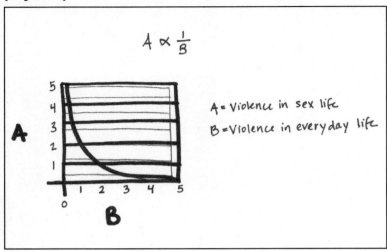

$$A \propto \frac{1}{B}$$

A = Violence in sex life
B = Violence in everyday life

[Figure 8]

La Brea Tar Pits Equation

$$Observation [sorrow_{elephant} + laughter_{incongrous} + (reaction^J - response^A)] = Realization$$

ACKNOWLEDGMENTS

THANK YOU TO my supportive and wise agent, Lindsay Ribar. Finding you was serendipity squared and not just because we both like sushi and *Six Feet Under*.

Liz Parker, you're bold, soothing, and intuitive. I couldn't have invented an editor with a clearer, more comprehensive understanding of my vision. I was totally prepared for you to tell me to kill Jordan on page five and turn Andrea into a man. Thanks for not doing that.

Thank you to everyone at Soft Skull Press. You're my publishing house dream date. If I weren't terrified of flying I'd have told you that in person by now.

The words thank you could never contain my gratitude to my mentor, Carol Anshaw. The moment you informed me the protagonist in my (since discarded) first novel sounded like SNL's "Mango" and I should look into teeth whitening, I knew you'd never lie to me. Thank you for your irreplaceable combination of frank critiques and unwavering support.

My love and appreciation to Martin and Maureen Rosenblum for support both financial and emotional and for never once suggesting I might have chosen to pursue a business degree.

Thank you to my best friend and aesthetic guru, Molly Dvora Rosenblum. In matters of fashion, music, gastronomy, and amusing noises I turn to you.

A world of thanks to my daily touchstone Deanna Wesolowski and also to the Mid-Missouri Reference Service (at least two of whom know more about the English language than I).

My gratitude to my readers:

Janet Desaulniers, your work inspires me. Who knows where I'd be if you hadn't seen something worthy in mine?

Justyn Harkin, I owe you more than a Starbucks gift card. Your input was worth the price of graduate school!

Aileen Keown Vaux

Erin O'Neil, for making everything seem manageable.

Dustin Weil

Terri Griffith

Holly Birnbaum

Many thanks to:

Robin Mullins whose faith in my writing preceded my own.

Barry Bursak

Victoria Holland

Jessie Ewing

Elizabeth Dean Prusko

Peg and Tony Remsen for a lovely, fruitful place to write.

Jessica Donheimmer, you showed up at a critical moment and helped me make the leap into the next phase of my life.

Krista Mathews Dean, without whom Roslyn might have been a barista, because coffee makes much more sense to me than law.

And finally, thank you to Patty V. Michels. You've provided love, support and laundry detergent. I am forever grateful.